PRAISE FOR Wife of the Gods

"[A]n absolute gem of a first novel and the sort of book that will delight not only hard-core mystery fans, but also those who visit the genre only casually in search of an occasional literary entertainment. . . . *Wife of the Gods* is not simply an extraordinarily well-crafted mystery; it's also an extremely well-structured and deftly written novel. . . . [Quartey] has a remarkable ability to credibly evoke the simultaneity of the modern and deeply traditional worlds in which so many of that continent's people coexist." —*Los Angeles Times*

"Like *The No. 1 Ladies' Detective Agency* suspense novels? You'll love *Wife of the Gods*." —*Essence*

"*Wife of the Gods* is a lush and well-written tale of murder most foul, set in an alien landscape, but laced with many of the same motivations and alibis you might expect to find much closer to home." —*BookPage*

"Already garnering unusual critical acclaim for a debut novel, Quartey's remarkable characters give the reader a worthy whodunit." —*Ebony*

"Move over Alexander McCall Smith. Ghana has joined Botswana on the map of mystery. . . . [This] newcomer is most welcome." —*Kirkus Reviews*

"Crisp, engrossing . . . [Quartey] renders a compelling cast of characters inhabiting a world precariously perched between old and new. Fans of McCall Smith's *No. 1 Ladies' Detective Agency* will relish the opportunity to discover yet another intriguing area of Africa." —*Booklist* (starred)

"[A] winning debut . . . Dawson is a wonderful creation, a man as rich with contradictions as the Ghana Quartey so delightfully evokes. . . . Readers will be eager for the next installment in what one hopes will be a long series." —*Publishers Weekly*

ALSO BY KWEI QUARTEY

Wife of the Gods

CHILDREN
of the
STREET

CHILDREN

of the

STREET

A Novel

KWEI QUARTEY

Random House Trade Paperbacks · New York

A Random House Trade Paperback Original

Copyright © 2011 by Kwei J. Quartey

Published in the United States by Random House Trade Paperbacks, an imprint of The Random House Publishing Group, a division of Random House, Inc., New York.

RANDOM HOUSE TRADE PAPERBACKS and colophon are trademarks of Random House, Inc.

Library of Congress Cataloging-in-Publication Data

Quartey, Kwei J.
Children of the street: a novel / Kwei Quartey.
p. cm.
ISBN 978-0-8129-8167-4
eBook ISBN 978-0-679-60411-2
1. Police—Ghana—Fiction. 2. Murder—Investigation—Fiction.
3. Ghana—Fiction. I. Title.
PS3617.U37C47 2011
813'.6—dc22
2010026476

Printed in the United States of America

www.atrandom.com

2 4 6 8 9 7 5 3 1

To all those who dare to care

Prologue

A day shy of his seventeenth birthday, Musa was a boy with the survival instincts of a grown man. Blood sprang from the stab wound in his back, but he did not die instantly. As his life drained, Musa had a running vision, like a video, of his short life. Life in his small hometown of Gurungu had been a depressing, losing battle as his family tried to grow millet in the unforgivable desert conditions of northern Ghana. It was what had pushed him to his seven-day trek to Ghana's capital city of smooth motorways and impenetrable traffic jams.

Penniless and lonely, Musa hadn't known a soul in Accra. With no education, no family connections, and no skills, he could hope for only a few jobs. He could be a street vendor, a luggage porter at a lorry park, a shoeshine boy, or a truck pusher—one of those guys who roams Accra with carts picking up metal scraps to take to the junkyards. He earned much less than a *cedi* a day.

Up before dawn, Musa never rested until after nightfall, laying his head down on city pavements, at storefronts, and

around marketplaces. He had only wanted his life to get better. He had sworn that, after working in Accra for a year, he
would go back to Gurungu with new clothes and some money
for his mother.

As Musa's eyelids fluttered closed, he must have wondered
if this was what his father had meant when he had shaken a
warning finger in Musa's face. *If you go to Accra, you will become nothing but a street child, and you will pay a terrible price
for it.*

PART ONE

1

The call had come in on a Sunday morning in June.

"For this one," Detective Sergeant Chikata had said, "I think they will need us."

On his Honda motorbike, Detective Inspector Darko Dawson sped by industrial buildings along Ring Road West. The dead body was near the Korle Lagoon. Dawson made it there in fifteen minutes. Even if his eyes had been shut, the pervasive, foul smell of the lagoon would have announced to him that he had arrived.

He turned onto Abossey Okai Road, which formed two bridges, the first of them over the refuse-choked Odaw River, which flowed into the lagoon. Agbogbloshie Market on Dawson's left and Kokomba Market on his right teemed with Sunday shoppers and hawkers trying to sell everything from bananas to sea crabs.

At the second bridge, over a much smaller channel of tarry, polluted water, there were umbrella-shaded market vendors, pedestrians, trucks, and cars mixed together in organized chaos. Dawson parked and locked his bike. Sprawling onto the riverbanks, a crowd of onlookers overflowed both ends of the bridge. Standing at over six feet, Dawson could see above most people's heads. Detective Sergeant Chikata and a uniformed man Dawson didn't know were about a hundred meters up on the south bank of the channel. Framed apocalyptically against dense black smoke billowing from somewhere upstream, Deputy Superintendent Bright and three members of his crime scene team, all in masks, gloves, and galoshes, were moving about knee-deep in the foul mire.

Dawson skirted the mass of the crowd and made his way onto the bank. It was carpeted with litter, much of it plastic bottles discarded without a second's thought after the contained water had been drunk. The rest of the junk included boxes, tin cans, abandoned clothing, trash bags, pieces of machinery, old tires, coconut husks, and unidentifiable bits of metal and plastic detritus. There was also the kind of human waste Dawson definitely did not want his shoes to touch, some of it exposed, some of it in "flying toilets"—tossed black plastic bags with excrement inside.

The impossibly good-looking Detective Sergeant Chikata, Dawson's junior in rank in the Criminal Investigations Department (CID) Homicide Division, looked up as Dawson approached.

"Morning, Dawson."

"Morning, Chikata."

"Body of a dead male spotted in there this morning."

"How did we get notified?"

Chikata introduced the bulky, flinty-eyed man next to him. "This is Inspector Agyekum. He was the Korle Bu station officer this morning."

Agyekum was Detective Inspector Dawson's rank equivalent, but as a general inspector he wore the standard, heavy, sweltering dark blue uniform of the Ghana Police Service (GPS) in contrast to CID's plainclothesmen.

"Morning, Inspector." Dawson shook hands, finishing with the customary mutual finger snap.

"I was starting my shift when a small boy came into the station," Agyekum took up. "That's him there with Constable Gyamfi." He pointed his chin farther along the bank where a police constable stood over a boy of about eight sitting on the ground with his head down and his arms folded tightly across his skinny body.

"Many people saw the body," Agyekum continued, "but because they fear the police, they just kept quiet. But the boy took it upon himself to run over to the Korle Bu station to report it."

"He's a brave young man," Dawson said, looking over at the boy with approval. "And then?"

"Constable Gyamfi took the report in the station and brought it to me," Agyekum said, "then the two of us returned with the boy. When I saw the body there, I decided to call the Crime Scene Unit."

"Very good," Dawson said. "Thank you."

Dawson knew Police Constable Gyamfi from a previous case a year ago. He waved at the constable, who smiled and half waved, half saluted in return.

"Mr. Bright says he's quite sure it's a homicide," Chikata said.

"Then it probably is," Dawson said.

Deputy Superintendent Bright, a trained serologist, was head of the CSU team. His hunches were seldom wrong.

Dawson moved a little closer to the water, which was the color of tar and almost the same consistency. He winced at its relentless stench, but people living within smelling distance were used to it, or maybe just ignored it.

Bright and his two crime scene guys squelched around looking for an unlikely clue. There was so much garbage it would be a miracle if they found anything useful. Only Bright's relentless thoroughness and commitment to excellence had deemed the search necessary. Others might have simply reeled the corpse in without bothering.

The garbage partially camouflaged the dead body, which was facedown. On casual glance, it could have been mistaken for a big clump of rubbish, and undoubtedly had been.

With glop sucking at his galoshes, Deputy Superintendent Bright joined Dawson and the other two men.

"Morning, Dawson." His voice sounded like the bass notes of a bassoon. "Please excuse my appearance and odor."

"Good morning, sir. I admire you for going in there."

Bright looked down at his soiled outfit with a grimace. "These are the last of our hazardous materials garb, so fortunately or not, I won't be doing this again for a while."

"Any findings, sir?" Dawson asked.

"Besides the body? Nothing. Still suspect foul play, however. I know a dumped corpse when I see one. And this one is in terrible shape."

"When are you bringing it in?"

"We're almost ready for that now."

"Can you wait a few minutes? I don't want the boy to see that."

"No problem, Dawson."

"Thank you, sir. It's good to have you around." Dawson turned and trotted up the bank.

2

The boy was still with Police Constable Gyamfi, who was in his mid-twenties but looked so young he could have gone undercover as a high school student. As Dawson approached, Gyamfi's face lit up with a smile of strong, white teeth—the kind that could snap the top off a beer bottle.

"Morning, Gyamfi," Dawson said as they clasped hands. "How are you? It's nice to see you again."

"Yes, sir, and you too."

"How're the wife and new daughter?"

"Very well, sir, thank you, sir."

"Good, I'm glad."

Gyamfi was a recent import from the rural town of Ketanu in the Volta Region. With Dawson's help and persistence, he had been transferred to the police force in Accra, not an easy achievement in the GPS. He was a good man with great integrity and promise.

Dawson looked down at the boy, who didn't return the look. He wore torn cutoff jeans, a soiled black-and-white muscle shirt that was too big for him, and slippers that were falling apart on his dusty feet. He was staring at a point on the ground in front of him. Dawson knelt down.

"How are you? I'm Darko. What's your name?"

The boy's eyes flitted up and away. "Sly."

Dawson held out his hand. Sly shook it after a second's consideration.

"Thank you for what you did," Dawson said. "You were brave to go to the police station. Do you know that?"

Sly nodded tautly. Dawson lifted his face with a touch to his chin.

"Are you all right?"

"Yes."

"I'm not going to do anything to you. I only want to be your friend."

Sly nodded again. Dawson stood and reached for the boy's hand, pulling him up. "Let's go for a walk."

"Okay."

"While we're gone," Dawson said to Gyamfi, "I want you to talk to these people in the crowd. We need to know if anyone saw anything this morning or last night in connection with the body. We need names, and we need a way to get back in touch with them. That might be hard around here, but do your best."

"Yes, sir."

"And always remember faces, Gyamfi. Try to make your mind a camera. You never know who you might run into later on."

Dawson turned away with Sly and steered him around the pack of spectators. As he and the boy walked past, every head turned to watch them. Dawson took a quick but good look at all the faces, practicing what he had just preached to his constable. In reality, the chance was remote that they would get usable information from anyone. Watching policemen at work was okay, talking to them was not.

Dawson and Sly were now walking along the curve of the Odaw River's east bank toward the shacks of the slum in the distance.

"How old are you, Sly?"

"Nine."

"From northern Ghana?"

"Upper West Region."

Dawson had made an educated guess. Most of Agbogbloshie's residents came from northern Ghana.

"Where do you live?"

"Here in Sodom and Gomorrah."

It was the bitter, ironic nickname for Agbogbloshie, Accra's most notorious slum. Drugs, prostitution, rape, forty thousand squatters, and practically every year a new but unsuccessful government plan to relocate them.

Dawson and Sly walked the beaten path through mounds of trash containing the ubiquitous plastic bags and bottles, carcasses of old TVs, trashed scanners, mobile phones, air conditioners, refrigerators, fax machines, microwaves, dead computer monitors and defunct CPUs. To their left was a mountain of electronic waste piled higher than Dawson's head.

"What were you doing this morning when you saw that dead man in the water?" he asked Sly.

"Burning cables."

That was what caused the dense black smoke all along the banks of the Odaw. The boys burned TV and computer cables to get at the copper wires, which they sold locally for fifty *pesewas* per kilo, or about eighteen cents per pound.

Ahead was a line of teenage boys that made Dawson think of an assembly line, only this was *dis*assembly. The first boy was breaking open the back of an old TV monitor using a rock. The second was degreasing some cables with a solvent. Farther along still, a cable-burning session was beginning. Five boys of ages ten to fifteen were crowded around a mass of prepped cables. All from northern Ghana, they addressed Sly in rapid-fire Hausa. Although Dawson wasn't fluent in the language, it was obvious they were asking who he was. Sly's response seemed to satisfy them because they nodded and smiled.

"I tell them you're my friend," Sly explained.

"Where did you learn English?" Dawson asked.

"I was schooling at my hometown before my father told me to come to Accra with my uncle."

"Are you continuing school here?"

"No."

"Why not?"

"My uncle says he won't send me to school. He just wants me to sell copper and make money."

Dawson said nothing to that, for now anyway.

The Hausa boys used insulation foam as kindling and a cigarette lighter to start the burn. Poking the cables with sticks brought the needed rush of oxygen and created a miniature inferno with a blast of deadly black smoke. Even though he was upwind from it, Dawson caught a good whiff and backed away slightly, thinking of the toxicity of the fumes. With his foot, he flipped over a piece of plastic from a computer monitor and found a label that read SCHOOL DISTRICT OF PHILADELPHIA. Junked, unusable equipment that the rich countries passed off as charitable donations ended up right here in Agbogbloshie.

"Ask them if any of them saw the dead person back there or heard anything about it," Dawson said to Sly.

The boy obliged. His friends, intent on their task, replied briefly.

"They didn't see anything," Sly said. "They haven't heard anything."

Dawson nodded. He hadn't expected much more than that. Fact was, if the dead person wasn't a friend of theirs or otherwise important, it just wasn't of that much interest to them. *Someone died. So what?*

"Let's go," Dawson said to Sly. A little farther along he put his hand on the boy's head like he was palming a soccer ball. "Burning that stuff is dangerous. There's poison in the smoke and you're breathing it inside your body. You understand?"

Sly nodded, but uncertainly. Dawson wasn't sure he really did get it. He ruffled his companion's short, wiry hair. "You're a good boy, Sly. Is your uncle at home?"

Sly was hesitant about something.

"You don't like your uncle?" Darko asked.

"Yes, I like him," Sly said.

But the changed tone of his voice, broken up like a bleat, told Dawson he wasn't telling the truth.

"Don't be afraid," Dawson said. "I only want to talk to him."

Roaming the open land bordered by the Ring Road on the west and the edge of the Odaw River on the east were a few grazing horses and a herd of placid, foraging cows, brought all the way from the northern territories by migrants who had lived as nomads. It was a bizarre mixing of rural lifestyle with the urban slum. *Only in Accra,* Dawson thought. Only in Accra.

Deep within Agbogbloshie, Sly walked with easy assurance, as if floating over the rocky ground. He skipped nonchalantly across gutters filled to overflowing with garbage encased in opaque, grayish black glop. He ducked under laundry hung out to dry on clotheslines crisscrossing like railway tracks. He took narrow, abruptly swerving passages between rows of rickety homes constructed of wood that just begged for a conflagration.

Life went on here with the same inevitability it does anywhere else. People worked and traded, children played, women got their nails done, men had their hair cut, and a group of shirtless teenage boys watched soccer on a communal TV.

Here and there, Dawson caught a whiff of marijuana, or "wee," as it was popularly known. From his nasal passages, it went like a blast to a pleasure spot inside his brain. He felt that tug of desire that told him he had not yet conquered his vice. *Five months completely clean.* One day at a time.

People asked Sly who his companion was. He gave the same answer every time. "He's Darko, my friend." It was best that way. They didn't take to policemen. If casual queries about the corpse in the lagoon yielded little to no useful information, it was still more than Dawson would get if people knew he was a detective.

They passed a small mosque that stood out as one of the few brick buildings in Agbogbloshie. A man inside was prostrate on his prayer mat.

"There is my house," Sly said, slowing down and pointing. "Where those boys are playing."

Four teenagers were kicking and heading a soccer ball back and forth to one another without allowing it to touch the ground. A man sat in front of a windowless, eight-foot-square wooden shack raised off the ground on short stilts.

"Is that your uncle?" Dawson asked.

"Yes."

Sly's uncle saw them approaching. For a moment he didn't

move, but he finally rose to his feet as they came closer. He was frowning—the puzzled kind of frown—and then he looked wary.

"Good morning?" He was average height with squinting eyes. His hair was graying at the temples and retreating from his dome forehead. He had tribal marks on both cheeks.

"Good morning, sir. My name is Darko Dawson."

"Yessah. I'm Gamel." His voice was like gravel.

Behind him, the door of his living quarters was ajar, and Dawson caught a glimpse of a thin foam floor mattress as holey as Swiss cheese.

"Have he do someting wrong?" Gamel asked, gesturing at Sly.

"No," Dawson said. "This morning he reported a dead body to the police."

"A dead body?"

Suddenly angry, Gamel began scolding Sly in Hausa. Without warning, he lunged at the boy, but Dawson blocked his move.

"Hold on, my friend," he said. "Come with me and let's talk. Sly, wait here for us."

Dawson and Gamel ducked into a tight space between his shack and the next. It reeked of urine. The two men stood barely six inches apart.

"What is your problem with Sly?" Dawson asked.

"I tell him say, if you talk to policeman you go bring plenty trouble for house. But the boy never listen."

"He did the right thing," Dawson said.

Gamel grew wary as realization dawned. "You are policeman?"

"Yes."

The whites of Gamel's eyes flashed like those of a shying horse. He took a confined step back.

"Relax," Dawson said, "I'm not accusing you of anything."

Gamel breathed again.

"Does Sly go to school?" Dawson asked.

Gamel hesitated. "No, sah."

"Why not?"

"I tell him say go to school, sah. He no like."

"How old are you, Gamel?" Dawson snapped.

"Forty-two, sah."

"How old is Sly?"

"Nine."

"Who do you think should be making sure he gets to school?"

Gamel looked away without answering.

"Is he even registered to attend school?" Dawson demanded.

"No, sah," Gamel said heavily.

"Okay, listen to me," Dawson said. "Sly should be in school. My wife is a teacher. Maybe we can help Sly register in a public school. We'll come back and see you in a few days."

Gamel nodded. "Yessah. Thank you."

"One other thing," Dawson added, moving in close. He put his hand on the other man's oily neck and brought his thumb around to rest on the larynx.

"If you beat the boy, I will hear about it and you'll be sorry you did it. You understand?"

Gamel nodded stiffly. "Yes, sah."

Dawson kept his hand on Gamel's neck for a moment longer before releasing him. "Good."

Dawson hurried back across the littered wasteland to the crime scene. Bright and his men were rolling the body onto a board rigged with a long rope at one edge. They returned to the bank and grabbed hold of the rope tug-o'-war style. With

Bright chanting, "One, two, three, *pull!*" they brought the body out of the muck and onto the bank.

For a moment, Dawson and the others stood staring at the corpse. It was hideously inflated with gases of putrefaction and coated with a patina of glistening lagoon slime. The face was puffed up three times normal, the chest and belly balloon-like. The smell was dizzying. Dawson choked and swallowed down nausea rising in his throat like a fountain.

Gritting his teeth, he crouched by the body, determined not to throw up. The person had no shoes, his clothes were blackened and soiled—a T-shirt, long shorts that guys in Accra wore—nothing out of the ordinary. Difficult to say how old he was, and so far, there was no indication of what exactly had killed him.

Dawson stood up, feeling ill. He looked at Bright. "Anything else, sir?"

Bright shook his head. "If you are done, we will transport the body to the Police Hospital Mortuary."

3

It was afternoon when Dawson headed home. Canvassing the Agbogbloshie neighborhood had been fruitless. If anyone had seen the dead body being dumped, they weren't saying.

Dawson turned onto the slight incline of Nim Tree Avenue. Lined on either side with fortunately clean gutters, the street ran in an east-west direction. At this time of day, Darko was riding into the sun. The sky, a pale, clean blue overhead, was bright and almost white at the horizon, making the street appear luminous.

Dawson's house at No. 10 Nim Tree was cream-colored with olive trim. The mango tree on one side had just begun to fruit. It was a tiny dwelling, yet it was still a million times better than the sorry GPS barracks where even a *chief* inspector could often afford only a single room. Policemen were not a rich bunch, and detectives were possibly the least well paid. Dawson and Christine could afford No. 10 only because their landlord was a member of her extended family. He gave them a generous discount and made up for it with his other property. That their low rent depended on family ties made Dawson a little nervous. Family and money could be a dangerous mix.

Every time he came home, Dawson felt a surge of thankfulness, like the swell of a wave. The little house was a sanctuary, armor against the wickedness of the crime he dealt with every day. A bit of a fortress too. His police sense had led him to burglarproof the house to the extreme.

Christine's red Opel, which was so small Dawson felt he could pick it up and carry it under his arm, was parked in front of the house, meaning she and Hosiah were home from the regular Sunday visit to her mother after church and Sunday school.

"I'm home!" he called out as he came in through the rear kitchen door.

"Hi, Dark."

Christine was in the sitting room on the sofa as she read the paper.

"Hi, sweetie." He kissed her on the forehead.

"Tough case?"

"Horrible. Dead man in Korle Lagoon."

Christine winced, barely a ripple on the fine sheen of her complexion.

"I need some help on something," Dawson said, sitting down beside her. Before he could get any further, Hosiah came running in and dived onto Dawson's lap.

"Hi, Daddy!"

"Hey, champ!" Darko sat his son up straight and snuggled him against his chest.

"Guess what I made," Hosiah said.

"A sports car?"

"No."

"A truck?"

"No," Hosiah said, laughing. "Come with me and I'll show

you. But you have to close your eyes first and I'll tell you when you can open them."

At his bedroom door, he said, "You can open your eyes now."

In the middle of the floor of the small bedroom was one of Hosiah's increasingly complex creations. A genius with his hands, he adroitly crafted model cars, trucks, and motorbikes out of empy cans and milk cartons, old matchboxes, bottle caps, rubber bands, and bits of cardboard. The end products were surprisingly fine toys, considering the crudity of the raw materials Hosiah worked with.

"Wow," Dawson said. "Is that a spaceship?"

"Yes." The boy held it proudly up to his father. "Look, Daddy. Here are the jets for takeoff. The pilot goes in here and he can see out of this window."

The window was a square of plastic cut out from a water bottle. Recently, Hosiah had been expanding his repertoire from land vehicles to airplanes, and now, for the first time, a spacecraft.

"So, how far can the spaceship travel?"

"Um. To the moon, I think. No, to the sun."

"Really? You know it's going to be very hot there."

Hosiah thought about that for a moment. "I'll put something on it so it doesn't burn."

Dawson watched as Hosiah constructed a "heat shield," his little round head bent in concentration. Dawson rubbed it gently. His son was seven now, suffering from congenital heart disease, yet full of a spirit that uplifted Dawson's every day.

Christine appeared at the door. "Are we still going to the park?"

Dawson looked at his watch. They would have gone earlier had he not been called out. "Yes, we can still go. Hosiah, tidy your room and then we'll go, okay?"

"Okay, Daddy."

Back in the sitting room, Dawson asked Christine, "How was he today?"

"Actually, he's done very well," she said.

"Good. So we'll play a little ball at the park but we'll take it easy."

"Right. What was it you were going to ask me?"

He told Christine about Sly and his uncle. "I want to get the boy into school."

"I'll see what I can do," she said, "but you realize, even if we get him registered, he might never go."

"I'll try to make sure that doesn't happen."

She smiled slightly.

"What's that look?" Dawson asked.

"You can't stand Uncle Gamel getting away with not sending the boy to school."

"You're right. I can't."

That night Dawson, a confirmed insomniac, lay on his back, with the blackness pressing against his eyes as he thought about their earlier excursion to the Efua Sutherland Park. It hadn't been too bad. He and Christine had played catch with Hosiah, throwing the ball as directly to his waiting hands as possible. That was better than playing soccer, where dribbling and running after the ball was more strenuous. They were walking a fine line between letting Hosiah be as active as a boy his age should be and limiting his exertions to what his heart, with its ventricular septal defect, could handle. His symptoms varied from day to day. He rationalized it as the defect changing in size. "The hole in my heart is small today, Daddy," he would say.

So far, Hosiah had never given an indication that he felt something was wrong with *him* as a whole. That was a relief for Christine and Dawson, but they knew their son's healthy adaptations, both physical and psychological, might not last forever.

His prescribed medications only patched the problem. The real solution, cardiac surgery, was staggeringly expensive. There was now a National Health Insurance Scheme, NHIS, but the very basic medical care it covered most certainly did not include heart surgery. For years, Dawson and Christine had been saving up, adding a generous contribution from an uncle of Christine's, but the target was still practically unattainable. They had applied for a personal loan at Standard Bank, Ecobank, and Barclays, but hadn't qualified at any of them. Besides, the interest rate was a horrible 21 percent.

Then, nine months ago, wonderful news had arrived. The GPS announced an official policy that it would pay all medical and surgical fees for its employees and their dependents. For a moment, Dawson's and Christine's hearts soared with the fantasy of submitting Hosiah's medical report to the police service employee financial office, which would approve the surgery. But then reality struck like a sledgehammer.

It turned out that the GPS would not prepay employees' medical or surgical expenses under any circumstances of illness, major or minor. All payments would be strictly on a reimbursement basis. That put Dawson and Christine right back at square one: they would have to finance Hosiah's operation at the Korle Bu Hospital Cardiothoracic Center and then present the receipt to the GPS. After that, there would be a long process of validating, cross-checking, and obtaining successive levels of approval, including the director general of GPS. And then, if they were lucky, they would receive the reimbursement after several months.

Another idea had come along about half a year ago. Edith Kingson, a senior clerk in the financial office at Korle Bu, had met Hosiah when Dawson once took him along to render a payment for a hospital visit. So delighted was she with the boy that she took Dawson aside and suggested he fill out a special "financial clemency petition" with an attached letter detailing Hosiah's circumstances. She would personally try to push it through, but Edith was at pains to warn Dawson she could not guarantee that anything would come of it.

She was right to have tried to keep Dawson's expectations low. In the six months since submitting the petition, he had periodically called Edith, but she had had no news for him.

Beside him, Christine normally slept so heavily that a thunderstorm would not wake her, but Dawson could tell from her breathing pattern that she wasn't in deep sleep right now. She stirred and turned over.

"Dark?"

"Yes."

"I can't sleep either."

"Surprising. For you."

Christine moved in closer, tucking her head into the hollow of his shoulder. Her skin smelled of sweet and spice. He felt the tension in her body slowly dissipate, and she drifted back to sleep long before he did.

He woke at five-thirty. Christine would surface soon. He showered and was getting dressed when his mobile rang from the bed stand. He went out to the sitting room to take the call. He knew who it was from the caller ID.

"Dr. Biney, good morning!"

"Good morning, Inspector Dawson! How are you?"

"I'm doing well. And yourself?"

"No complaints, my good man. Forgive me for calling this early, but I wanted to catch you before you start your day."

"No problem at all."

Asum Biney was a superb doctor and now one of the best of the very few forensic pathologists in the country. He was the director of the Volta River Authority Hospital in the Eastern Region, where Dawson had first met him. He gave several days of his time every month to hospitals in Accra and elsewhere, routinely starting at dawn and heading home late at night.

"To what do I owe the honor, Doctor?"

"I'm doing a few days at the Police Hospital Mortuary because one of the docs is out on sick leave. I noticed this new case you have—the fellow discovered in the Korle Lagoon?"

"Yes. It's very bad."

"Indeed, and even with refrigeration, the decay will continue. We should get to it today as soon as possible."

"Bless you, Dr. Biney. I was preparing for a nasty fight to get the case on before the end of this *week,* never mind today."

"Well, I'm glad I could save you the agony. I'll have the staff put it on for eight this morning."

"I'll be there."

Dawson went to Hosiah's room, where Christine was getting him up.

"I have to go." He kissed them both. "See you tonight."

"Bye, Daddy."

"Careful, Dark." Christine said that every day. She meant it.

"I will be."

4

The phlegmatic Sergeant Baidoo, a man of few words and Dawson's favorite CID driver, steered the made-in-India Tata police jeep over the rough, unpaved road that led to the Police Hospital Mortuary (PHM). It was a depressing gray stucco building browned off with decades of dust. It needed to be either remodeled and expanded or razed and rebuilt. Dawson liked the second alternative.

Baidoo parked under the flowering flame tree that lent a welcome patch of color to all that dreariness. Reception was to Dawson's left as he went in. Straight ahead against the far wall were two old coffins piled one on top of the other. They had been there for years, part of the furniture now. He turned left to reception, where there was a sign on the wall that read JESUS CHRIST DIED FOR YOUR SINS. On seeing Dawson, the young lance corporal at the desk behind the counter sprang to his feet.

"Morning, massa," he said, using the alternative word to "sir." Maybe it was a legacy of the British colonial police service, when black officers referred to the white officers as their "masters," but now *massa* was comfortably used by the junior ranks to address their superiors.

"Morning, Brempong," Dawson said. "How are you?"

"Fine, massa."

"Is Dr. Biney in?"

"Yes, massa. He's inside."

"Thank you."

"Yessah."

Dawson went through the double-door entry labeled STRICTLY OUT OF BOUNDS. With no forewarning, the autopsy room was directly behind that, which had caught Dawson off guard the first time he had come to PHM. There were only two autopsy tables for a backlog of corpses possibly a hundred times that. Four mortuary attendants were in constant motion, like traffic at a busy intersection. Dr. Biney was at the right-hand table. He was masked, but when he looked up and saw Dawson, his eyes crinkled at the corners with his smile.

"Inspector Dawson! Welcome."

"Thank you, Dr. Biney, it's good to see you."

"I'm just finishing up with this case, and we'll do yours next. Would you like to suit up while we get your case ready?"

Dawson branched left to the changing room, where he gladly put on the most important item, his mask. The gown went on second. He took a breath before returning to the autopsy room proper. The odor in the room was subtler and less assaulting than that of, say, Korle Lagoon, but it was oddly more penetrating, as if it got under one's skin.

Between Dr. Biney and his attendants, it was a frenetic but coordinated dance. On finishing their case on the left-hand table, two attendants dumped the organs back into the body and transferred it to a gurney. As they wheeled it out, a new case was being wheeled in. Simultaneously, on the second table, one attendant was readying the next case for Dr. Biney with a vertical incision from neck to pelvis. No matter how many times Dawson had been here, he had never grown completely accustomed to the matter-of-factness with which the team worked, and he still flinched inwardly at the harsh bang of bodies on the gurney metal. Relax, he kept telling himself. *They don't feel anything.*

As they waited for his case, Dawson chatted with Dr. Biney—not empty pleasantries: the two men were always genuinely glad to see each other.

"Here we go," Biney said, as Dawson's case was wheeled in. "Ready?"

The body had been washed in the adjoining room, so it looked a trifle better than it had the day before, but the amount of decay was just as severe and the smell was no less sickening. The top layer of skin was blistering and sloughing off, revealing a curiously white layer underneath. The abdomen was extremely distended, rounded like a cathedral dome.

"The putrefaction hasn't stopped completely," Biney said, catching Dawson's look. "Biology will do what it wants, refrigeration be damned."

Dawson grimaced, trying not to gag. "This one is hard to take."

"Yes, it is. Has your investigation turned up anything so far?"

"Nothing. We have no idea who he is."

Dr. Biney turned to George, a wizened veteran of PHM and the most experienced of the mortuary attendants. "Did you see anything of interest while washing the body?"

"Please, yes, Doctor," George said deferentially. "First thing we noticed was this."

He held up the corpse's right hand.

"Curious," Dr. Biney said, stepping in to examine it. "The thumb and all fingers except the index are hacked off."

"Fresh wounds?" Dawson asked.

"Very likely. At or around the time of death."

Dr. Biney looked at Dawson, who turned the corners of his mouth down. "I have no idea what it means."

"Neither do I," Dr. Biney said. "Anything else, George?"

"Yes, Doctor," he said, lifting the corpse's bloated top lip.

"Missing upper right cuspid," Dr. Biney said. He peered closer. "Looks like the whole tooth is out, not just broken off. I can't tell how long it's been missing, though. I'll make a note of it on my report. Was that all, George?"

"Please, yes, Doctor."

"Carry on, then."

As George began the incision, Dr. Biney turned to the counter next to the sink. "We have his clothing over here, Inspector. By the way, get ready for the release of gases from the body. It won't be pleasant."

The clothes were dry now—a worn T-shirt and long shorts with a safety pin at the waist where buttons should have been.

"Look at this," Biney said, carefully spreading the T-shirt out with the back facing up. "Here on the right side, a hole, slightly rectangular, and some staining around it—presumably blood."

"Stab wound?" Dawson said.

"Ah, you're always sharp, Inspector," Biney said. "Stab wound is exactly what I'm surmising."

Dawson coughed and choked as Biney's warning about the abdominal gases materialized. Even the hardened George muttered an exclamation.

"Not for the faint of heart," Biney said, returning to the autopsy table. Dawson followed after a moment's hesitation.

"So what I can tell you at this point," Biney said, as George began removing the chest plate, "is that he was fifteen to seventeen years old."

"Fifteen to seventeen?" Dawson echoed, shocked. "Oh, that changes the whole picture. He's a boy, really. I thought he was much older."

"The decomposition lends that impression, but on the bone survey with our brand-new, secondhand X-ray machine, courtesy of the government of Denmark, I see nice young bones, and the epiphyses still open, so he probably had another couple of inches at least to grow."

"Doctor," George said, peering into the boy's chest cavity. "Look at this."

Biney joined him. "Goodness. Massive hemothorax. The right lung is practically swimming in blood. Suction it out, would you, George? Inspector, you'll want to see this."

Dawson watched as Biney removed the right lung.

"There's a laceration on the posterior surface associated with severe disruption of the lung tissue," he said. As Biney explored, the other attendants gathered to look on with interest.

After a minute or so, Biney said, "It's a deep laceration, far into the tissue of the lung. Let's examine the right posterior chest cavity. George, would you wash it out, please?"

After a couple of rinses, Biney could get a better look.

"The muscles of the fifth intercostal space are disrupted, and here you can see splintering of the sixth rib, where the weapon struck it with considerable force on the way in. Turn the body on its left side, please?"

The attendants did so, holding the corpse steady as Dr. Biney examined the back.

"Because of swelling and decay, it's hard to spot it at first, but here is the external wound corresponding to the internal injury. See that, Inspector?"

"I do."

"In turn, the external wound matches the tear in the victim's shirt where the knife struck. I estimate that the blade was six to eight inches long."

"Vicious," Dawson murmured.

"Yes, indeed. Stab wound to the back resulting in perforation of the right lung, massive hemothorax, and death."

"Time of death?"

"I hesitate to assign a specific number, but remember this: the body was lying in a warm, wet environment saturated with bacteria. Under such conditions, this degree of putrefaction could have developed in just hours."

Dawson stared at the murdered boy's face. "I don't know how we're going to identify him. He would be unrecognizable even to someone who knew him. The missing tooth might help, though."

"Or a forensic artist," Dr. Biney said. He chuckled ironically. "I'm just dreaming."

Dawson smiled. There was no such thing as a forensic artist in Ghana.

As they washed their hands, Dr. Biney said, "Inspector, I believe you have your work cut out for you."

"Doctor, I believe you are right."

5

Dawson ducked into Papaye for a quick lunch—piping hot rice and chicken washed down with ice-cold Malta, the soft drink he loved. If he were on death row, he would choose Malta as his last meal—oversweet, fizzy, rich with malt and hops. While he was waiting for his meal to be brought to the table, he phoned Chikata to tell him about the autopsy.

"It will be tough finding out who this guy is," the detective sergeant said.

"I know, but we have to keep trying," Dawson replied. "Get two detective constables, go down to Agbogbloshie, and ask around for a missing boy of about seventeen, about five-six in height with a missing upper right tooth."

"*Ewurade.* You're sending me back to that stinking place."

"Wear a mask."

"These people are just not going to talk, Dawson."

"You never know. Miracles happen."

"But not in Accra," Chikata said with a derisive snort.

"Get to work and stop complaining," Dawson said, ending the call.

Chikata was a spoiled brat. He could be lazy as well. His uncle, Theophilus Lartey, was chief superintendent of police, or *chief supol*. That made him a senior officer and Dawson's superior. Chikata thought that gave him the right to take liberties. In truth, it was nepotism that had got him into CID's Homicide Division with Dawson, and it might well be nepotism that got him promoted.

Dawson was on his last gulp of Malta and considering having some more when his phone rang.

"Dawson," he answered.

"Inspector! How are you?"

"I'm fine, Wisdom."

Dawson knew the voice well. It was thin and brittle, like snapping plantain chips in one's fingers. Wisdom Asamoah was one of the *Daily Graphic*'s leading reporters. He and Dawson had a long history together, sometimes at each other's throats.

" I want to know about the man in the lagoon," Wisdom said.

"How did you hear about it?"

"I have eyes and ears everywhere, Dawson."

"We have a Public Relations Office for press inquiries, remember? Call them."

"Come on, Dawson. PRO is too slow for me. By the time they get me the information I need, I'll be in the afterlife."

"I can give you something, but you can't use my name."

"You know you can trust me, Dawson."

"We don't know who the victim is yet, but it's a homicide—"

"How was he killed? Drowned?"

"Not drowned."

"How, then?"

"Not drowned."

"Okay. You're not saying. How old a person?"

"Estimated sixteen or seventeen."

"Oh, so a teenager, eh? Dr. Asum Biney did the autopsy?"

"Yes."

"No witness accounts of any kind?"

"No, nothing."

"When are you going to release photos?"

"We can't. Too much decomposition."

"Ah. You need a forensic artist."

Dawson was surprised. "How do you know about that?"

"I watch *Forensic Files,*" Wisdom said with a laugh.

"Well, this is Ghana. We don't have most of that fancy American stuff you see on TV."

"Can I make you an offer, Inspector Dawson?"

"What kind of offer?"

"What if I get hold of a forensic artist, you release the victim's autopsy photos to me, I forward them to him and have him draw a likeness of the victim? You would get that back so you can use it for police purposes, and I would get it to publish it in the *Graphic.*"

"How would you find a forensic artist?" Dawson asked suspiciously.

"I know one—Yves Kirezi. I met him years ago when I covered the Rwanda genocide. He's helped identify thousands of genocide victims by re-creating their appearance after they had been beaten beyond recognition, so you know he has to be good at what he does."

"Are you sure he would be willing to do this?"

"We are good friends, Inspector Dawson. That's what I'm trying to tell you."

"All right, then. Let me know if and when you reach him. Thank you, Wisdom."

Dawson needed to visit the pump station belonging to KLERP, the Korle Lagoon Ecological Restoration Project. It stood on the west bank of the upper lagoon, directly opposite Agbogbloshie on the east. You couldn't talk about Agbogbloshie and its cursed waterways without bringing in KLERP. It had been around for ten years or more, and was part and parcel of the saga of a troubled slum that just would not go away.

By twisting the arm of one of the other investigators, Dawson managed to snag Baidoo and the only Tata jeep immediately available out of the two assigned to the Homicide Division. Otherwise, Dawson would have had to wait hours before the other vehicle returned from whatever mission it was on.

Traffic was heavy along High Street. As Baidoo inched forward with unflappable patience, Dawson's phone rang. He felt a surge of both dread and anticipation as he saw it was Edith Kingson calling. This might be it.

"Edith, how are you?" he said sweetly.

"I'm very well, thank you, Darko." Her voice was as clear and sparkling as crystal, but now she hesitated slightly and his heart sank.

"It's not good news, is it?" he said.

"No," she replied sadly. "I'm so sorry. They turned it down. They said your financial situation was not dire enough to justify clemency. I tried to argue on the basis of Hosiah's bad medical situation and the kind of future he was facing. I argued until Director Hanson even got annoyed with me."

Dawson felt as though a ten-story building had just collapsed and crushed him. His breath left him, and for a moment his vision darkened and he couldn't speak.

"Darko?"

"Yes," he said hoarsely. "I'm here."

"Again, I'm terribly sorry. If you like, you can always re-submit the petition and I will try once more for you."

"Thank you, Edith," he said softly. "For all your help. I appreciate it."

He pocketed his phone and stared despondently out the window. Traffic had begun to clear as they passed James Fort toward Cleland Road. Agbogbloshie was in the distance to their right; the beach was visible on their left. Ahead, new road construction was raising a cloud of dust. Underneath the section of Cleland that became the Winneba Bridge, the sea met the Korle Lagoon with spectacular and sometimes violent churning, like two opposing cultures forced to mix. Dawson kept his head firmly turned away so that Baidoo wouldn't see his tears welling up.

They turned right on Ring Road West. About half a mile up, Baidoo pulled into KLERP's yard, where two small, one-story office buildings stood, one of them a trailer. A black 4 x 4 with darkened windows was leaving about the same time.

"Wait for me," Dawson told Baidoo, hopping out.

The merciless noon sun was almost directly overhead, and the asphalt underfoot felt like it was on fire. Dawson walked up the steps to the trailer and knocked on the first door. He heard a faint "Come in." He pushed the door open. It was a small office chilled to Arctic temperatures by a gale-force air conditioner. A doe-eyed woman with vermilion lipstick and an expensive hair weave was sitting at the only desk in the room.

"Good morning," Dawson said.

"Good morning. You are welcome."

Dawson explained who he was and the reason for the visit.

"Please have a seat," Doe Eyes said. "I will see if the director is available."

She left the room. Dawson sat down on a chair to the side, looking around while tapping his foot on the hollow-sounding floor. Pasted on the wall were pictures of the top KLERP executives, two of whom were Europeans.

Doe Eyes came back. "Please, the director has just left."

Dawson guessed it had been the said director in the 4 x 4.

"Can I speak to someone else?" he asked her.

She hesitated. "Please, one moment."

She disappeared again, returning two minutes later. "Please, come with me."

Dawson accompanied her outside to the trailer's third door. He waited again as she went inside, certain that at least one step in this process could have been eliminated. The door opened, and Doe Eyes said Dawson could come in. She held the door for him and then she left.

This room was even more frigid than the first. At one of the two desks was a young man in a tie working at his laptop. He stood up.

"Good afternoon, sir."

"Afternoon. Darko Dawson, CID."

"Cuthbert Plange," the man said, shaking hands. "I'm in charge of client relations here. Please, have a seat."

"Thank you," Dawson said, choosing the closest chair. "I'm investigating the death of a boy found in one of the Agbogbloshie channels yesterday."

"Ewurade," Cuthbert said, shaking his head and sitting back down. He had full lips and thick speech, like a cotton-stuffed pillow. "This Agbogbloshie. You never know what can happen next. How did the boy get there?"

"That's what we're trying to find out. You have a good view of the lagoon from here. Was anyone here early Sunday morning?"

Cuthbert shook his head. "Not at all, sir. We close the station down Saturday evening around six, lock the gates, and open up again Monday morning. Sundays are sacred."

"Church wins every time," Dawson commented.

"Oh, yes." Cuthbert smiled. "Have you ever visited our plant before, Mr. Dawson?"

"No, I haven't."

Cuthbert stood up. "Then come along. I'm happy to show you around. We'll go to the pump station first."

After they had been in the air-conditioned office, the heat outside hit them like a cricket bat. They walked across the parking area down east of the second building and around the corner. The whir of the pump and the powerful swish of water got louder, and the sewage smell became stronger. Cuthbert led the way to the base of the pump. Towering above them in a brick housing was a huge, spinning piece of machinery that looked like a giant corkscrew.

"It's called an Archimedes' screw," Cuthbert told Dawson, raising his voice above the din. "It may not seem that its turning action could pump water up, but it does—at a good two cubic meters per second from the base to the top of the tower."

They climbed a platform beyond the pump for a panoramic view of the surroundings.

"Where was the boy found?" Cuthbert asked.

"That's what I'm trying to figure out," Dawson said, frowning. "I was on the Agbogbloshie side of the canal yesterday. Everything looks different from this angle."

"Let me help you get your bearings, then, sir." Cuthbert

looked south. "The outlet of the lagoon to the sea underneath the Winneba Bridge is over there—where you just came from. That's a mangrove island you see in the middle of the lagoon."

He turned the opposite direction now.

"The Odaw River comes from several miles north. Once it crosses Abossey Okai Road, it becomes Korle Canal, which is the only portion we can see from here because of the way it curves out of sight. Agbogbloshie, where you were yesterday, is on the opposite bank from us."

Dawson gazed across at the landscape of trash and wooden shacks seen through the haze of smoke from the burning copper wire.

"Some people don't even realize we have a river in Accra," Cuthbert continued. "At any rate, the poor Odaw has become part of Accra's open sewer. Garbage, human waste, domestic waste, factory waste—you name it, they dump it, and after it's accumulated all that nastiness, it arrives here."

"Not pretty," Dawson said. "There must be, what, millions of plastic water bottles and water bags in there."

"Not to mention toxic waste and chemicals. We have two excavators to take out as much of the solid waste as possible as it arrives, but it's tough to keep up."

"What's that dam that goes from this side to the other bank?" Dawson asked, indicating the broad, partitioned concrete wall spanning the canal.

"That's the interceptor. It stops solids from getting into the lagoon. It also has twenty flap gates to regulate water levels during flood season."

In front of the interceptor, a boom lay across the breadth of the lagoon to help trap floating material. At the boom, the garbage was so dense it looked like a solid mass. Egrets, light enough to stand on it, pecked around for morsels. *What food could they possibly find in there?*

"Now, look carefully, Inspector, sir," Cuthbert said. "Slightly upstream from the interceptor, you can make out the Agbogbloshie Canal as it joins the Korle Canal. It's difficult to spot because it's so much smaller than the Korle Canal."

"I see it now," Dawson said. "And that's where the body was found."

"Aha. Now you've got your bearings."

Because the Agbogbloshie Canal was upstream from the interceptor, Dawson now saw that the dead body could not have got there if it had been dumped in the sea or even the lagoon. Even if an extremely high tide had washed the corpse in, the interceptor would have done exactly that: intercepted the body before it got to the Agbogbloshie Canal. Which brought up the next logical question.

"Could the body have floated down the Odaw River into the Korle Canal and then the Agbogbloshie Canal?" Dawson asked.

"I doubt it, sir," Cuthbert said, shaking his head. "More likely it would have ended up at the boom with all the rest of the floating debris. Maybe, just maybe, that could happen if there was an extreme flood situation, but that hasn't occurred recently."

"So the body had to have been dumped right where it was found."

"Yes, sir."

Dawson turned and gazed as far as he could see down the lagoon. "It could be a beautiful place. But then there's that." He gestured toward Agbogbloshie. "Seriously, Mr. Plange, what are we going to do about it?"

"The government is moving all these squatters out."

Dawson was incredulous. "Moving them out? To where?"

"To a place outside of the city. Everything. The yam market, the timber market, everything going."

"I'll believe it when I see it."

Cuthbert looked intently at Dawson. "I understand your skepticism, Inspector, and I've heard it a lot. Many people say to me, 'Aren't you just wasting your time dredging this place when trash is being dumped faster than you can remove it?' But my answer is, Can we really afford not to try? One day in the future when I'm old and gray, I'll come down here and look at the beautiful, clear water of the lagoon where people are fishing, swimming, and sailing, and I'll feel thankful and proud that we never gave up."

6

The sky opened up that evening and dumped a torrent on the city. Just in time, Dawson cleared out the channels he had constructed to divert rainwater from the house.

With the first jagged flash of lightning, electric power went out on Dawson's block and in the entire area between Awudome Circle and Kaneshie Market. It was lantern time. Dawson and Christine had decided to have *kenkey* with fish, the latter prepared by Christine without salt because of Hosiah's dietary restrictions. They went traditional, using their fingers to eat from one large common bowl. It was a social and intimate way to take a meal, even more fitting by lantern light.

"This is all it takes to make me happy," Dawson said between mouthfuls. "Kenkey and fish. And Malta."

"The way you love kenkey, you'd think you were a Ga," Christine said.

The Ga, Accra's original people, had a legendary love of kenkey, but Dawson was half Ewe and half Fante. Nevertheless, he was fluent in Ga, as well as Ewe, Fante, and Twi, which took care of most of the lower half of Ghana. He had only a rudimentary knowledge of Hausa, one of the major languages spoken in the north.

As they talked, Dawson was putting up a cheerful front, but a lump formed in his throat every time Edith's words from earlier that day came back to him. *I'm so sorry. They turned it down.*

When was he going to tell Christine? Tonight?

Hosiah let out a cheer as the lights suddenly came back on. While Christine washed dishes, Dawson took him to have his bath in preparation for bed.

As Dawson was toweling him dry, Hosiah asked, "Daddy, if the hole in my heart gets bigger and bigger, will I stop growing?"

"No, that won't stop you from growing."

"I want to be big and tall like you."

"You will. Probably even taller."

He was thrilled. "*Really?*"

"Mm-hm. Your ears dry?"

Hosiah checked. "Yes."

"No little tadpoles inside?"

Hosiah cackled as he went to brush his teeth. *I want to be big and tall like you.* What if he never made it? Dawson turned away, pretending to fuss with the towels. His forehead was furrowed and his lips tight as he gulped his emotions down.

"Daddy?"

"Yes, champ?" Dawson's voice wobbled just a bit.

"Do you catch a lot of bad people?"

"I try to." He came to the boy's side. "Don't forget your back teeth."

Hosiah said something unintelligible through toothpaste foam.

"Finish brushing first," Dawson said.

When Hosiah was toothpaste free, he asked his question again. "What happens to the bad people when you catch them?"

"We send them to jail for a while, and then one day they go before a judge and he decides if they were really bad and need to go to prison."

"Oh."

"Come on. Story time."

On the way to the bedroom, Hosiah asked, "How come when I'm bad I don't get a judge too?"

"You know why?"

"Why?"

Dawson suddenly swept Hosiah up onto one shoulder, and the boy shrieked with laughter.

"You know why?"

"Why?" Hosiah shouted.

"Because I'm the judge too."

Dawson delivered him to bed in a giggling bundle. Hosiah cuddled against him as he read, for probably the one thousandth time, an Ananse the Spider story.

"Was that good?"

"Yes."

"Okay. Lights out. Mammy will come up in a minute."

He kissed Hosiah twice.

In their own bedroom as they got ready to turn in, Dawson asked Christine, "Can we go to Agbogbloshie together tomorrow afternoon to see what we can do about getting Sly into school?"

"Sure, if you like." She got into bed. "Oh, wait a minute. I have to pick Hosiah up early from school. They have a half day."

"What about your friend? She can't take him for the afternoon?"

"No, she's busy." Hesitation. "The only alternative is for Mama to watch Hosiah till we get back."

Dawson got into bed as well but didn't respond.

"Dark," she pleaded. "You can't punish her anymore."

Almost a year ago, Dawson's mother-in-law, Gifty, had taken Hosiah to see a traditional healer to "cure" the boy's heart ailment. She had done this without the consent of either Dawson or Christine. In the process of the healer's "cleansing ritual," Hosiah was accidentally struck on the head, opening a gash in his scalp. Dawson had never forgiven Gifty.

"Look," he said, "it's not as if she hasn't been able to see Hosiah at all."

"But that's strictly my taking him over to visit her together. You don't want me to leave him there alone with her. You know she loves having him for the day. This is killing her."

Dawson blew his breath out. "All right," he said resignedly, "maybe I'm being too hard on her. You can drop Hosiah off at her house tomorrow."

"And from now on she can babysit him when needed?"

"Yes, I suppose so."

Christine gave him a big kiss on the cheek. "Thank you, sweetheart. She's going to be thrilled."

Like a lightning bolt, a thought flashed through Dawson's mind and made him cringe. *What if my mother-in-law outlives Hosiah?*

"What's the matter?" Christine asked him at once. "What was that look?"

He brought her closer.

"Dark, what's wrong?"

"Edith called me today," he said.

"I see." Christine became very still. "So they turned the petition down."

Dawson nodded.

They both stayed silent for some time.

"What are we going to do?" she asked, sounding empty.

"It's not the end of the road," Dawson said. "There's always something around the corner."

Christine sat up, suddenly angry. "We're not going to sit around and let our son die." Her voice cracked. "This stupid government that does nothing but steal our money. They think we're going to let him die just because of them?"

She jumped out of bed, eyes blazing.

"Christine—"

"Idiot bureaucrats at the hospital with no soul," she said, her voice trembling. "Just because of them?"

Dawson scrambled up himself and hurried around to her side of the bed.

"And yes," she continued in fury, "that incompetent Ghana Police Service you work for. Do they want us to let him die?"

She began to weep, her lacerated cries wrenched from her throat. Dawson put his arms around her, but she struggled to pull away. He held her firmly and wouldn't let go.

"I'm with you, Christine," he said. "You have to remember that. I'm with you. And I won't let you or Hosiah down. Ever."

At last her body relaxed and molded into his, and she cried until her energy was spent.

7

After the overnight rain, the roads were in no condition for Dawson's motorbike, so he took a cab to work. The commute was a nightmare. Several intersections and whole segments of streets were flooded, a reflection of the sorry state of Accra's drainage system. Traffic was at a standstill in every direction. Taxi drivers, including Dawson's, were being their usual aggressive selves, which didn't help people's tempers any.

His phone rang.

"Morning, Wisdom."

"Good morning, Inspector. Where are you?"

"Stuck at Nkrumah Circle."

Wisdom grunted. "Best of luck. I spoke to Yves last night. He says he'll do it for us."

"Okay. When do you need the photo?"

"Today. Can you send me a high-quality scan?"

"Scan! We hardly have any computers at CID and you're talking about scanners?"

"The whole CID, not a single scanner? I don't believe it."

"Since it troubles you so much, why not buy one for us?" Wisdom chortled.

"I can photocopy it for you," Dawson said. "That's the best I can do."

"Why can't I get the original?"

"Release an original photo to you from police files? I don't think so, my friend."

"Okay, okay. So where can I pick up the copy?"

"I'm going to Agbogbloshie later today. I can meet you on the way there, say in front of the Ghana Customs building. I'll call you before I leave."

Chikata was even later to work than Dawson was.

"Ah, this Accra flooding," he said with disgust as he sat down next to his boss at a worn, pockmarked desk. "Anyway, good morning, Dawson."

"Morning, Chikata."

They shared a large, open office with nine other detectives ranging in rank from constable to inspector. When Dawson got to be *chief* inspector, he would move to a more exclusive room somewhere. For now, this old and bare room on the seventh floor of the CID building was the home base Dawson and his colleagues loved to hate. The air-conditioning consisted of louvered windows, which on one side of the room provided a view of the car park below and on the opposite side opened to the outside corridor.

The noisy office was as busy as an ant colony. Some detectives were taking reports from witnesses or crime victims. Others streamed in and out through the always open door. There was also a good deal of aimless chatter that all the investigators had learned to tune out as they conducted interviews.

"Any leads from yesterday in Agbogbloshie?" Dawson asked.

Chikata shook his head. "I took two constables with me. We spread out and asked as many people as we could, about a hundred and fifty in total. But nothing."

"A hundred and fifty? Not bad. And no one knew of a missing young man of the description you gave?"

"No one was even interested."

"Maybe people will care more when we circulate a forensic artist's sketch."

Chikata was surprised. "Since when do we have a forensic artist?"

"*We* don't, but Wisdom Asamoah found one for me."

Chikata pulled a face. "That nosy guy."

"Ah, but it's the same nosiness as ours," Dawson said with a shrug, "and as long as we're getting something out of it, I don't care."

Around four, Dawson flagged a taxi down to make the trip to Agbogbloshie via his meeting place with Wisdom at the customs building. He called Wisdom to let him know he was on his way. The taxi crawled along Independence Avenue while captive traffic was swamped by hawkers trying to peddle plantain chips, apples, world maps, DVDs, books, tools, belts, and even three bewildered little puppies. While the taxi was stationary, Dawson beckoned to a vendor and bought a bag of iced water—the same item responsible for much of the scourge in the Korle Lagoon.

Dawson's phone rang. The caller ID said DARAMANI. He hesitated before answering. Daramani, who came from arid northern Ghana, had been a petty thief and marijuana dealer Dawson had arrested years ago. He was considerably rehabilitated now, holding down a job and not stealing.

When Dawson had first raided Daramani's place in Nima, he had found a marijuana stash of exceptional quality. Possession and use was illegal in Ghana. It also happened to be Dawson's Achilles' heel. He disliked alcohol, but wee was almost impossible for him to resist. Standing in Daramani's ragged living quarters, Dawson was the arsonist in a tinderbox or the child molester in a nursery school. He did what he should never have done and took some of the marijuana for himself.

For a while after Daramani had served time, he became an informant of sorts. That was the ostensible reason that Dawson kept in touch with the thief, but the marijuana was the real attraction.

"Hello, Daramani," he said into the phone.

"*Ei,* Dawson, why you no visit me these days?"

"You know why."

"Because of the wee?"

"Yes. I don't want to smell it or even be anywhere near it."

"*Ao,* Dawson, my brodda," Daramani said regretfully. "So no more?"

"No more. I've given it up."

"I see. Anyway, how are you?"

"Fine."

"And your wife and your boy?"

"They're fine too. You still have your job in Maamobi?"

"Yes, but life make too hard for Ghana nowadays."

"I know, but don't go back to your old habits."

"No, not at all."

They said good-bye and Dawson pocketed his phone. He had an odd fondness for Daramani, yet the man and his marijuana were a compartment of Dawson's life that he couldn't share with the people in his work or home life. That was why he wanted to leave it behind and kick the habit. Five months. Still clean. Still vulnerable.

The Ghana Customs, Excise and Preventive Service Building was a good meeting place. One couldn't miss the red-roofed, sky blue structure against Jamestown's mostly cream and brown. A few meters away on the same side of the street, the rusty Jamestown post office seemed like a sad, neglected child.

Wisdom was late. Dawson let the cab go and sought shade on the covered veranda of the customs building until the reporter showed up. When Wisdom arrived he parked with two wheels of his *Graphic* car up on the sidewalk and hopped out.

"Inspector, *εte sεn*?" he greeted in Twi as they shook hands.

"*Eyε.* And you?"

Wisdom had one of the largest heads Dawson had ever seen, with a wide gap between the eyes. All that brain taking up space, Dawson supposed.

"So, you have something for me?" the newspaperman said.

Dawson handed him an envelope. Wisdom peered into it as if something might jump out at him, and then he withdrew the autopsy photocopies.

"*Ei!*" he exclaimed, wincing. "My God. This is serious."

"I hope your Yves can work on it soon."

"He will. Trust me, he's a good man."

"Thank you for the help, Wisdom. I need to get to Agbog-bloshie. Can you give me a lift?"

"But of course, Inspector."

Walking alongside Christine in Agbogbloshie, Dawson could not help thinking that this was not such a good idea. It wasn't just the mud, it was the sewage spread and garbage

scattered everywhere after having been flooded out of rudimentary gutters.

"You remember the way?" Christine asked him, going
around a puddle.

"Yes."

"I'm glad. Because I'd be lost by now."

Glancing at her with a smile, Dawson thought his wife
looked like a bright jewel in a pigsty here in Sodom and Gomorrah. She had brought some papers to be filled out to start
the process of getting Sly into a school.

A few more twists and turns, and they arrived at Gamel
and Sly's hovel. Dawson knocked, praying they were still
there.

A young woman with heavy black eyeliner opened the
door and peered out. "Yes?"

"Is Gamel here?" Dawson asked.

"You say what?"

"Gamel. Is he here?"

She was puzzled. "Please, no Gamel here."

Dawson's heart sank.

"What about a small boy called Sly?"

She shook her head.

A thirtyish man with massive shoulders was sitting on an
upturned crate a few meters away. "They have gone," he said,
without much interest.

Dawson turned to him. "Gone to where?"

The man shrugged. "I dunno."

Dawson blew out his breath like a deflating balloon. He
looked at Christine.

"Sorry, Dark," she said sympathetically.

"I had a funny feeling they might not be here," he said, re-
signed. "Oh, well. I tried."

"You did," Christine said. "That's what matters."

But as they walked away, Dawson made a mental note: what mattered even more was that he continue to try. He would keep looking for Sly. Something about the boy had struck a chord.

8

Over the next three days, there were no leads. Dr. Biney's official report didn't add anything to what Dawson already knew from attending the autopsy. It would take ages to get back the test results from Korle Bu Hospital's new DNA center, which was of limited capacity. Many of its samples still had to be sent out for analysis in South African labs and at the University of Southern California—a costly and time-consuming exercise.

Dawson, preoccupied over Hosiah, felt out of sorts, as if he might be heading into a blue mood. But it was Friday, and the prospect of the weekend brightened him somewhat.

Saturday, Dawson, Christine, and Hosiah visited friends in Lartebiokorshie. They had a son of around Hosiah's age, so he had someone to play with while the adults talked. As they chatted on the veranda of the house, Dawson's phone rang.

"Yes, Wisdom?"

"Dawson, Yves just sent me his rendition of the boy. You wouldn't believe how fine it is."

"Have you emailed it to me?"

"Yes, I have. And my boss wants it in the paper as soon as possible, so you'll see the article tomorrow."

"Okay, no problem." Before he hung up, Dawson said, "Thank you, eh?"

"Who was that?" Christine asked.

"I'm afraid I have to leave," Dawson said. "Something new on the case has come in."

"You really have to go right now?"

"Yes, I apologize."

Christine didn't look happy.

The email was waiting for Dawson on his laptop at home. He had bought the slightly used computer in multiple payments for a total of GHC450, which was a good bargain.

"Oh," he said under his breath as he saw the images. "Outstanding."

Yves Kirezi had created two black-and-white images, one showing the lagoon boy with a serious expression, the other showing him smiling to reveal the right upper missing canine tooth. "LB"'s eyes were deep and energetic. His face was open and generous, the kind that makes people want to approach and chat. How had Yves captured that?

Dawson sent a reply to Wisdom thanking both him and Kirezi. He got on the phone to Chikata.

"Meet me in Agbogbloshie in two hours."

Chikata almost choked. "What?"

"We have the sketch. I want to start showing it around."

"Ah, Dawson. Sir. *Today?*"

"We've lost a week already. No more time to waste."

"I know, but . . ."

"Are you drunk?"

"No."

"Good. So see you in two hours."

Dawson had a couple things to get done in those two hours. First he bought the cheapest possible ream of paper from a small store near Central Post Office. Next, laptop slung over his shoulder, he hotfooted it to Salaga Internet to print LB's image and get a hundred copies made. At Salaga, bringing in his own paper dropped the price drastically, knowing the owner dropped it even more, which was a good thing, because Dawson was perilously low on cash. No one else in CID would spend his or her hard-earned wages on any part of an investigation in such a personal way. Dawson was either a saint or a fool. His colleagues would vote the latter.

Have you ever seen anyone, or do you know anyone, who looks like this boy?

That was the standard question Dawson and Chikata asked as they handed out the lagoon boy flyers. They split up, Chikata venturing into Agbogbloshie Market east of Abossey Okai Road to canvass the always-observant market women, while Dawson took Agbogbloshie west of the street.

He came across a group of six teenage boys languishing by a defunct kiosk in front of a puddle of water. Dawson greeted them as they sized him up. The biggest one stood. Introducing himself, Dawson shook hands. The boy's name was Abdel, a name typical of northern Ghana. Chances were his native tongue was Hausa.

"Do you speak Twi?" he asked Abdel hopefully.

"Yes."

Dawson handed him a flyer. "Do you know this boy?"

His companions crowded round the picture, leaning

against one another with the casual intimacy of pals. There was an avid discussion in Hausa. Dawson understood snatches of it.

"We don't know him," Abdel said finally.

"But Abdel, my friend," Dawson said, "I heard some of you say you might have seen him before."

Abdel was surprised. "Do you hear our language?" he asked in Hausa.

"A little bit," Dawson replied in kind.

The boys all smiled at him instantly, appreciating his effort.

"Why are you looking for him?" Abdel asked, returning to Twi for Dawson's benefit.

"I'm not. He's dead. I'm trying to find out who he is."

Abdel translated again for his friends. They got shifty-eyed and uneasy, and one of them muttered "Police." They were suspicious of Dawson, and even if one or more of them might have recognized the lagoon boy, their instincts were telling them that this was trouble.

"Okay," Dawson said lightly, giving them a few more flyers. "Please ask some of your other friends, or your families, if they know this boy. If you hear something about this, please try to call the number there."

He thanked them. *"Nagode."*

But as he walked away, Dawson felt it was a lost cause. There was no chance these kids would call him. He prayed Chikata was having better luck.

9

Chikata hadn't done any better. People were either evasive or just not that interested. He and Dawson called it a day.

Monday morning, Dawson was cautiously hopeful that things would begin to move in the right direction. LB's image would be ready for the evening TV news broadcast. Dawson saw to it that the picture went up in all the waiting areas of the CID building, alongside the other Wanted and Missing Person posters.

Last night, he had read Wisdom's well-crafted *Sunday Graphic* feature entitled DEATH IN THE LAGOON: IS THIS WHAT IT WILL TAKE? Rather than just reporting LB's death as a crime, Wisdom had made it a sociological study of Korle Lagoon and its surrounding areas.

By Tuesday, Dawson was praying for some kind of lead—anything at all. By Wednesday he was telling himself to settle down to reality. Things never happen as quickly as one would like. It could be months before they got any leads. The case could go cold too. The piles of folders and papers on his desk were a reminder of that.

After lunch on Wednesday, just as it was beginning to seem like another routine day, Constable Simon, who worked on the second floor, came up to Dawson's desk.

"Please, massa, can you come? We have a problem downstairs."

"What is it?" Dawson asked, getting up.

"A certain girl came asking for you," Simon said, "but there's something wrong with her. While she was waiting, she just collapsed on the ground and started to cry."

Chikata stood up as well. He and Dawson followed Simon out the door and down the narrow stairs to reception on the second floor, a relatively open area at the intersection of the three wings of the sand-colored building. The two receptionists and a growing crowd of people were standing around a scrawny teenage girl, who was on the floor weeping.

Crouched beside the girl was a stout young woman imploring her in Twi, "Akosua, please, get up. Don't cry, Akosua, eh? Please."

She was trying to scoop Akosua into her arms, but the girl was unwieldy, as limp and floppy as a rag doll. In between sobs, she was saying something that Dawson could not make out at first.

Simon looked at him and said, "Massa, it's your name she's calling."

"*My* name?" Dawson said, craning forward. "Are you sure?"

Simon was right. In Twi, Akosua was moaning, "I want Mr. Darko, I want to talk to Mr. Darko."

He knelt down beside the woman. "Are you her friend?"

"Yes, please. My name is Regina. You are Inspector Darko?

The one they said in the newspaper we should call if we have information on the boy in Korle Lagoon?"

"Yes."

"Please, yesterday Akosua and I saw the drawing of the boy. It looks like her boyfriend. She has been looking for him for more than one week. She won't eat, and she can't sleep. I have to force her to drink even just a little bit of water. As soon as she saw the picture, she said, 'That is Musa,' and she started to cry. She almost fainted when we were waiting for a tro-tro to bring us here."

Dawson looked quickly around. First order of business, get Akosua off this stage and away from this audience. Covering her face with her hands, she had quieted down now, only whimpering slightly, breathing quickly and deeply.

Dawson touched her shoulder. "Akosua, I'm Darko. Can you stand up?"

She nodded, still hiding her face, as though scared to face the world.

"Come on, then. I'll help you."

Dawson took her arm and supported her as she shakily got to her feet. To Constable Simon, he said, "Please get her some water."

To talk to her, he needed a relatively quiet and private place, which could be difficult to find at CID. One of the secretaries in the Public Relations Office was standing nearby. Dawson knew she worked in a small office with only one other woman.

"Can we use your room for a moment?"

She nodded. "No problem, sir. It's free."

The audience began to disperse, the spectacle of the day over.

Akosua, still unsteady on her feet, leaned against Regina as they followed Dawson down the corridor. Chikata accompanied them into the office, where there were two desks, one with a computer that was switched off. Dawson wondered if it worked. Many of CID's computers were old, burned-out fixtures.

Chikata moved the chairs from behind the desks, offering them to the young women. Akosua was trembling. Her eyes were bloodshot and as painfully swollen as those of a pummeled boxer. Now, Dawson could get a good look at her. While Regina was around twenty, twenty-one, Akosua couldn't have been more than about seventeen. She was built very slightly, with a mousy, anxious face. She had a small tribal mark on her left cheek. Her hair was badly cut and straightened, but she had made an effort to gather it back and look sophisticated. Her dress, a Ghanaian print, was on the shabby side with oil stains. She wore cheap plastic slippers. Yet Dawson could see the care she had put into her appearance.

Physically, she and Regina could not have been more unlike each other. Regina was richly made, her body forcing her blouse and tight jeans to conform to her curves. Akosua looked like she ate once every other day.

Constable Simon came in with a bottle of Voltic water.

"Thank you, Simon," Dawson said.

"No problem, massa. Please, do you need anything else?"

"No, thank you. You can go."

Dawson snapped the seal on the top of the bottle and handed it to Akosua. "Have water. You need it. Take your time."

For the first time, Akosua looked up at him and met his gaze. "Thank you," she whispered, taking the bottle.

Regina, supportively holding her friend's free hand,

watched as she tilted her head back and drank thirstily, her glottis loudly registering each gulp.

"*Ei!*" Regina exclaimed with a half laugh. "Take a breath, Akosua."

The girl did, stopping only briefly, and then finished up the bottle.

Dawson took it from her. "Better?"

Akosua nodded, wiping her chin with the back of her hand. "Please, yes. Thank you."

Dawson perched on the side of the desk, the one with the computer. "So. You wanted to talk to me. Here I am."

She might have felt intimidated by him or been shy, or both. She looked uncertainly at Regina, who took up the slack and said, "Please, Mr. Dawson, we came to look for you yesterday afternoon, but they said you weren't here and we should come back today."

Dawson didn't comment, but his *not* hearing about who had come looking for him was a common occurrence. More often than not, the receptionists did not take a message, verbal or written, nor did they pass it on. "Come back tomorrow" was an all-too-frequent response to the visitor in search of a CID officer.

"I'm sorry I was so hard to find, Akosua," Dawson said, addressing her rather than Regina, trying to coax her out. "You say the drawing of the boy resembles your boyfriend?"

"Yes, please," she said softly, her hands wringing in her lap.

"What is his name?"

"Please, his name is Musa Zakari. I haven't seen him for ten days. As soon as I saw the picture in the newspaper, I knew it was him."

Regina pulled out a mobile from her jeans pocket. "Mr.

Darko, I took some pictures of Akosua and Musa some weeks ago, if you want to have a look. Then you can see how he looks like."

Dawson and Chikata came around so they could see her phone screen. Akosua looked on as Regina went through each of four photographs, all containing Musa. One of them really got Dawson's attention. Musa was standing behind Akosua with his arms around her, his smiling face nuzzling against her neck as she leaned against him. Comparing a drawing to a photo was often difficult, and the facial features were not a dead-on likeness to Kirezi's sketch. But the *smile*. It was the smile with the same missing cuspid that did it. Somehow, Kirezi had captured it perfectly.

"That's a fine picture of you and Musa," Dawson said to Akosua.

She smiled tentatively, a smile marred by sadness.

"How did he lose his tooth?" Dawson asked.

Akosua cleared her throat. "Please, about three months ago, some thieves at Agbogbloshie Market beat him and stole his money. His mouth was bleeding and his tooth was loose, and it was paining him so he pulled it out and he was going to throw it away, but I said no, don't throw it away—give it to me, and he said, Ah, but what will you do with it? And I said I would make a necklace with it, so when I wear it I know I have you with me even if you are not there."

Without warning, tears erupted, running down her cheeks, and a whimper escaped her.

Regina gave her friend a handkerchief and then rubbed Akosua's back soothingly. "You're doing well," she said.

Dawson squeezed the girl's hand encouragingly. "I know this is tough. Try for me, eh? I'm very glad you came to see me."

She pressed the handkerchief against her eyes. Dawson

gave her a chance to recover. He asked her gently, "Did you make the necklace with the tooth?"

Akosua nodded, taking a grimy piece of paper carefully out of her pocket. She unfolded it gingerly, revealing a thin strand of leather with a single strung item—a tooth. Dawson picked up the necklace and examined it. The tooth, one of the cuspids, was dazzling white and smooth as pearl. In a minute hole drilled through its base was a small metal loop, to which the leather string was attached. Dawson felt that surge of excitement that came with a significant break.

"You made this, Akosua?"

She shook her head. "Regina's husband—he makes jewelry at the Arts Center."

"Oh, very good." Dawson acknowledged Regina. She smiled, looking proud.

Dawson looked up at Chikata. "Can you get me one more chair?"

"Sure." Chikata left the room.

"When was the last time you saw Musa?" Dawson asked Akosua.

"The Saturday before last."

"That's the fifth of June, the day before the body was found."

"Yes, please."

"Where did you see Musa that day?"

"We went to Nima Market."

"At what time?"

"In the evening about six o'clock."

"Did Musa live in Nima?"

"No, please. He stayed at different places. He was a truck pusher, so he stayed anywhere he had work."

"He lived on the street?" Dawson asked.

"Yes, please."

"Did he have any family?"

"Please, no. He came from the north. He didn't have anyone here."

Chikata came back with a borrowed chair. Dawson sat
down at a comfortable angle from Akosua. His previous position, sitting on the edge of the desk, which forced her to look
up at him, had seemed dominating. He wanted her to feel at
ease.

"What you've done," he said, "bringing us Musa's tooth, is
a very good thing, Akosua, because we can test it to see if it be-
longs to the person in the lagoon. If it does, then it means that
the person in the lagoon was Musa."

"Yes, please."

"But we have to keep the tooth for some time," Dawson
went on. "We won't break it. We just have to remove a small
piece from it, so small that you wouldn't notice. You get me?"

"Yes, please."

"About the fight you say Musa had with the thieves—did
you see it happen?"

"No, I wasn't with him."

"How old was Musa?"

"Sixteen. He was going to be seventeen."

"And how old are you?"

"Seventeen too."

"Do you know anyone who didn't like Musa?"

She shook her head. "Everyone liked him."

"That evening when you and Musa went to the market,
what time did you leave each other?"

"About seven o'clock. One friend came to help Musa take
something to Maamobi."

"Did you know that friend? His name?"

"I know his name is Daramani, but I don't know him well."

Daramani. Dawson stiffened, but then he reassured himself. There were undoubtedly countless Daramanis in Accra, not just the one he knew.

"Do you know where this Daramani lives?"

"He lives in Nima. I went to his house with Musa one time."

Nima. Where Dawson's Daramani lived.

"About how old is this Daramani?"

"I don't know," she said, adding, "older than me."

"Do you like him?"

"I don't like him." Akosua squirmed. "He was always looking at me like he wanted to be with me."

"Do you think he was jealous of Musa?"

"I don't know."

"If we take you to Nima, can you show us his house?"

"I think so. But I don't want him to see me."

"Okay, no problem."

Dawson stood up. So did Chikata.

"You stay here," Dawson said to him abruptly.

Chikata was puzzled. "Why shouldn't I go with you?"

"It doesn't need two of us to go to question this man. You've got a lot of paperwork to finish. Come along, Akosua."

As they left the room, Dawson could feel Chikata's stunned look burning a hole in his back.

Nima was bustling with furious midweek commerce, men and women weaving through the crowds with loads of merchandise while they dodged horn-blaring cars. Truck pushers forged paths through the jammed traffic, their unwieldy carts piled with scrap metal, engine blocks, old TVs, and computers. The sidewalks were packed with traders bursting beyond the boundaries of Nima Market. With no space for pedestrians on the pavement, vehicles and people shared the street in a constant battle for dominance.

Akosua was in the backseat. Dawson, in the front next to Baidoo, wasn't much bothered by the chaos of Nima. What was taking his attention was the turmoil in his own head. *You panicked.* Afraid that Akosua's Daramani was the same as the one he knew, terrified that his "other life" might be exposed, he had ordered Chikata to stay behind. Dawson suddenly felt corrupt and ashamed.

"I think we can get down here," Akosua said. She pointed to their left. "His house is somewhere over there."

Baidoo inched over and somehow created a parking space next to a paint and hardware store. Dawson and Akosua got out, weaving to the other side of Nima Highway. He let her lead him through the narrow walkways of the market, where the vendor stalls were packed on either side and space between one person and the next was a matter of a few inches. Whenever there was a cry of *Agoo!* behind them, they moved instinctively to one side to give way to someone pushing or carrying a load of grain or produce so heavy that, if he broke stride for even a second, it would be a disastrous loss of momentum.

Under the pitiless sun, the smell of raw sweat merged with the pungency of heaps of cinnamon, cumin, and thyme, sharp and fresh enough to make Dawson sneeze. As they moved from the sweetness of the spice market to the olfactory assault of the stink-fish section, Dawson was watching which way Akosua was going. In Nima, there was always more than one route anywhere, so it was too early to say if she was moving in the direction of Daramani's place. She took a sharp right, which Dawson knew would move them out of the main body of the market. Gradually, it became quieter as they reached purely residential areas of both brick and wooden structures. Some alleys were paved; others were of red dirt only. The gutters were a flashback to those of Agbogbloshie—looking like them and smelling like them.

Akosua stopped and looked around.

"Lost?" Dawson asked her, aware of a silly spark of hope that she might not find the place.

She mopped her perspiring brow. "This way, I think," she said, starting off again.

It happened she was taking a route straight through the prostitutes' row called 4-4-1. It was inactive now but would spring to life in the evening. Akosua made another turn, but Dawson gently restrained her.

"You don't want to go that way."

They had come face-to-face with one of Nima's addicts' lanes, where four guys were using wee and cocaine. They looked like they hadn't eaten in weeks, lifeless eye sockets in gaunt faces. Somewhere at the other end of the alley, where there was a squalid public toilet, a drug dealer could be selling to some well-heeled guy who had just driven up in an SUV, or maybe even to a policeman.

Akosua reversed her direction, getting her bearings back. Down an alley shaded on one side and sunlit on the other, as they passed a dreadlocked guy in a flaming skull T-shirt, Dawson's heart sank. This was the way to the wee-smoking ex-thief, ex-convict Daramani Gushegu he knew. *Make her turn, make her turn. Please.* He was praying she would change direction, but she didn't. Instead, Akosua stopped again.

"I don't want him to see me," she said to Dawson.

"Okay, no problem. Just tell me which house it is, then you can go back around the corner and wait for me."

"Number three on the left. The yellow one."

She disappeared. Dawson approached the house. Daramani's place was incompletely painted—the yellow had apparently run out. There was a small window with fraying mosquito netting. An antenna was attached to the edge of the corrugated tin roof. It seemed Daramani now had a TV. He must be moving up in the world, despite his complaint that "life make too hard for Ghana nowadays."

Dawson looked up and down the alley before knocking on the fragmenting wooden door. No one responded. Dawson tried it. Locked, although, quite frankly, he could have got in if he wanted to. *No, you're in enough trouble already.*

He hesitated, then wrote a note asking Daramani to call him. He slipped it under the door.

10

Dawson asked Baidoo to drive to Agbogbloshie to drop Akosua off. On the way there, Dawson tried Wisdom again and got him this time, explaining the new development with Akosua and the picture on her friend's mobile.

"I will email the photo to you," Dawson told him.

"I need you to crop it to show Musa's face by itself," Dawson said, "and send it back."

"Can we publish it after we've cropped and enhanced it?"

"As soon as we get DNA confirmation that the lagoon boy and Musa are the same person. Not before."

"Where are the DNA samples going—South Africa?"

"No, we can get them done at Korle Bu."

"Hmm, good luck."

"Don't be so cynical. Also, I need another favor from you."

"Anything, my dear Inspector."

"Please make a print of the uncropped photo—with Akosua in it—so I can give it to her to keep."

"I can do that. Shoot the pic over."

"Thank you, Wisdom."

As he ended the call, Dawson asked Akosua how long she would be able to keep her friend's mobile.

"I promised to take it to her this evening," Akosua said.

Dawson thought about this for a moment. He might need to get back in touch with Akosua. He stole a look in his wallet and winced. He was down to almost nothing. He'd be lucky if he made it to the next paycheck.

"Stop at the Ecobank ATM up there," he told Baidoo, "and then take us to the Vodafone shop near Nkrumah Circle."

Dawson bought the cheapest available bare-bones phone for GHC35, but since Akosua had never had her own mobile before, she was thrilled, thanking Dawson profusely. A small amount of prepaid time came with the SIM card. Dawson begged her not to run through it making jubilant calls to her friend Regina.

"This is for us to get in touch with each other," he pressed. "You hear?"

"Yes, please."

Before they dropped Akosua off on Abossey Okai Road in Agbogbloshie, Dawson thanked her again for coming forward and promised he would let her know when he received the photo print of Musa and her together.

"Where now, massa?" Baidoo asked.

"Korle Bu Hospital."

Dawson had never been to Korle Bu's brand-new DNA lab, which had been installed in a remodeled space in the Central Lab. The technicians and medical director had both been trained in South Africa.

"Detective Inspector Dawson from CID," he told the receptionist. "I'm here to talk to the one in charge of police DNA samples."

Lifting her eyes languidly from her computer screen, she said, "Is he expecting you?"

"No, but he will be if you tell him I'm here."

"Then please, you can have a seat," she said, indicating the chairs behind him.

"Thank you, but I don't have time to have a seat. This is police business. I need to see the person in charge now, please?"

Looking insulted, she got up and left, returning sulkily a few minutes later with a man in a white lab jacket.

"Good afternoon." He had a wide face and a boyish voice.

"Afternoon. I'm D.I. Dawson."

"Jason Allotey at your service. Do you have a case registered with us?"

"Yes," Dawson said. "It should be in your system."

"Please, come with me, Inspector."

Dawson followed Jason around the corner to the lab proper, which, though compact, was very impressive. It was colder than the inside of a refrigerator. The floor gleamed white. Three spotless sequencing machines with matching flat-screen computer monitors stood on a central stainless steel counter. Along the sides of the room were glass cabinets, centrifuges, pipettes, reagents, and test tubes.

Jason went to one of the computers. "You know the case file number?"

Dawson rattled it off from memory. Jason matched him by typing it in just as fast.

"Okay, yah," he said. "I know this one. The guy found in the lagoon. We are working on two blood samples sent to us from the Police Hospital Mortuary. No results yet, Inspector."

"I brought you a present," Dawson said, producing the plastic bag containing the tooth necklace.

Jason peered at it. "Whose tooth?"

"The victim—or the person we believe is the victim—lost a tooth, and his girlfriend made a necklace out of it."

"Wow." Jason's face lit up as if someone had just dropped the Asantehene's gold in his lap. "This is a dream source of DNA."

"Just one thing, though," Dawson said. "She wants the tooth back in one piece."

Jason went over to the microscope to examine it, leaving it in the bag.

"Yeah, we can get material from it without any problem."

"And without putting a big hole in it?" Dawson asked.

"Eh? You say a big hole?" Jason looked offended. "We deal in microns here, Inspector."

"Sorry," Dawson said, sufficiently chastened. "So, how long to find out if we have a DNA match?"

"For you, two weeks, Inspector."

"Two weeks! Why does the test take so long?"

"It's not the length of the test, Inspector, it's how many tests are waiting in line to be done. You know we have a back-log of a whole bunch of specimens that were originally going to South Africa and the U.S."

"Do you like tilapia?"

"Oh, by all means! Why?"

"I'll bring the best tilapia to your house if you speed it up for me."

"*Ei!*" Jason exclaimed in wonder. "Personal delivery from a detective inspector?"

"Yessah. Sharp-sharp."

Jason laughed happily and slapped hands with Dawson, ending with a crisp finger snap.

"You will have your DNA analysis, Inspector," he said.

On his return to CID, Dawson stayed in the car park to call Daramani. There was no answer. He waited a few minutes and tried again. Still nothing. He sucked his teeth with impatience. His need to talk to Daramani was eating him alive. Not only did Dawson need to question him about the lagoon boy but he wanted to ask Daramani to keep his mouth shut about their friendship and, above all, their mutual vice. As he went back upstairs, he heard the words *conflict of interest* reverberating around his head. He felt himself getting into trouble. Just like in quicksand, his every move was drawing him in deeper, making it impossible to pull away.

11

Midmorning the following day, Thursday, Dawson got a call from Christine. He knew at once from the tremor in her voice that something was wrong.

"I'm going to pick Hosiah up from school," she told him. "They just called me to say he's not feeling well."

"What do they mean, 'not feeling well'?"

"They said it's his breathing."

Dawson's stomach swooped. "Okay, I'll meet you there."

"No, wait for me to call you back. I'm much closer to the school than you—I can be there in twenty minutes."

"All right."

Chikata walked in drinking chocolate milk. "What's wrong, Dawson?"

"Hosiah. His school says something's wrong with his breathing. I'll have to leave soon."

"No problem, boss. Take care of the boy, I'll handle everything here."

Thirty anxious minutes later, Christine called back. "I

have to take him to Korle Bu, Dark. He's okay when he sits or lies still, but he's short of breath when he moves around."

"I'll be there."

The outpatient pediatric waiting area at Korle Bu Hospital was a hall open on two sides and filled with rows of long wooden benches. With space cleared for future laboratories and treatment areas, the lobby was both expansive and crowded. Mothers and fathers sat with their crying babies, waiting the obligatory eternity before they would be called into one of the three consultation rooms.

Dawson spotted Christine and Hosiah sitting at the end of a middle row. Hosiah's eyes lit up when he saw his father approaching. They simultaneously reached for each other, and Dawson lifted his son up into his arms.

"How you doing, champ?"

"I'm okay."

"Is the breathing better?"

"A little."

But Dawson could see and hear how rapid his respiratory rate was.

"Here," Christine said. "Let's change places. I can stand for a while."

They switched, Dawson sitting down with Hosiah on his lap. "Lean back against me. There. Comfortable?"

Hosiah nodded.

"How long will we have to wait, Daddy?"

"I don't know, Hosiah. I hope it won't be long, but there are a lot of people."

It wasn't until three hours later that they were called into the consultation room. Dr. Asem, the pediatrician, was a youngish male who was managing to look cool and unflustered even under the sweltering, stressful conditions. He went quickly through Hosiah's medical record.

"So," he said. "Short of breath today?"

"Yes," Christine said. "With exertion, but not at rest."

Asem listened to Hosiah's chest and lungs with his stethoscope, nodded, and folded it up into his jacket pocket.

"Moderately fluid overloaded. Have you been salt-restricting him?"

Dawson glanced at Christine. "Trying."

"Need to do more." Asem pushed back on his mobile stool, putting his head out the door to call for a pulse oximeter.

He returned to Hosiah to check his hands and fingernails. A nurse came in with the pulse ox, and Hosiah automatically extended his right third finger for her to attach the device. He knew the drill.

"Ninety-three percent, Doctor," the nurse said.

"Not terrible," he said to Dawson and Christine, "but not good either. I think if we admit him and diurese him overnight, he should be fine by tomorrow."

Hosiah looked up apprehensively at his parents. Dawson instinctively put a reassuring hand on his head.

"Daddy, I don't want to stay here," he said.

Dawson leaned forward, speaking softly to him. "I know you don't, Hosiah, but it's so we can get you better. Both Mammy and I will be right here with you." He wiped away his son's tears. "And tomorrow we'll go back home, okay?"

Hosiah nodded, trying not to cry.

Asem dashed off admission orders in completely illegible handwriting and put the note in Hosiah's chart. "Take this with you to the Emergency Department to get the IV started, and then he'll go up to the general medical ward on the second floor. Okay?" He smiled at Hosiah. "You'll be okay. You're not afraid, are you?"

"No," Hosiah said defiantly. "Not even of needles. My daddy is, though."

Dr. Asem laughed. "Is that true?" he asked Dawson.

"I'm afraid so," he said sheepishly.

As they stood to leave, Dawson softly told Christine, "Go on ahead with Hosiah, I'll join you in a few minutes."

Once his wife and son had left, Dawson turned to Dr. Asem. "In your honest opinion, is Hosiah's condition getting worse?"

Asem inclined his head left to right as he considered the question. "Might be a little bit. On the other hand, maybe his sodium balance is just off. You have to be really careful with that salt."

"We will," Dawson promised.

"Is surgery on the horizon?" Asem asked.

"As soon as we find a way to pay for it."

"I pray that it will be soon. Remember that if Hosiah ever develops the complication of pulmonary hypertension, it's too late for surgery."

Dawson bit his bottom lip. The warning was harsh but true.

"Thank you for your help, Dr. Asem."

There were twenty-eight beds in total on the general medical ward, infants on one side of the floor, children on the other. Dawson, Christine, and Hosiah were all too familiar with the large, common room shared by all the patients. That was the way it had been for a long time at Korle Bu, and with the exception of a new private wing for people with a lot of money, that was the way it would be for some time to come.

As the diuretic began to take effect, Christine and Dawson helped Hosiah with the urinal just as other parents did their own children.

Night came. By 2:00 A.M., Hosiah had settled down, sleeping without much trouble. His pulse oximetry reading was up to 95 percent. Christine had been dozing off and on with her head resting on the edge of the bed. Dawson allowed his eyes to drift closed for short periods, but he was still on constant watch over his son.

"Christine," he whispered. "Why not go home and get a few hours? He seems to be doing fine."

She rubbed her eyes. "You'll be okay?"

"Yes, we'll be fine. Are you going to work tomorrow?"

"I'll go in for half a day. Hopefully he can come home in the afternoon."

"He should be able to."

She nodded and stood up. "Okay. But call me if . . . you know, if anything comes up."

"Of course."

She kissed him on the cheek and softly kissed Hosiah as well, and then she was gone.

PART TWO

12

Friday morning, Detective Sergeant Chikata was enjoying being "in charge" while Dawson was temporarily away. He went up to his uncle's air-conditioned office to spend some time with him. Chief Supol Theophilus Lartey was a small man with large aspirations and good connections. He was undoubtedly on his way up to deputy commissioner of police, and ultimately commissioner.

In turn, Chikata was eyeing inspector rank, where Dawson was now. As he chatted with his uncle, Chikata asked him about the prospects for promotion.

"I also want to see you move up, Philip," Lartey reassured him. "Very much so. One thing you have to remember, however, is that, although I have influence, I'm not the only one who has a say in your promotion. You understand me?"

"Yes, Uncle."

Lartey put his fingertips together, making a steeple. "What senior officers my rank and higher are looking for in a junior officer is *exemplary*"—he emphasized each syllable—"performance, something I can turn to them and say, Look how well this young chap is doing. This is someone we need to push up the ladder. You see?"

Chikata nodded. "Yes, Uncle."

"Now," Lartey continued, "you are doing well, but let's see you standing out, excelling above the average officer. I think you get what I'm trying to say, not so?"

"Yes, Uncle. I understand what you mean."

"What's new on the lagoon case?" Lartey asked.

"We have one possible lead."

Chikata told his uncle about Daramani. "Dawson went to Nima on Wednesday to find him, but he wasn't there. If Dawson comes back this afternoon, then maybe we can go to Nima again."

"You didn't accompany Dawson to Nima on Wednesday?" Uncle Theo asked with a frown. "Why not?"

"That's the same question I asked him. He told me to stay behind and do paperwork, but I didn't understand why. We always have paperwork."

Lartey shook his head. "Dawson can be a little strange at times. But here is an example of where you could have shown your initiative. You knew Dawson was going to be away yesterday afternoon and you knew he wasn't able to find this fellow Daramani on Wednesday. So why not say to Inspector Dawson, 'Please, in your absence, let me go again to Nima to look for the man?' Do you see how that creates a good image for you?"

"Yes, Uncle, I do see that."

Lartey smiled at him. "Good man. I think everything is going to go well." He looked at his watch. "Shall we go to lunch?"

Hosiah had responded well to the treatment at Korle Bu, and by midmorning, after the doctors' teaching rounds, he was ready for discharge. Gladly, Dawson took his son home. Christine would be back from school by noon or so.

Hospitals were exhausting. Dawson and Hosiah fell asleep together on the sofa. Only Dawson opened his eyes when Christine came in.

"How is he?" she whispered.

"Much better," Dawson said. "Just tired."

He gently repositioned Hosiah on the sofa by himself and got up.

"You must be tired too," Christine said. "Are you going into work?"

"No, I'm calling it a day."

"Do you want some lunch? I bought something from Awo's."

"Oh, perfect."

Awo's Tilapia Joint, directly across the street, was a favorite of theirs. It made Dawson think of his tilapia promise to Jason Allotey in the DNA lab. Hopefully, he was making progress with Musa's tooth.

Lartey treated his nephew to lunch at the Dynasty Chinese Restaurant on Oxford Street. As Chikata dug into his kung pao chicken, his mobile rang. On the line was a sergeant in the CID Charge Office.

"Do you know some woman called Akosua Prempeh?" he asked Chikata.

"Yes, why?"

"She's been calling here over and over again," the sergeant said, obviously irritated. "I don't even know how she got our number, but she says she has to speak urgently to you or Inspector Dawson. Please, can you call her?"

"No problem. What's her number?"

A minute later he reached Akosua.

"Please, Mr. Chikata," she said, voice breathless and shaky, "I'm at Nima Market and I have seen Daramani."

Chikata sat up at attention. "You can see him right now?"

"Yes, please. He is buying some tomatoes."

"Has he spotted you?"

"No, please."

"I'll get there as soon as I can. Try not to lose him, but be careful. I will call you back in five minutes."

Chikata pocketed his phone. "Uncle Theo, I'm very sorry, but I have to go. Akosua has spotted Daramani. I'm going to try to accost him."

"Good job, Philip. This is exactly the kind of thing I want to see from you."

Dawson checked his phone and realized he had forgotten to switch his mobile from vibration back to normal mode on his return from Korle Bu. To his dismay, he saw he had missed two calls from Akosua while fast asleep on the sofa. He quickly called her number. No response. Dawson wondered what she could have been calling about. He speed-dialed Chikata, who didn't respond either. He'd try both of them after lunch. For now, he forgot about them as he dug into a luscious plate of baked tilapia smothered in Awo's mouthwatering tomato and onion sauce.

It was after lunch that Chikata phoned.

"I tried calling you earlier," Dawson said.

"Yes, I see that," Chikata said. "Sorry I couldn't take it. I was questioning that guy, Daramani."

Dawson sat bolt upright. *"Daramani?"*

"Akosua spotted him at the Nima Market earlier on today. She tried to call you but didn't get you, so she got in touch with me through CID. At that time she had kept Daramani within sight, so I told her to follow him if she could while I was on my way there. We stayed in contact on the phone, and by the time I got to Nima, he had gone into the public WC—the one on Alata Street. So I just waited for him to come out."

Dawson swallowed. "Where are you now?"

"At CID. I brought Daramani back with me so we could interview him."

Dawson's heart began to race. "Has he said much to you so far?"

"He says he knows you. In fact, he says you're his friend."

Dawson's mouth went dry.

"At first I thought he was bluffing," Chikata continued, "but then he told me he knew your wife's name is Christine and your son is Hosiah."

A sheen of cold sweat burst out over Dawson's forehead. "I'll be there as soon as I can."

When he got to CID, neither Chikata nor Daramani was in the detectives' room. Instead, one of the corporals had a message that Dawson was to report to the chief supol. His heart sank. This was getting worse by the minute. He went down to the second floor with the sick feeling of a pupil going to the headmaster's office.

"Sit down," Lartey said as Dawson came in. "Philip picked up this man Daramani, who I understand knew the Korle Lagoon victim."

"Yes, sir," Dawson said. "That's what the victim's former girlfriend told us."

"Mm-hm, yes. Now, when Philip was questioning him, Daramani claimed he's a good friend of yours, and even named your wife and son correctly. Is it true he's your friend?"

"He knows me, I know him," Dawson said. "Maybe you call that a friend, I don't know, sir. I arrested him years ago, and after he had served time, he acted as an informant for a while. After that, I kept an eye on him to make sure he stayed out of trouble."

"That's laudable, I suppose, but why the interest in him in particular?"

Dawson shrugged. "Sometimes I see potential in the unlikeliest people."

"You brought him in on marijuana possession, correct?"

"Yes, sir."

"Have you seen any, em, potential—as you call it—realized in this gentleman?"

"Well, he's stayed out of trouble, learned better English. And now he has a better job."

Lartey tapped the end of his pen on his desk, looking skeptical. "I see. And the marijuana? Tell me about that."

Dawson had to be careful. *Was this a trap?* What had Daramani told them?

"He knows all too well it's against the law," Dawson said.

"Has he stopped using it?"

"If not, he could be arrested all over again."

"So if you were to catch him smoking marijuana, you would of course arrest him."

"Use, possession, and sale of marijuana is against the law," Dawson said firmly. "He knows that and I know that."

"Yes." Lartey stared at him for a moment without blinking. "Do you understand how your relationship with Daramani is a conflict of interest in this investigation?"

"Yes, sir, I do."

"Did you not realize on Wednesday that you knew Dara-mani when the young lady showed you his place of residence in Nima?"

"Since he wasn't there, I couldn't be one hundred percent sure it was the same person. People move around."

"But you planned to make it known as soon as you discovered it to be true."

"Not doing that would jeopardize the investigation."

"Correct." Lartey leaned back. "In that regard, I won't have you interrogate this man, nor do I advise you have any further contact with him while we are investigating him. Is that understood?"

"Of course, sir. Who will do the interrogation, then?"

"Chikata will."

13

There is only one official interrogation room at CID Head-quarters. It is reserved for "cases of national significance." The murder of a presumably unimportant teenager in the slum of Agbogbloshie did not make the grade. Normally, Daramani would have been interviewed in the detectives' room like everyone else, but Lartey had decided to use an assistant superintendent's room that was empty for the moment while the ASP was on assignment in Tamale. Even though Lartey was going to "sit in" on the interrogation, it was Chikata who would be doing the talking.

Dawson didn't think that was a good idea. Chikata was too inexperienced, and he didn't have the skills. But Dawson knew what was happening. The detective sergeant wanted to "prove himself," and his uncle was going to let him have a good try.

They proceeded to the ASP's room down the hallway. Dawson followed them, but as they reached the door, the chief supol turned to him and said, "So as not to bias the suspect's answers, it would be better if you're not present in the room."

So Daramani is officially now a suspect?

"All right, sir."

Uncle and nephew entered the room. There were two tables, one piled with papers. Daramani, tall and lean in his chair, sat at the other with his back to the louvered windows where Dawson stood observing.

Chikata sat down opposite Daramani, Lartey stayed out of sight, sitting behind Daramani.

"Your full name is Daramani Gushegu?" Chikata began in Twi.

"Yes, please."

"And you live in Nima?"

"Yes, please."

"Do you know one Musa Zakari?"

"Please, yes, I know him."

"How do you know him?"

"He is a truck pusher, and I met him one time at Nima side."

"How long ago?"

"Maybe . . . some six months, something like that."

"Do you know where he is right now?"

"No, please."

"Do you know that a man resembling Musa was found dead in Korle Lagoon?"

Daramani drew back. "No. Serious? When?"

"It will be two weeks ago this Sunday. You never saw it in the newspapers?"

"No, please. But is he the one in the lagoon for sure?"

"Do you know his girlfriend, Akosua Prempeh?"

"Yes, please. I know her."

"When was the last time you saw Musa?"

"Please, I saw him . . . two weeks ago."

"What day?"

"Hmm." Daramani thought back. "Friday. No, Saturday."

"Where did you see him?"

"Nima Market."

"Was he by himself?"

"No, please. He was with Akosua."

"What time was that?"

"Evening time. Like six o'clock."

"And then what happened?"

"He asked me to help him to take metal pieces to one man in Maamobi, so I said okay I can help you."

"How did you take the metal scraps there?"

"With a cart from my friend in Nima."

"What's your friend's name?"

"Yaw."

"After you used his cart to take the stuff to the man, what did you do?"

"We went to my house."

"You and Musa?"

"Yes, please."

"What did you do at your house?"

"We were just talking."

"And smoking marijuana?"

"Please, no. I don't smoke that."

Chikata grunted, looking skeptical. "Okay, we'll see when we search your house. How long did Musa stay with you?"

"Maybe . . . two hours."

"And then?"

"Then he left."

"To go where?"

"Please, I don't know. Sometimes he goes to Agbogbloshie side."

"Do you like Akosua?"

"Eh?" Daramani was caught off guard.

"Akosua. Do you like her?"

"Yes, please, I like her."

Careful, Daramani.

"In what way do you like her?"

"She's a nice girl."

"Would you like her as a girlfriend now that Musa is gone?"

"But please, are you sure he's dead?"

"If he was dead, would you like to take Akosua for your girlfriend?"

"Please." Daramani shook his head. "She's his girlfriend, not mine."

"Akosua already told me how you used to look at her, that you wanted her."

"Me?" Daramani said, pointing at himself. "Not at all."

"Look, don't be afraid. If you were jealous of Musa because of Akosua, you can tell me. It's okay."

Daramani stared blankly at him.

"I know you northern men always want to get Ashanti girls, but it's hard to get them," Chikata said.

"Eh?"

"Accra women and Ashanti girls," Chikata persisted. "That's what you northerners like."

What a ridiculous statement.

"Please, as for me," Daramani said, "I like girls from the north."

Chikata kept a steady gaze on Daramani. "We're going to search your house. If we find anything bad, even if we find a little bit of marijuana, you're going to jail, and the more lies you tell, the longer you'll be in jail. Do you understand?"

"But, please, I'm not telling lies."

"You were the last person to be seen with Musa, do you know that?"

"I don't get you."

"You were with him on Saturday night," Chikata continued, "and the next morning he was found dead. Did you go
with him to Korle Lagoon that night?"

"Please, no."

"You were jealous of him and Akosua, and you wanted
Akosua for yourself, not so?"

"*No.* Jealous of him and Akosua, why? Musa is my coun-
tryman."

"Where did you kill him?" Chikata said. "We know you
did it. Did you kill him near the lagoon? *Where?*"

Daramani turned his palms up and lifted his shoulders. "I
didn't kill him! What do you want me to say?"

"You *did.* Someone saw you."

"What? *Who?* It's a *lie.*"

Dawson rested his brow against the wall for a moment,
eyes closed. This was horrible.

"You liked that Akosua so much," Chikata said, lowering
his voice, "and when you saw Musa with her that Saturday at
the Nima Market, you decided to kill him."

Daramani put his head between his hands.

"So after you left your house," Chikata continued, "you
went with him to Agbogbloshie and late at night you killed
him. We know that's how it happened. If you confess, it will
be better for you. You're going to jail. Why not tell the truth
now and we can help you?"

"Please," Daramani said wearily. "I am telling you the
truth."

Chikata pushed his chair back abruptly and stood up.
"Okay, we will see about that."

He and Lartey came out, shutting the door behind them
and joining Dawson. The three of them went up the hallway a
few meters to be out of Daramani's hearing.

"I believe he is our prime suspect," Chikata said.

"You didn't give him a chance to establish an alibi," Dawson pointed out. "You do that first and then you follow it up. If the alibi proves false, you come back to him and challenge him."

"His alibi is implied," Lartey interjected quietly. "Daramani says Musa was with him in Nima for two hours and then Musa left. That means Daramani is claiming he was in Nima when Musa was killed."

Dawson looked away. He didn't agree. *And thank you for cutting me down in front of my junior officer.* He wasn't going to waste any more time arguing. What was the point? The chief supol would defend his nephew to the death no matter what Dawson or anyone else said.

"Go and get the search warrant, Philip," Lartey said.

Chikata left the two men.

"I think your detective sergeant *does* have a case, Dawson," Lartey said, lifting his chin imperiously. "You are probably blinded by your bias toward your, em, friend. It's a normal human tendency."

"Yes, sir."

"And one word of advice to you. Be very careful who you mix yourself up with—not just on duty but off duty too. The kind of company this Daramani keeps—truck pushers, Agbogbloshie people—is unsavory." Lartey made a face, as if bile had just erupted into his mouth. "It isn't fitting for you to associate with such base elements of society. You understand what I'm saying?"

"Yes, sir."

"Good. That's all for today. You may go."

14

Dawson didn't go home immediately. Instead, he took a walk. He would have liked to escape to some wilderness setting with fresh air and beautiful vistas, like Mount Afadjato or Wli Falls, but the streets of Accra would have to do for now. He turned away from noisy Ring Road, heading past the vehicle yard to the relatively quieter neighborhood roads behind CID Headquarters. Here, where a street called Myohaung formed a shady alcove, policemen and women parked official vehicles while stopping for a meal from the outdoor food vendors.

Pulling out his shirttails, Dawson thrust his hands in his pockets as he walked along Myohaung Street. Curious about the name, Dawson had once researched it, finding out it referred to the part Ghanaian troops played in defeating the Japanese at Myohaung, Burma. Over 65,000 Ghanaians had fought abroad with the Allied forces during the Second World War. One of these days, Dawson would tell Hosiah about such historical details, which western textbooks often left out.

And Dawson? What would his contribution to the world

be? What would he leave behind when he was gone? Would his name be in a textbook or on a street sign somewhere? Did it matter? Conflicts with Chief Superintendent Lartey often brought on these existential crises for Dawson.

Sometimes too, in these situations, Dawson thought about his mentor Daniel Armah, the detective who had first investigated the disappearance of Dawson's mother when Dawson was a boy of twelve. What would he have become if he had never met Detective Armah? Now retired and living in Kumasi, Armah had been a sergeant back then. It wasn't so much Armah's abilities as a detective that had inspired Dawson to go into the same field. In fact, Armah never did find out what had happened to Dawson's mother, and in that sense, some might have said that Armah failed. But no matter, it was the care Armah had shown to Darko the boy that had been so moving, care Darko never received from his own father.

Was Chief Supol Lartey right that associating with "people like Daramani" was unfitting for Dawson? Did Dawson have some kind of moral failing? Defensively he thought, *I could be a worse man.* After all, he was a good father and husband, was he not? But if that was the case, he should completely drop the vice that he strenuously kept hidden from his family.

As Dawson turned in to Rangoon Lane, he felt the existential crisis fading for now, but he knew it would be back sooner or later.

Chikata and Issifu, another detective sergeant, were gloved up and searching Daramani's small, messy dwelling. Chikata went first for the thin foam mattress on the floor. Issifu was looking through a box of clothing. There was a hot plate on the floor with some battered cookware.

Turning to the clothes hanging from a nail in the wall, Chikata dug through all the shirt and pants pockets. He checked the two pairs of ragged tennis shoes on the floor. Nothing so far. There was a portmanteau in the corner packed with bottles of beer and plates. Chikata took the items out one by one. He found the odd fork and knife on the bottom as well as something flat wrapped in a newspaper. Chikata removed it. It was a hefty knife with a razor-sharp edge. The blade, about eight inches long, caught the meager light in the room and flashed it back. Chikata took the knife to the doorway to examine it in the late afternoon sunlight. The blade was clean except for some water spots, but along the bolster between handle and blade, there was a red stain that Chikata could have missed had he been careless. And indeed, the murderer could have missed the same spot as he washed the blood off the knife he had used to stab Musa Zakari in the back.

15

When Dawson returned home, Christine was getting dinner ready. Hosiah was watching TV in the living room. Dawson's spirits lifted the instant he saw his son. He picked him up high in the air, suspending him there for a few seconds before bringing him down again.

"How's my boy?"

"I'm fine, Daddy."

"Hungry?"

"A little bit."

"Remember what we said about salt in your food makes your breathing harder?"

"Yes, Daddy. I know I can't have any salt now."

"Good boy. TV off in five minutes for dinner, all right?"

Once Hosiah was in bed, stress and lack of sleep began to take their toll on Dawson and Christine. They washed the dishes and put them away with energy flagging fast.

Christine sat down heavily at the table. "By the way, what was all that about, having to run off to CID today?"

Dawson took the chair next to hers. "It had to do with the case I told you about—the boy in the lagoon. First we got a preliminary identification on him as a Musa Zakari, and then we found out that a friend called Daramani had been seen with the victim a day before he was found dead. They brought Daramani in for questioning, and it turns out he and I know each other."

"Who is he?"

"A guy I arrested years ago for stealing. After he'd done time, I kept in touch with him."

"I don't remember your talking about him. What was the interest in him about?"

Dawson rested his palm in hers and fiddled with her fingers. He sighed.

"What's going on, Dark?"

"We don't talk about this, but I know you know I have a weakness for marijuana."

"I do."

"I used to get together with Daramani and smoke it."

"Used to?"

"I've given it up. I haven't smoked in five months now."

"Really?" She jumped to her feet and wrapped her arms around him. "Sweetheart, I'm so proud of you."

Dawson laughed. "Thank you."

"Has it been tough for you?"

"Sometimes the desire pops up. Kind of like a quick jab. But I'm making it."

"Is it when things get tense at work? Is that what makes you want it?"

"I don't know, quite honestly." He looked at her. "How do you feel about it? Why don't you ever say anything?"

She pursed her lips contemplatively, and that made Dawson suddenly want to kiss her. "Maybe I don't say anything because I find it difficult to deal with and to sort out," she said. "I mean, I don't like the idea of your using wee, and something about it just doesn't go with your personality. But I don't see that it makes you any less a good person. On the other hand again, it is a drug, which makes you a drug user, and that sounds so ugly."

"I agree with you. Look, obviously I'm not proud of it, otherwise I would come home in the evening and announce to you and Hosiah that I've had a good smoke today. So that's why I decided to stop."

She nodded. "I'm glad. I think sometimes I worried that . . ."

"That what?"

"That it was Hosiah and me making you so stressed you had to smoke for relief."

He chuckled, pulling her over to him and wrapping his arms around her. "You're so silly." He kissed her. "That's not it at all. I couldn't live without you and Hosiah. I love both of you more than anything or anyone in the world. You know that, right?"

"News to me," she said teasingly and then laughed. "Yes, of course I know that. We love you too."

He kissed her again.

"Look, Dark," she said, "I want you to kick the habit, and I want to support you. I don't know if there's anything in particular I can do, but if there is, will you please tell me?"

"Thank you, Christine. I will."

"So anyway," she said after a moment, "back to Daramani. What happened in the end?"

"Lartey didn't want me interrogating him because of conflict of interest and all that, so he had Chikata do it. He made a mess of it trying to make the case that Daramani killed Musa because he was jealous of him and his girlfriend."

"Did they release Daramani?"

"You must be joking. He's in jail right now, and Chikata went and got a search warrant for his place."

"Do you think they can get a conviction?"

"I doubt it. He didn't do the deed, that much I know."

"Are you going to try to intervene?"

"I don't think I'll need to. This is not going anywhere. Let's go to bed."

It was as they were about to turn in that Chikata called.

"It's him, Dawson," he said, his voice flat with finality.

"What are you talking about?"

"Daramani. We found a knife hidden in his room."

Dawson's heart faltered a couple beats. "A knife. What kind of knife? Dinner knife, pocketknife, what?"

"A *big* knife. Eight inches long, and it looks like there's blood on it. We'll send it for DNA testing, but I know it will match Musa's. Daramani tried to get out of it with some crazy story that he killed a chicken a couple weeks ago to make a stew." Chikata laughed. "He must think we're stupid."

"Why is that so difficult to believe?" Dawson asked testily. "It's still cheaper to buy a live chicken in Accra than a packaged one from a store. Daramani doesn't buy his food at ShopRite, you know."

"I know that," Chikata said dismissively, "but come on, what a story. Chicken blood."

"Wait for the DNA, that's what I'd advise you."

"Dawson, you always brag about your instincts, but when it's *my* instinct, you don't give me any credit."

Dawson wanted to say "Because you don't *have* any instinct" but changed his mind.

"Wait for the DNA, Chikata," he said. "That's all I can say. Good night."

They've delivered the scrap metal to the man in Nima, and now they're heading back toward Daramani's place. At night, Nima is full of shadows and dark places. Daramani takes Musa through an alley as a shortcut. When they emerge on the other side, Daramani is the only one pushing the cart. The cargo on the cart is wrapped in a tarpaulin. It's Musa, dead with a knife in his back. No one pays the slightest attention to Daramani as he pushes his cart down the street in the direction of Korle Lagoon.

Dawson sat up in a cold sweat. He looked around in the darkness. Those first few seconds after his nightmares, the brief transition from the dreamworld to the real, were the scariest.

He got up, changed his wet pajama shirt, and sat on the side of the bed. Christine stirred and turned but didn't wake up.

Dawson thought about the dream, visualizing Daramani pushing a cart with the dead Musa on it. In the middle of the night, it seemed plausible. In the morning it would not. He cupped his chin in his palm. Why was perception always so different at night?

His mind bounced around. Chikata had wrestled the case away from him. Just like that. Dawson felt impotent. What good was an inspector who gave the case away to his sergeant? Maybe he wasn't really cut out for this work. He sighed. That tiresome existential crisis was back.

16

Saturday morning, Christine and Hosiah went shopping with Granny Gifty, leaving Dawson to do a few things around the house. About noon, he headed to Nima, picking up a *Daily Graphic* on the way. All Saturdays had a certain quality about them, a feeling of release from the chains of the workweek, the freedom to relax and browse. In neighborhoods like Nima, there was an increase in crowds moving back and forth and an upswing in buying and selling: fabrics, food, clothes, shoes, pots, pans, building materials, tools, cosmetics, and electronics.

Dawson made his way to Daramani's place. He tried the door, hoping in vain that Chikata had carelessly left it unlocked after his search. Two doors down, a woman was washing clothes in a wide metal bowl with a pot of stew bubbling beside her on a charcoal grill. Dawson greeted her.

"Do you know Daramani who lives there?" Dawson asked her, pointing to his door.

She flicked perspiration from her forehead. "Yes, I know him."

She was probably in her forties. Her voice was raspy, like sandpaper. Her name was Sheila.

"I'm from CID," Dawson said. "I'm trying to find out a little bit about him. Can you help me?"

She might cooperate, she might not. It was luck of the draw.

"If I can help you, I will," she said.

"Thank you. Were you here the night of Saturday before last?"

She shrugged. "I'm always here at night."

"Do you remember seeing Daramani with another man around ten o'clock?"

She shook her head. "By that time, I'm inside. But maybe my son saw something. As for that boy, he stays up too late playing cards with his friends."

"Is your son here?"

"Yes, but he's sleeping." She got up. "Please, let me wake him up for you. Lazy boy."

The ratty door, which didn't fit in its frame, slammed behind Sheila as she went inside yelling, "William! *William!*"

Glancing through the dirty, unraveling mosquito netting in the top half of the door, Dawson made out one larger and one smaller room, but they were both small.

Sheila returned in a huff. "He sleeps until late, then he gets up and listens to that crazy music, and then he goes out with his friends." She shook her head. "Oh, Ewurade."

William came to the door and propped it open as he leaned against the jamb. Chunky, around twenty, he was wearing a red T-shirt with I ❤ AMSTERDAM written across it in blue and white.

"Good afternoon, William."

"Good afternoon, sir."

"The gentleman wants to know about Daramani," Sheila

said to her son. "Two weeks ago on Saturday night, weren't you playing cards with your friends?"

William nodded. "Yah. Every Saturday."

"Where do you play?" Dawson asked him.

"We take a small table over there." He pointed to a small alcove on the farther side of Daramani's door, where there was a little shop selling snacks and cold drinks.

"How many of you altogether?"

"Three. Me and Alex and Houdine."

"And you played from what time to what time?"

William chewed thoughtfully on the inside of his cheek. "From about ten to after midnight."

"Did you see Daramani during that time?"

William's focus suddenly shifted as a buzz came from his pocket. He pulled out his phone and read the text message with a salacious grin.

"The gentleman is talking to you, William!" Sheila cried, appalled. "Don't disrespect! Can't you leave that thing alone for even one second?"

"Sorry," William said, sheepishly pocketing the phone. "Please, what did you say, sir?"

"Between ten and midnight, did you see Daramani?"

"Wait. Let me think. There was one night he came with another guy . . . I think it was that same Saturday night. Yah, I remember they had a cart, and we asked them what they were doing and they told us they had taken something to some man in Maamobi."

"Did they go into Daramani's house together?"

"Yes. We asked them if they wanted to play cards, they said no, but could we watch their cart and we said okay, no problem."

"About what time was that?"

"A little past eleven—we hadn't been playing that long."

"The guy with Daramani, do you know his name?"

William shook his head. "No, he didn't say."

"What did he look like?"

William shrugged. "Shorter than me, and skinny."

"Did you notice a gap in his teeth?"

"I don't really remember that." He smiled slyly. "If it's not a girl, I don't pay so much attention."

"Oh, my Lord, help me," Sheila said, rolling her eyes.

Dawson had an impulse to smile himself. "Did you see the friend come back out from Daramani's room at any time?"

"Around midnight, I think."

"By himself?"

"Yes. He took his cart and left."

Good. "And Daramani didn't come out again?"

"Oh, yah, he did."

Not so good. "Do you know where he went?"

"No."

"Did you see him come back?"

"No, but you should ask my two friends. They wanted to play another round, but I was tired, so I went to bed and left them out here."

"How can I get hold of them?"

"Alex has a mobile. I can call him, if you like."

"If you please, yes."

William speed-dialed the number, waiting as it rang. He shook his head. "No answer. Maybe he's sleeping."

Sheila looked at Dawson. "You see now? They're all like that."

"I'll text him too," William said, dispatching a lightning-quick SMS.

"Thank you, William. If he doesn't respond in the next

couple minutes, leave a message that I'm trying to get in touch with him. I'll give you my CID office number, if you would let Alex have it too."

Dawson exchanged numbers with William, chatted for a little while more in case Alex answered, but he didn't.

"Thank you, Sheila. Thank you, William." He shook hands with them in turn. "You've been very helpful."

Dawson left them in high spirits. Not every question was settled yet, but things had the right feel now. He was back in stride.

17

Monday morning after he arrived at work, Dawson read the *Daily Graphic*'s front-page article headlined ARREST MADE IN LAGOON MAN'S KILLING, with an account of the discovery of "incriminating evidence in the Nima habitation of one Daramani Gushegu, a previous associate of the deceased victim." The presumed name of the victim had been withheld pending results of DNA testing.

Chikata's name was all over the article, whereas "Detective Inspector Darko Dawson, his immediate superior, was not available for comment." Dawson laughed at that. Had they really tried to reach him?

Alex had still not called.

Chikata came into the office looking pleased with himself. Some of the other detectives who had read the newspaper account began congratulating him in a playfully teasing fashion.

"Ei, Chikata! So now you're the big man in town, eh?"

The detective sergeant grinned, showing his beautiful white teeth.

"How was your weekend?" he asked Dawson.

"Fruitful. But I'm sure not as fruitful as yours."

Chikata caught the sarcasm. "Dawson, I'm sorry. I'm sorry this Daramani is, or was, a friend or whatever he is to you, but what do you want me to do? If the man has done something wrong, then we have to investigate it. Isn't that right?"

"Did I say otherwise?"

"But then why are you annoyed with me? You don't want me to be the one to find out anything, or what? It has to be only you who gets the glory?"

"Not at all." Dawson's desk phone rang. "One second. Let me get this. Hello?"

"Is this Mr. Dawson?"

"Speaking."

"This is Alex, William's friend. He told me to call you."

"Thank you very much, Alex. I really appreciate it. Did William explain what I wanted to talk to you about?"

"Something about his neighbor Daramani—that's the name, right?"

"Yes. From what William told me, Musa, the friend who was with Daramani, left his place that Saturday around midnight, is that correct?"

"Around there, yeah."

"And then Daramani left a little later. Do you remember about how long after his friend had left?"

"I don't know, maybe about thirty minutes."

"And then William went to bed, right?" Dawson asked. Chikata was eyeing him with curiosity, wondering what the conversation was all about.

"Yes," Alex said.

"But you stayed behind with your other friend, Houdine, playing cards."

"Correct."

"Until what time?"

"Almost two, and then we packed up."

"You must really like cards."

"We like beer even more. We play cards and drink and have fun."

"Understood. So here's my question: did Daramani come back before you and your friends called it a night?"

"Yeah, he did."

"What time was that?"

"One-something. Maybe one-fifteen, one-twenty or so."

"Did he go straight back to his place?"

"Yeah. Well, not exactly straight. He was drunk, paa."

"Ah," Dawson said. "Interesting. Alex, if I need to get in touch with you again, can I always reach you at this number?"

"By all means."

"Thank you very much."

As Dawson hung up the phone, Chikata asked, "Who was that?"

"Guy called Alex," Dawson said. "He and two friends were playing cards near Daramani's place when Daramani showed up with Musa the Saturday night before Musa was found. One of the friends, William, lives two doors down from Daramani."

"Eh? How do you know all this?"

"I went to Daramani's place on the weekend to look around. That's where and when I met William."

"Wait, wait, I don't get you. This guy William said what?"

"Daramani and Musa came along a little past eleven after delivering the scrap metal," Dawson explained. "At the time, William was playing cards near Daramani's place with Alex and one other friend."

"Okay. Go on."

"So the three of them see Musa leaving from Daramani's place around midnight, and then Daramani himself leaves about twelve-thirty. Just after that, William goes to bed, but Alex and the other friend, Houdine, are still playing cards. Around one-twenty in the morning, they see Daramani coming back. He goes straight to bed. Alex and Houdine finish up around two."

Chikata was absorbing all this.

"If Daramani murdered Musa," Dawson continued, "he must have done it at or near Korle Lagoon, because without some kind of vehicle, which Daramani doesn't have, he couldn't have moved the body very far. So the question is, how did he leave his house in Nima at twelve-thirty, get to Agbogbloshie, kill Musa, dump his body in the lagoon, and get back to Nima at one-twenty?"

"He could have taken a taxi there and back."

"It's about twenty minutes from Nima to Agbogbloshie. Forty minutes for the roundtrip. Where's the time to commit the murder?"

Chikata's eyes darted back and forth as his mind searched for an answer.

"Any ideas?" Dawson probed.

"Daramani could have left his house again after Alex and Houdine had finished playing cards at two o'clock."

Dawson shook his head. "I doubt it. According to Alex, Daramani was so drunk he could barely walk a straight line."

"Em, maybe these guys—Alex and William or whoever—are really Daramani's friends and are covering for him."

Dawson tilted his head side to side, considering. "Hmm. Seems unlikely, but maybe you're right, who knows? Oh, well, we'll see."

He went back to his paperwork, and Chikata stared at the wall for a moment. Abruptly he got up and left the room. Ten minutes later, he was back.

"My uncle wants to speak to you," he told Dawson tersely.

With Dawson in the execution chair in the boss's office, Lartey said coldly, "I understand this weekend you went after information regarding Daramani."

"Yes, sir. Two separate witnesses have given me concurring accounts that make it very difficult to see how Daramani could have killed Musa."

"While Daramani is under suspicion of murder, Dawson, you may not conduct any investigations. Didn't I make myself clear on this?"

"I'm confused, sir. Are you saying I'm off the case?"

Before Lartey could answer, Dawson's phone rang and he looked at the ID. "Oh, sorry, sir, I have to answer this. It's from Korle Bu DNA Lab. Hello, Dawson speaking."

"Inspector, this is Jason Allotey."

"Yes, hi, how are you, Jason?"

"I'm fine. You owe me some nice tilapia."

"You've completed the DNA?"

"Yes. Record time. You have a positive match with the lagoon guy."

"You are incredible, Jason. Thank you very, very much. I will personally deliver the best tilapia in town."

"Excellent. I have a question for you, however. Is CID investigating avian murders these days?"

"What do you mean, avian murders?"

"The blood on this knife D.S. Chikata sent us isn't human. The red cells are nucleated. In other words, the blood of a bird. You still want DNA testing?"

Dawson chuckled at first. Then he progressed to a full-throated laugh.

Lartey stared at him. "What's wrong with you, Dawson?"

"Jason, would you mind speaking to Chief Superintendent of Police Lartey?" Dawson handed his boss the phone.

After listening for a moment, the chief supol was visibly displeased.

"Thank you, Mr. Allotey," he said tightly. He handed the phone back without a word.

As Dawson returned to the detectives' room, Chikata was coming out. He gave his boss an anxious, searching look.

"My uncle just called me, and he doesn't sound too happy. Is he annoyed about something?"

Dawson feigned ignorance. "Not that I know of."

Chikata hurried away. Fifteen minutes later, he returned looking devastated. He went quietly back to work.

After a few minutes, he cleared his throat. "My uncle says I should ask you what the next step is and what my orders are. Sir."

"Your *orders*?"

"Yes, sir, Dawson, sir. He said you're in charge and I shouldn't do anything without your prior approval. He also said Daramani should be released immediately because the case against him is very feeble. Sir."

"Oh." Dawson blinked. "Okay. Well, what we need to do now is get Musa Zakari's name and photograph to the Public Relations Office for wide media release. Also there should be a statement that charges against Daramani have been dropped. Oh, and remind Wisdom Asamoah he's supposed to give me an extra print for Akosua."

"Yes, sir."

"We don't think Musa had any family in Accra, but someone might come forward if they see the photograph in the papers or on TV. We also need to look for people who knew him, like his fellow truck pushers in Agbogbloshie and around Accra. So we go to the places they congregate, show them the new picture of Musa, and see if anyone knew him. We're looking for enemies too. These guys are living in a very tough world. Maybe one of them hated Musa for whatever reason. Maybe cutting off his fingers was an act of spite, who knows?"

"Yes, sir. I'll start on those things. What are you going to do?"

"I'm going to look for a Dr. Allen Botswe at the University of Ghana. He's a criminal psychologist. I want to ask him what he thinks of Musa's case."

"Yes, all right, sir."

As Dawson got to the door, he turned to add, "And Chikata, stop calling me 'sir.' I'm not the bloody headmaster."

18

Professor Allen Botswe, Ph.D., had suggested meeting Dawson around three o'clock at his house in East Legon. Dawson had a good idea of what to expect. This neighborhood southeast of the University of Ghana campus was populated by mansions priced at 400,000 cedis up to a million, roughly the same figure in U.S. dollars. How and where did Botswe get all that money? Not on a University of Ghana salary, for sure. Dawson had done his homework. Botswe was the only criminalist in the psychology department. He'd made himself a name as an expert on cultural aspects of murder in Ghana and West Africa. Every year, he was invited to be guest professor or speaker at universities in Europe, the United States, and Canada, engagements that paid handsomely.

The autopsy photos in a messenger bag slung across his back, Dawson started out to East Legon on his Honda. There was rain in the forecast, but he thought it was going to be much later on. As he passed the airport on his right, Dawson felt the bike shudder slightly. The machine was getting long in the tooth, with various mechanical hiccups showing up of late. Just past the Tetteh Quarshie Interchange, the Honda stalled out completely. Dawson cursed as he repeatedly tried to get it started again.

He let the Honda cool off for about ten minutes. He tried again. This time it responded. Still sputtering, it made it to the destination, but barely.

Dr. Botswe's house was enclosed within high walls topped with razor wire. The entrance was a towering wrought-iron gate. Dawson rang the outside bell. A man peeped through a viewing space in the right-hand wall.

"Good afternoon, I'm Inspector Dawson."

The man nodded, pulling the gate open. Dawson rode in. The Honda gasped, shuddered, and shut off prematurely.

"Good afternoon, sir," the man said. "I'm Obi. You are welcome."

Dawson shook hands with him. "Pleased to meet you, Obi. How are you?"

"I'm blessed, praise God." His voice had a grainy texture, like *gari*. He was a compact, powerful man of about thirty-five with a shiny, shaved head. "Is your motorcycle giving you problems?"

Dawson pulled his helmet off, resting it on the seat. "It's getting old, is the problem."

Obi smiled broadly but sympathetically. "Oh, so sorry. Please, if you can come with me. Doctor is expecting you."

Parked at the perimeter of the circular, redbrick driveway was a glistening silver, late edition Benz with an interesting license plate: AB-7777-P. Dawson assumed the AB was by design: *Allen Botswe.* One paid extra for a personalized plate—a *lot* extra. The professor also had a stunning black Infiniti SUV in the two-car garage. *Filthy rich,* Dawson thought.

The front door was solid mahogany with a decorative

etched-glass inset. Obi waved his proximity card across the reader to the side, pushing the door open after a faint click. The vestibule was deliciously cool. A giant chandelier hung from the high, vaulted ceiling. On the marble floor stood four massive Ghanaian sculptures. The paintings on the walls were from different parts of West Africa. Against a mauve accent wall was a bronze representation of Sankofa, the bird that turns its beak to retrieve the egg on its back. *It is not taboo to go back and fetch what you forgot*—so the saying went.

They passed a spiral staircase on the way to the expansive sitting room. On the far side of that was a floor-to-ceiling bay window. A pair of sliding French doors opened onto a mani-cured garden with a gurgling fountain. Dr. Allen Botswe, who was sitting in a plush leather armchair reading a book, looked up.

"Please, Inspector Dawson is here to see you," Obi said.

Dr. Botswe put down the book as he stood up and strode over to shake hands. He was short, dapper, late forties, Dawson guessed. His black and gray beard was exquisitely trimmed, just like his landscaped garden.

"Allen, Allen Botswe," he said. "Good to meet you, Inspec-tor Dawson."

"Likewise. I appreciate your seeing me."

"Not at all. It's my pleasure." He spoke with just a touch of sibilance, like a straw broom sweeping concrete. "Please, do have a seat."

Dawson chose the low-backed ebony chair with stitched, buttery soft, chocolate-colored leather.

"May I offer you some refreshments?" Botswe asked.

"Do you happen to have Malta?"

"Do we, Obi?"

"Yes, please."

"Have Irene bring Malta for the inspector, and I'll have a Heineken."

Obi crossed to the adjoining formal dining room, disappearing through a door on its far side. Dawson imagined him trekking for miles to some region of the mansion in another time zone.

Dawson tried not to stare too obviously at all this opulence as he and Botswe made small talk. Irene, a tiny woman in her early twenties, came in with a tray of Malta, Heineken, and frosted glasses. She set it down on the table between the two men, poured the drinks, and backed away a few steps.

"Please," she said to Botswe in barely a whisper. "Do you need something else?"

"No, that will be all for now, Irene. Thank you." He gave a permissive wave. She curtsied before leaving.

"She's one of our newer ones," Botswe said casually to Dawson, raising his glass. "They come and go rather faster than I would like. Obi is our only Rock of Gibraltar, really. He's been with us for twelve years, trains all the staff, keeps an eye on them, and whips them into shape, that sort of thing. All-round handyman as well, takes care of the repairs and the garden."

Dawson nodded, more concerned with his Malta. When it came to the complexities of supervising the servant classes, he had nothing to contribute.

"Anyway, enough of that," Botswe said, as if reading his mind. "How can I help, Inspector?"

Dawson told him what he knew about the young man found dead in the lagoon, now identified as Musa Zakari. Botswe listened with rapt attention, nodding at intervals.

"Outstanding detective work," he commented, at the end of the account.

"Thank you, Dr. Botswe. I know you've written extensively about ritual murder in Ghana and other West African countries, and that's why I'm here. There's something specific about Musa's murder that I want to consult you about."

"Excellent," Botswe said, sitting forward.

Dawson handed him the autopsy photos.

"My goodness," Botswe said. "This is extreme decomposition."

Dawson detected just the tiniest trill in the doctor's voice.

"Hello, what's this?" He looked up at Dawson. "Fingers amputated?"

"Yes, except the index."

"Associated with the murder? Or do we know that?"

"Dr. Biney, the pathologist, thinks so."

Botswe leaned back, one hand contemplatively on his chin. "Hmm. Any other mutilation? No removal of the genitalia, or the tongue?"

"No."

Botswe rose. "Come with me, Inspector. Let's go to my study. Please, by all means bring your Malta with you."

They passed the dining room into a carpeted corridor. The professor's study had a muted, anechoic quality to it, like a library. In a way, it was, what with the wall-to-wall-to-wall bookcase. A king-size mahogany desk was polished to a hard, reflecting shine. Botswe's framed degrees and awards—Dawson counted ten of them—told a tale of academic brilliance. The University of Ghana, Kwame Nkrumah University of Science and Technology, Oxford, Yale, and several prestigious societies. On another wall hung three framed pictures of Botswe with a woman and three teenage children.

A large window looked out onto the garden at an angle slightly different from that of the sitting room. Obi was spreading a tarp over the garden furniture to protect it from the looming rainstorm. Judging by the sky, it would arrive sooner than Dawson had been expecting.

From the bookshelf, the professor selected a hefty textbook titled *Magic, Murder and Madness: Ritual Killing in West Africa,* by Allen Botswe, Ph.D. He brought it back to the desk and pulled up a chair for Dawson.

"This is probably the most focused on ritual murder that I have." Botswe opened the book to a page about one-third through. "We can go back as far as the eighteen seventies, when British colonials gave accounts of human sacrifices made to the gods by the Ashantis. Here's a rare depiction by an unknown artist of a sacrificial ceremony."

Botswe gave Dawson a few moments to examine the picture before going to another page. "In more modern times, one of the most well-documented early cases was the Bridge House Murders of March 1945. The body of a ten-year-old girl was found on the beach a short distance from Elmina at a popular bathing spot. Her lips, cheeks, eyes, and privates had been removed. The poor little girl died from hemorrhage. The story goes that these body parts were to be used to make medicine, so called, to help someone win a chieftaincy dispute."

"A human life just for a chieftaincy dispute," Dawson said.

"People go to extraordinary lengths," Botswe said. "Five men were charged, found guilty of first-degree murder, and hanged. In the twenty-first century, we still have examples of ritual murder. Although Nigeria has probably received most notoriety on the subject, Ghana has had its share."

"What makes a killing a ritual one?"

"It shows some aspect of strong belief systems that have no scientific basis. It may be for the purposes of creating a magic potion, as in the Bridge House Murder, or to appease the gods, or in some cases, there's the belief that a particular ritual will bring wealth."

"Are there parts of the body that are focused on more than others?"

"Yes, some are invested with greater magical powers than others. If you read accounts of these killings, it's clear that heads, breasts, lips, eyes, and genitalia are more valued than limbs or limb parts."

"So what's your feeling about the Musa Zakari case?"

"We can't completely rule out that the fingers had some ritualistic significance to the killer," Botswe said, "but in the absence of some *other* body part removed in addition, I'm not that persuaded it's a ritual murder in the usual defined sense."

"If that's the case, can you suggest what else it could mean?"

"Nothing specific comes to mind except that either the fingers have special meaning to the killer or he's trying to say something with the murder. For instance, we point with the index finger. When we want to indicate 'number one,' we hold up the index finger . . . Oh, wait a minute."

He and Dawson stared at each other.

"Could he be saying this is only number one in a series?" Botswe said.

"If that were the case, wouldn't he cut the index first, then the middle finger, and so on until they're all removed, not the reverse? That would be like counting backward."

Botswe was stroking his beard. "Or," he said slowly, "another alternative—and this is just a wild notion—is that he's making reference to the opposite phenomenon, as in a *reincarnation,* or rebirth. Among some African peoples, death is an end to one life only and a gateway to another. In other words, man must be reborn because reincarnation is a spiritual necessity. So let's say this man kills repeatedly, each subsequent death is represented by the appearance of one more finger until all five are back."

"It never even occurred to me," Dawson said with some admiration. "I suppose that's why I'm the ignoramus and you're the expert I came to consult."

Botswe smiled. "My fancy theory may hold no water whatsoever. I hope it doesn't."

They spent a little more time with each other. As they walked outside together, Dawson was praying the Honda wouldn't embarrass him by not starting. Which was exactly what it did. Botswe and Obi watched him as he tried multiple times to coax some life out of the bike.

"Obi can put it in the back of his pickup and take you home," Botswe suggested, glancing up at the sky. The sun had disappeared. "Looking at those rain clouds, I don't think you want to be out riding in any case. There may be lightning."

"I can take you," Obi said to Dawson. "No problem."

"Thank you very much."

Obi went out to the street, returning in a well-used black Toyota pickup that looked out of place in Dr. Botswe's lavish environment. Dawson and Obi loaded the bike, tethering it upright and steady on the truck bed.

"Thank you for your help, Dr. Botswe," Dawson said, shaking hands again. "I'll be in touch."

Once Obi and Inspector Dawson had departed, Dr. Botswe sat on the terrace overlooking the garden. Smart man, that detective, the kind you watched what you said when he was around. Botswe had sensed the gears and cogwheels working in the inspector's mind.

After a while, he went back inside to the study. At his desk, he thought for a moment about life when Peggy had been alive. She was gone forever, leaving an unhealed gash straight through Botswe's heart. His children and grandchildren were his treasures, but he didn't see them often enough. His only constant companions were his work and his wealth. He applied himself assiduously to both to distract him from the pain and emptiness.

He logged on to his computer and worked for about thirty minutes on his latest paper: "Fight for Survival: Street Children and Crime." His mind strayed. He saved his latest edit and brought up the photos he had been looking at before the inspector arrived. Gruesome. Mutilations of all kinds from war atrocities, crime scenes, vehicle crashes, and autopsies. His work had brought him to this awful attraction. *What would Peggy have said about his obsession?*

He logged off quickly and stood up. He knew there was something wrong with him. He was, after all, a psychologist. Then again, those in his profession were often the most psychologically flawed.

As Obi drove past the Tetteh Quarshie Interchange, he said to Dawson, "The doctor is a lovely man."

"I understand you've worked for him about twelve years."

"Yes, please. When I first came, I was poor. I didn't know anything at all, at all. But I struggled to learn. Windows, doors, electricity, water—I can fix anything. That fountain in the doctor's garden, I made it myself."

"I think you need to come to *my* house then," Dawson said with a laugh.

Obi chuckled. "Please, you just tell me, I will come."

"Thank you. I'll remember that."

"But how the doctor treats me," Obi continued, becoming serious again, "it's like I'm his family. He is the one who bought me this truck three years ago, and even before that, he helped me get furniture and a new gas stove for my house."

"He has a good heart, obviously."

"Oh, yes. Every day I thank the Almighty for guiding me to the doctor."

"The pictures of the woman and three kids in his office—that's his family?"

"Yes, please. But four years ago, the wife died. He has been sad ever since that day. He loved her very much."

"What happened—to the wife, I mean?"

"Accident. A terrible one like you've never seen. She was driving to Cape Coast."

"And the children?"

"They are all in different places abroad, but the oldest one says she will come back to Ghana soon. I know the doctor wants her to stay in his house."

"He's lonesome."

"Oh, yes—very lonesome. When his children come to see him, and the oldest one brings the grandchildren too, he is so happy." Obi laughed, as though his boss's joy was being channeled through him.

The expected rain began in earnest. Dawson asked Obi to drive his motorbike to a repair shop in Asylum Down. Once his bike had been dropped off, Dawson insisted on taking a taxi despite Obi's repeated offers to give him a ride home.

"You've done more than enough, my friend. Thank you."

He gave Obi a generous tip for his trouble.

19

Comfort Mahama was sixteen. She was copper-colored, a coveted hue, with a tiny waist that flared to those big, bouncy, round buttocks that drove men crazy. Starting late Monday afternoon, she loitered around the Timber Market waiting for customers.

Most of the time, she was a head porter at Agbogbloshie Market up the street, carrying neck-breaking loads of merchandise for people. It just didn't pay enough. In her mind, Comfort was doing what she needed to do to survive. There was no right or wrong about being an *ashawo,* no good or bad.

She glanced at the gathering storm clouds. Rain ruined business. Her gaze shifted, roaming languidly across the crowded market scene—people haggling over plywood or paint, a woman selecting herbal preparations from the fetish section, porters lumbering through with planks of wood on carts. One of them, a ragged boy of about seventeen, came up to her after delivering his consignment and offered her fifty pesewas.

She shook her head. He must be joking.

He called her a nasty name and moved on. Comfort flicked her head with contempt and stuck her tongue out at his back.

A few meters away, down a row of timber, a fight had broken out between two porter boys over who was to get the job transporting a pile of plywood. No one seemed to want to stop the brawl. Quite the contrary, a small crowd was collecting to watch. One of the boys was much bigger than the other, who was getting thrashed. After a few minutes of being thoroughly beaten, he begged for mercy, picked himself up, and limped off swollen and battered.

Comfort looked away. These fights were entertainment only because there was nothing better to watch. She shifted her weight slightly, aware of a burning sensation in her loins. She was using some medicine from the fetish market, but it didn't seem to be working. She still had a yellowish discharge.

Someone hissed at her and beckoned. She sauntered over. He was about nineteen, she guessed, not bad looking.

"I like you," he said, smiling and showing a gap in his teeth that suited him.

"Four cedis."

"Oh, it's too much!"

"How much you want to pay?"

"One fifty."

They haggled until they agreed on two fifty and then took a walk. The commercial area of the market thinned out. Standing outside a tent rigged up to a wall was a gaunt man. Flash, as people called him, might have been in his twenties, but he looked like forty. He was wearing orange trousers and a bright blue shirt open almost to his navel. Comfort wondered where he got his ridiculous clothes. No one dressed like that.

This turf belonged to a guy called Tedamm. Everyone

knew Tedamm. Flash collected user fees from the ashawos and paid Tedamm the larger portion.

Comfort handed him seventy-five pesewas. He looked at it as if it wasn't money.

"You short fifteen pesewas," he said.

"*Ho!*" she exclaimed. "But you charged seventy-five last time."

"Price go up."

Sullenly, she topped off the fee.

"Wait small," Flash told her.

She ignored him while he stared at her without blinking the whole time they stood there. She hated the man. They waited for the muffled groans from inside the tent to die down. The girl came out first, her face dispassionate, then the man, zipping himself up.

Flash nodded permission to Comfort, and his eyes followed her as she went in with her customer.

Afterward, Comfort reflected she would have to do better than this. Two fifty minus the tent user fee didn't leave her with much. The first drops of rain began, which promised even more misery. She started out to Nkrumah Circle to pick up some more customers. It was a long walk, but she could charge more there than at the Timber Market.

By the time darkness fell, the downpour was in full force. She took partial shelter under the roof of a vendor's kiosk. After a while, a van sidled up to her. She looked in through the passenger window. The man inside nodded at her. She got in, they pulled off. Soaked, she was grateful to be out of the rain.

"How much?" he asked her.

"Fifteen."

"Ten."

"Twelve."

The man nodded. "Okay."

As he drove through the industrial area, he gave her a towel to wipe her face and neck. He turned in to a deserted alley behind a school near Awudome Circle.

"Get in the back," he told her.

He joined her, lying down with her on a cloth he had spread on the floor. The rain drummed on the roof. There was a little light through the front window from a lamp on the side of a building. As he hovered over her and pushed her legs back, she saw he had a curious scar. It ran from the front of his scalp down into his forehead. His eyes were unfocused and cold. She shuddered.

"Where are you from?" he asked.

"Juaso. Volta Region."

He was putting on a condom, which surprised her.

"Why did you come to Accra?"

"To make money."

"Your father used to beat you in Juaso?"

Second surprise. *How did he know?*

"Yes," she whispered. She adjusted her position for his access.

"He beat you very badly."

"Yes," she whimpered.

"Because you're a bad girl?"

She didn't understand what he was talking about.

"Say it. 'I'm a bad girl.' "

"I'm a bad girl."

As his pace increased, he told her to repeat it over and over again. He grabbed her wrist with a grip of steel, pulling her hand up to his forehead, where his scar was.

"Touch it," he gasped. *"Touch it."*

The scar felt firm, yet gelatinous and mobile, like worms in a bag. Comfort snatched her hand away as the man let out a hoarse groan of climax.

"Where do you sleep?" he asked her as they drove away.

"At the railway station."

"I'll take you there," he said. "I don't want you to sell your body to anyone else."

It was the strangest thing any man had ever said to her.

When he dropped her off, he said, "I'll come back for you." She wasn't sure what he meant.

Seven o'clock Monday night, Ebenezer trudged the final wet mile to the railway station area off Kwame Nkrumah Avenue. Like everyone else who lived on the streets, he hated the rain and the mess it caused. His shoeshine box was slung over his right shoulder. The brushes and tins of shoe polish made a comforting clattering noise against one another. Over a year ago, when he was fourteen and he had finally saved enough money as a refuse carrier, he bought a shoeshine box and supplies. Two weeks later, another street boy stole it all while Ebenezer was asleep. It was so painful and infuriating that he had wept. Not in front of the other kids. He did it when he visited the pit latrine, crying as he crouched in position.

That experience had toughened him. Wiry, Ebenezer didn't take abuse from anyone. Another thief had once tried to snatch his second shoeshine box, the one he had now. Ebenezer beat him with such heavy blows that he begged for his life.

Now, things were looking up. Ebenezer was the leader on his shoeshine corner in Lartebiokorshie. He was in charge of three other guys. To use his supplies, they paid him a percentage of their earnings.

His feet ached. Dusty during the day, they were now caked

in red mud. Walking was a matter of putting one foot in front of the other while pretending the pain wasn't there. Not even a week of toil on the farm in Jakwa, his home village in the Western Region, would have made his feet hurt so much. Accra's streets were hard and unyielding.

By the time he got to the railway, the rain had stopped. He crossed Kwame Nkrumah Avenue to Station Road. There was barely a streetlight, except for the odd fluorescent lighting outside a storefront or warehouse. Darkness shrouded the crumbling old UTC building, which had been one of Accra's best department stores long before Ebenezer was even born. People were still milling around the streets or talking, eating or playing cards, but later, as people slept on the pavements in front of the stores, everything would become as quiet as it was dark.

Rounding the corner to Knutsford Avenue, Ebenezer collided with someone, making him take half a step back. He stiffened, ready to do battle as he saw who it was. Tedamm was eighteen. He had been around for a long time. He was taller than everyone else. Angular and muscular, he looked as if he had been carved from rock. His eyes took on a hard glint as he saw Ebenezer.

"Hey, small boy, how are you?" Tedamm said with contempt. He took a mock swing at Ebenezer, who brought up his fists defensively in front of his face.

As usual, Tedamm's boys, Antwi and Ofosu, were following him around like stray dogs hoping for scraps. They had no minds of their own. They did whatever he told them.

"What were you doing shoeshining on my corner today?" Tedamm asked Ebenezer.

"It's not your corner."

"It was mine long before you came to Accra from your village."

"You weren't at that corner when I came to Accra."

"It's still my corner."

Ebenezer shook his head. "No."

"You think you're tough? I can pick you up by your head and break your neck in two."

His boys smirked.

Ebenezer started to leave, but Tedamm stepped in his way. "Get off my street corner. You hear me?"

"Try and stop me if you like," Ebenezer said.

Tedamm and his boys watched him as he went past. Ebenezer set his jaw. Now it was war. Him against Tedamm.

Ebenezer's home base was on the front veranda of the Prince Line Travel Agency on Knutsford Avenue. Every evening, street kids moved in as businesses closed for the day. Ebenezer shared his base with four good friends. They loved one another like brothers and had nicknamed themselves the Brooklyn Gang.

Besides Ebenezer, three of the boys were already back for the night. He slapped their palms in greeting and sat down next to tiny Mawusi, who was listening to music on a radio not much bigger than his hand. All of them had pitched in to buy the radio. They guarded it with their lives.

It was Mosquito, the fifth in the group, who was missing. Ebenezer asked where he was. Issa, a truck pusher and the official leader of the group, didn't know. Issa was almost eighteen, getting to be an "old man" now.

They talked and ate, sharing one small bowl of rice. That was all there was. They knew how to pace themselves so that they ate equal portions. No one cheated. They left some for Mosquito.

"Eben, you're first watchman tonight," Issa told him.

Every night it was the same routine. They took three equal

shifts to keep watch over one another until daybreak. You couldn't just happily go to sleep without someone keeping guard. That was exactly how Eben had allowed his shoeshine box to be stolen.

The four stretched out on the bare pavement. Mosquito would pick out his own spot when he arrived. Eben stayed seated for a while to rest his feet, but then he got up to pace back and forth so he could stay awake. He wondered where Mosquito was.

Eben needed to relieve himself. He would make it quick, even though the chance was small that someone would come along and attack the sleeping boys while he was away for only a few minutes. With a few strips of newspaper in his pocket, Eben trotted to the end of Knutsford Avenue, where it dead-ended at a chain-link fence on Kojo Thompson Road. Next to the fence was a broken-down *bola* truck that hadn't been moved in more than a year, its rear loader collecting garbage that was going nowhere. Eben slipped behind the vehicle, pulled down his pants, and crouched.

When he was done, he threw the soiled newspaper in the truck.

"*Ssss!*"

Eben turned to see who was hissing at him to attract his attention. He saw someone standing in the shadows at the opposite corner of the street.

Mosquito limped back to the base. He had hurt his ankle today while running after a tro-tro as it pulled into the Novotel Lorry Park. One had to fight to be the first to offer to carry passengers' luggage for a fee. Mosquito was hungry and exhausted. He was looking forward to seeing his mates, having something to eat, and getting some sleep.

Issa started awake as Mosquito touched his shoulder. He sat up quickly.

"Where Eben dey?" Mosquito asked.

"I don't know," Issa said, voice thick with sleep. "He was on guard. Maybe he went to the toilet."

Mosquito walked to the end of the street to check near the bola truck.

"Eben," he called out softly. There was no answer. He went around the other side of the truck. Eben wasn't there. Mosquito returned to Issa, who was propped up on one elbow waiting.

"He no dey?"

"No," Mosquito replied. It was almost ten-thirty, ninety minutes into Eben's shift from nine to midnight.

Mawusi stirred. "What wrong?" he mumbled.

"Where Eben dey?" Issa asked him.

"I don' know," he muttered and went back to sleep.

"Maybe he pass to the other side," Issa said to Mosquito.

They started off in the other direction, toward Kwame Nkrumah Avenue and the UTC building. It was pitch black, but they could make out the shadows of scores of street kids sleeping along the sidewalk.

"You hurt your foot?" Issa asked, noticing Mosquito's limp.

"Yah."

At Station Road, they went in opposite directions, calling out Eben's name. They searched Kinbu Road, then Tudu, going up as far as the Cocoa Marketing Board (CMB) building. Eben was nowhere to be found.

20

Tuesday morning, Accra woke up to a light drizzle. Dawson rose at 5:00 A.M. just so he could avoid the worst of traffic. At 5:30, when the neighborhood cocks began to crow like clockwork, he left the house and walked along Nim Tree to the main road, where he flagged down a cab. He arrived at CID by 6:00 and felt pleased with himself.

Barely an hour later, he got a call from Chikata and had to head right back into the rush-hour traffic he had wanted to avoid.

On Kwatei Kojo Street in Jamestown, a ditch-digging project had been going on for months. Every time it rained and the ditch was flooded, progress ground to a halt. The workers, who had been digging without the aid of heavy machinery, had arrived early Tuesday morning to empty the flooded channel. As they did that, they came across a dead body.

Chikata had roped off Kwatei Kojo at each end. The re-

sulting diversion was causing traffic backups on the surrounding roads, including High Street. Furious drivers leaned on
their horns while a traffic policeman tried to redirect them.

The CSU hadn't arrived yet. Dawson and Chikata looked
down at the body. Its head was completely submerged in the
mud, and only part of its left side was visible, with the left
hand sticking up like a rigid wave good-bye.

"Who found the body?" Dawson asked.

"They did," Chikata said, nodding toward a group of five
men with pickaxes, shovels, and buckets. "They were about to
start digging the channel out when they saw it. One of them
called Joy FM, who broadcast the report on the *Super Morning
Show*. I heard it before I left the house and stopped here on the
way to CID."

The country's reputed emergency numbers 1-9-1 and 1-9-
2 could be so unreliable that it was sometimes more effective
to call a radio station, which would then broadcast the emergency in the hope that the appropriate personnel were listening.

"Well done, Chikata," Dawson said quietly.

He saw the sergeant glance at him with pleasant surprise
that he had just earned praise, and Dawson realized guiltily
that he seldom gave it.

"Here comes CSU," Chikata said.

The CSU vehicle skidded on the wet road to a stop. The
crew got out, led by Deputy Superintendent Bright, the in-
domitable boss of the team.

"Morning, morning," he greeted Chikata and Dawson
cheerily.

"Morning, sir."

Bright peered into the ditch. "Interesting," he said. "Seems
we're always in the mud these days."

After quite some discussion, Bright and his men got down in the ditch and began to maneuver the corpse onto a sheet of tarpaulin.

"Hold on!" Bright said suddenly. "Wait. There's something wrong."

His assistants stood back, muddy, wet, and breathing heavily from their exertions.

"What's the matter?" Dawson asked.

"Is this the front of him or the back?" Bright said, staring at the body.

"What are you talking about?" Chikata asked.

"His face is facing upward," Bright said, "but . . ."

"He's on his belly," Dawson finished.

"Ewurade," Chikata muttered.

"His head is on backward," Bright said.

In the morgue, Dr. Biney shook his head in disbelief. "I've never seen anything like it."

The boy was lying on his belly, yet he was faceup. He was about sixteen. His wiry physique told of years of hard manual labor.

"There's a stab wound to the lowest one-third of the right thorax," Biney said. "This squared-off mark here is from the hilt of the knife, which means it was plunged deep. See these bruises around it? A bit tough to make out, but I call them satellite bruises. What do they tell us? They show the assailant rocked the knife around to inflict maximum damage. On internal examination, I think we'll find a collapsed lung and possibly a damaged diaphragm and lacerated liver."

"Is that the probable cause of death," Dawson asked, "or is it the broken neck?"

"Hard to say. If there was any life left in him after the stab wound, breaking his cervical spine made certain he was finished off. Or vice versa, for that matter. A violent death, for sure."

"By knife," Dawson said. "Like Musa."

"Are you connecting the two murders?"

"Speculating."

The murdered boy didn't have Musa's repulsive putrefaction, but the sight of a broken neck caused Dawson to cringe just as much, or even more. It shifted his thoughts to his brother, Cairo, rendered paraplegic at the age of thirteen. Mama had sent him to the corner kiosk to buy a tin of sardines. As he started across the street, she remembered one other item and called out to Cairo, who turned at her voice. He never saw the oncoming car, which hit him hard. He went up over the roof and down the back, severing his spinal cord. One moment he was the athlete of the family, who could outdribble anyone at soccer, the next he was a paraplegic totally dependent on the care of others.

"You'll want to look at the victim's belongings," Biney said, bringing Dawson abruptly back to the present. Moving to the counter by the sink, he showed Dawson the boy's clothes: a pair of brown trousers, a greenish shirt with only one button, and athletic shoes worn down beyond the sole.

"And there's this," Biney said. "It's still drying off, but I think it could be very useful to you."

He showed Dawson a business card, crumpled, moist, and soiled by mud, but still legible.

STREET CHILDREN OF ACCRA REFUGE (SCOAR)

Genevieve Kusi, Director

No. 2 Goodwill Road, Accra New Town

There was a phone number as well, which Dawson entered in his mobile. On the reverse side of the card, written several times in a halting scrawl, crossed out, and rewritten, as though the inscriber had been trying to perfect his signature, was the name *Ebenezer*.

21

SCOAR was in a slate-colored, two-story building. At the ground-floor reception, Dawson was asked to have a seat while waiting for Mrs. Kusi. Although the area had open windows on both sides, no air was moving through. The afternoon was as thick and warm as soup. Adult supervisors and kids of all ages went back and forth and in and out. The long bulletin board on the opposite wall carried community announcements, notices of job opportunities, and photos of smiling young men and women who had made it to the mainstream as seamstresses, carpenters, or wood carvers. A poster said:

Refuge Room Hours: 0800–1700. NO SMOKING, DRINKING, FIGHTING, OR STEALING

"Inspector Dawson?"

He turned at the sound of her voice, and his breath caught. She was only an inch shorter than he was, which made her tall for a woman. In her early thirties, she was beautifully dressed in sleek black slacks and a white silk blouse that clung possessively to her succulent breasts. Her skin was flawless molten dark chocolate. She had smooth, impossibly aligned braids and little or no makeup.

He stood up.

"Good morning," she said, smiling. Brilliant teeth. "I'm Genevieve Kusi."

They shook hands. Hers was soft and slim, nails short but manicured. Dawson's eyes begged to drop to her neck and below.

"Welcome to SCOAR," she said. "Please, come this way."

They went a short way down the hall to her office. Genevieve offered Dawson water, which he gladly accepted. It was a small but immaculate room. He noticed two small speakers above the door, facing her desk.

She sat opposite him in one of the three chairs in the room. He caught sight of her painted nails on perfect toes and tore his eyes away.

"So, how can I help you, Inspector?" Her voice was rich and warm.

"A young man was found dead in Jamestown this morning," Dawson said. "There was a business card on his body bearing your name, so I thought you might know him."

He handed her a photograph of the boy—just the face.

Her hand shot to her mouth in shock. "Oh, my goodness. That's Ebenezer Sarpong." She looked up. "You say he's *dead*? How? What happened to him?"

"He was murdered some time last night or early this morning."

"*Murdered.*" She gasped. "My God."

"Did he work here?"

"No, he was a street kid—a shoeshine boy. He hung

around with a group of boys who called themselves the Brooklyn Gang. Ebenezer came to the center once or twice a week. At first it was just to get some rest in the Refuge Room, but recently he had joined our computer classes." She shook her head. "This is the kind of nightmare we dread."

"How so?"

"We provide a refuge for homeless children here at SCOAR during the day, but we are closed in the evening. That means they're all on their own at night. There are thieves out there and fights over territory, possessions, and girls. We always fear that something like this might happen."

"I noticed you have all ages of children here, from babies up to late teens. Where are they all from?"

"From the more than sixty thousand homeless street children of Accra. Some of them travel from all parts of Ghana to find work here. There are also kids who make a conscious decision to leave their homes right here in Accra to live on the street—perhaps because of abuse. And then there are the children *born* on the street. We call them Second Generation."

"Sixty thousand," Dawson echoed. "And how many kids do you deal with here?"

"We have an average of about a hundred and twenty. A drop in the sea, I know. The problem is far bigger than we are."

"Was Ebenezer from Accra?"

"A village in the Western Region, I believe."

"Is there anyone who might have wanted to kill him? Maybe a turf rival?"

"I don't personally know of anyone, but we should talk to Patience, my main fieldworker. She knows so many of the street children. I'm not sure if she's here right now—she may be out in the field."

Genevieve put her head round the doorway and asked a teenage boy to find out where Patience was.

"Yes, madam," he said, scampering off.

A few minutes later, a plump, bespectacled woman appeared. Her face was round, open, and accepting. Dawson liked her at once.

"Come in, Patience," Genevieve said. "I'm glad you're here. This is Detective Inspector Dawson. There's some bad news."

Dawson shook hands with Patience. She pulled a chair over from the corner.

"What's happened?" she asked. Her voice was sweet and clear.

"I'm sorry to tell you that we found Ebenezer Sarpong murdered this morning," Dawson said.

Patience jumped back in her chair as if prodded with a naked electric wire. "Oh, Ewurade, *no*. Where?"

"Jamestown."

Patience's face showed her anguish. "He was one of our most promising youngsters. Learning to read and write through our computer program—" She stopped as her voice caught and her eyes moistened. "I don't even want to know how he was murdered. All I hope is that he didn't suffer."

"Inspector Dawson was wondering if Ebenezer had any rivals who might have wanted to harm him," Genevieve said.

"At least one," Patience said. "A young man called Tedamm. Basically the town bully among the kids, older and stronger than most of them. Over the years he's maneuvered himself into a position of power. One of the things he does is make children pay him a percentage of their earnings in return for his getting them a job on the streets."

"A one-time fee?" Dawson asked.

"Oh, no, Inspector. Every week or every month."

Dawson raised his eyebrows. "That could be profitable."

"And woe betide you if you don't pay what you supposedly owe. Tedamm hurts people. There aren't many boys who can stand up to him."

"He had a feud with Ebenezer?"

"Ebenezer led a crew of shoeshine boys in Lartebiokorshie. Tedamm claimed they were on his turf. Ebenezer wasn't intimidated, though. He was plucky."

"Is Tedamm capable of murder?" Dawson asked.

Patience's big eyes were direct. "In the world of homelessness, poverty, and desperation, you fight for survival, and there are no polite limits to the fight."

"I need to talk to Tedamm," Dawson said.

Patience exchanged a quick glance with Genevieve. "You can join me when I go out in the field in a little while, Inspector. We can ask around for him."

"Thank you. I would like to do that." He sat forward slightly. "About two weeks ago, a dead young man was found in Korle Lagoon."

"I remember the newspaper article," Patience said. "He was a truck pusher."

"Correct. His name was Musa Zakari. Is that familiar?"

"Not to me."

She looked at her boss, who shook her head. "Nor me. But just to be sure, we should check with Socrate Tagoe, our webmaster and photographer. He might know."

22

Dawson had imagined that Socrate would be thin and owlish. He was wrong. Standing around five-ten, Socrate probably weighed two hundred and fifty pounds. His office was too small for him, a laptop, a desktop, a printer-fax, piles of paper-stuffed folders, and boxes of CDs and DVDs.

"Socrate is our webmaster," Genevieve said as he and Dawson shook hands, "but he's also happy to get out there and photograph our street children, aren't you, Socra?"

He tried to smile as his eyes moved away from hers, collided with Dawson's for an instant, and swerved back. Dawson instinctively understood that the man really *didn't* enjoy going out to photograph street children. He was doing it for Genevieve, but if he had his way, he would spend all day sitting in front of his computer. He was no Patience.

"Socrate," Genevieve said, "have we ever had a boy here by the name of Musa Zakari?"

He rubbed his chin. "That name doesn't sound familiar to

me, but I can check my records." His voice was nasal and pinched.

"Thank you," Genevieve said. "You do that while I show Inspector Darko around."

Genevieve's and the other administrative offices were on the ground floor. There was one common office with space enough for four caseworkers, although SCOAR had only two at the moment.

"Budget cuts," Genevieve explained. "Things are tight."

"Everywhere," Dawson agreed.

"Most of our funding is from European organizations, but their trust in us has waned over the years."

"What do you mean by that?"

"As you said, finances are tight everywhere. Donors don't want to pour their aid into some bottomless pit anymore. They're saying to us, if you're not rehabilitating a certain number of children or getting a certain number of kids successfully into school or a trade, what's the point in our giving you money? In many ways, I understand their point of view. On the other hand, because we're often dealing with transient children, some of the results the donors demand are unrealistic."

Round the corner, Genevieve and Dawson went into a classroom where four young teenagers—three boys and one girl—were absorbed in front of computer screens learning word games under the supervision of a young female teacher. The boys, one of whom was bare-chested, all wore low-sagging basketball shorts. The girl had on a sleeveless red blouse and a wraparound skirt.

"These are poor children who live on the streets of an African city," Genevieve said to Dawson, "yet they love computers and video games as much as any pampered boy or girl in the U.S."

"Do you have Ghanaian traditional activities for them as well?" Dawson asked.

"Yes—for instance, we have drumming and dancing lessons on Fridays."

"What was Ebenezer most interested in?"

"He was completely illiterate when he came to Accra, but he learned basic reading and writing during the time he was here. He was a good drummer as well."

Dawson became aware of how close to Genevieve he was standing. She was wearing a light fragrance, but he also caught the pure scent of her skin—different from Christine's but just as intoxicating. He moved back slightly, afraid of the attraction.

"Come this way, Inspector," Genevieve said. "There's much more to show you."

Next door to the classroom was a small, rudimentary clinic run by a nurse, who was busy giving advice to a teenage mother cradling her baby.

"It's young pregnancies like hers that often make school an impossible prospect for teenage girls," Genevieve said as they went up to a room on the second floor with five sewing machines, two of them in use by girls training to be seamstresses. Beyond that was a woodshop, where two boys were carving traditional masks out of fresh mahogany.

The Refuge Room, the subject of the poster announcement downstairs, was the largest space so far. The front section had no furniture, just scores of floor mats on which a dozen or so children were lying down. Others were in the back recreation area playing table tennis and *oware* while the rest watched a DVD.

"This is their escape from the cruel streets," Genevieve said. "Sometimes the kids stage small performances or poetry or rapping contests."

"You do a lot of good work here," Dawson said. "I'm really very impressed."

"Thank you."

"Are there ever any fights here?"

"Rarely. Much less often than you might expect."

"Is it possible that Musa Zakari also visited the center but you don't remember him?"

"Possible, but unlikely. We know our kids intimately."

"And Tedamm? Has he ever been here?"

"I think that boy is too busy causing havoc out there to come here."

As they went back downstairs, a thought occurred to Dawson.

"Do you know a nine-year-old called Sly? He comes—or came—from Agbogbloshie."

"No, I'm sorry, I don't," Genevieve replied. "And I think I would remember the name Sly. Who is he?"

Dawson related how he had met the boy and then how Sly and his uncle had disappeared. In Socrate's office, someone was sitting next to him in front of the computer. His appearance was striking. A pale, sharp depression in his skin ran from the front part of his scalp to the middle of his forehead.

"Austin!" Genevieve exclaimed, beaming.

He gave her a huge smile. "Hey, Sis. How are you?"

They embraced.

"Meet Inspector Dawson. Inspector, my brother Austin."

Shaking hands, Dawson concentrated on the man's eyes, avoiding his forehead. A bad accident, maybe? He was older than Genevieve, and there was little, if any, resemblance. A half brother, perhaps.

"Austin is doing his Ph.D. in social systems among migrant groups in Accra," Genevieve said, pride in her voice. "And that of course includes our street kids."

"Congratulations," Dawson said to Austin.

"Originally my idea," Genevieve boasted, impishly. Austin smiled affectionately at her.

"Does the study include crime within these social systems?" Dawson asked.

"Oh, yes, very much," Austin said emphatically. His speech was rapid and tumbling, as though something was flogging it to go faster. "Crime is an integral part. I gather from Socrate that you're investigating the murders of two street teens, one of whom used to frequent this center?"

"Right."

"I would like to discuss the cases with you when you know a little more, Inspector. Would that be possible?"

"I don't see why not. How far back in time do you go in your study?"

"About fifty years. Urban crime patterns have changed, and much of it has to do with the increase in migrant and transient populations."

"I assume you've met Dr. Allen Botswe?"

"More than met—he was one of my professors last year. Great man. How do you know him?"

Dawson explained.

"Small world," Austin commented.

Dawson turned to Socrate. "Did you find Musa in your records?"

"No, sir. I didn't."

"Thank you for trying."

Patience put her head in the door. "Inspector? I'm ready to go out to the streets if you'd like to join me."

23

As she drove to their first stop, Patience explained to Dawson how, on a day like this, she would visit several of the street children's gathering places.

"Rule of thumb is," she said, "where there's commerce, there are kids, because that's where they get jobs. Carrying loads, cleaning, sweeping, assisting traders, and washing cars—things like that. Lorry stations, for instance, where boys hang around looking for luggage or farm produce to carry, and the big marketplaces. And that's where I try to engage them and talk to them about drugs, sex, alcohol, prostitution, AIDS, and such."

"Those are the problems that must keep you awake at night," Dawson said.

"Yes." She smiled at him. "It's as if you know me already. The sad thing for me is how many people like to say these kids are *responsible* for filth and disease in the city—not that they've come to a place that already has its vices, which the kids pick up. There are so many aspects about the attitude toward these children that I find ironic and troubling. For instance, it's often working class people who find street children so distasteful. Something else I hear is contempt for the boys and girls from northern Ghana specifically. I've heard people make reference to them as animals, which is very shocking to me."

"Speaking of the north," Dawson said, "I'm looking for a nine-year-old boy called Sly. Do you know anyone by that name?"

Patience shook her head. "No, I'm sorry, I don't."

She knew the Brooklyn Gang had their base near the railway station, so Patience had decided to visit the adjacent market called Kantamanto. She parked in the secure lot next to Merchant Bank across the street, where she charmed the security guard into letting her car stay without paying a fee.

Dawson crossed Kwame Nkrumah Avenue with Patience and went through the gated entrance to the station's huge, unpaved, dusty courtyard. For a part of town where space was scarce, there was a surprising amount of unused land around the defunct building. It was completely enclosed by a brick wall. Thirty meters to the right along the south wall was a pair of latrines, one for men and one for women—simple wooden stalls with bright blue doors, twenty pesewas for their use.

Walking past the latrines took them across a wide gutter to a slightly higher piece of land adjacent to the east wall, which ran alongside Nkrumah Avenue on its other side. Halfway along the wall, which went as far as one end of the railway building, there was a garbage dump.

The railway tower clock was permanently stopped at 5:32. The station, painted light salmon and gray with a corrugated tin roof, seemed sad and wistful. It could have been a beautiful showpiece of old architecture, even a museum, if only someone would renovate it. Dawson could guarantee that nobody would. The building would sit there and rot over the decades.

Squatters' laundry and mosquito netting were suspended between the columns along the station's veranda, and to complete the domestic picture, there were pots and pans scattered around. In an area that must have once been a passenger waiting room, a pastor was holding forth through a distorting microphone to a small congregation sitting on blue plastic chairs. Church wasn't just for Sundays.

Passing through another room where a young man was sleeping with his feet oddly propped up against the wall, Dawson and Patience emerged on the station platform. A group of *kayaye* sat talking and giggling with one another, their northern Ghana origins obvious from their heavy eyeliner and facial tribal marks.

Dawson and Patience crossed the tracks to the gray brick wall on the other side, where there was a prominent sign, DO NOT URINATE HERE, USE PUBLIC URINAL, a warning that was lost on a young man peeing a few meters away. Far up the tracks was a railway car with nothing to do but rust away.

Kantamanto Market was on the other side of the wall. Dawson and Patience entered the noisy world of buyers and sellers, porters and truck pushers. They passed by a loudspeaker blaring highlife. Raising her voice above the din, Patience told Dawson they were going to stop at Akuffo Junction, an area popular with the street kids.

When they got there, Dawson saw just why that was the case. It was a video game hangout—a narrow, noisy, and airless room with boys from six to eighteen squeezed together on a long wooden bench in front of a row of eight screens. All eyes were glued to the videos flashing before them, but only about every third boy had the use of a console.

"They pay for ten-minute segments," Patience explained.

"It can be expensive, so some of them split the cost two or three ways and take turns playing within each segment."

"I don't see how you can compete with the video games for the kids' attention," Dawson commented.

She laughed. "I can't, and I don't try. I work on the ones waiting their turns outside."

Patience spotted a cluster of boys loitering on the steps of a shop next door. She walked over to chat. She knew each one of them by name, lightheartedly teasing them and joking with a kind of affectionate toughness. She introduced Dawson casually to them. They had agreed beforehand that she would avoid telling them he was a policeman, at least at the beginning.

"Who knows Ebenezer Sarpong?" she asked them in Twi.

"Brooklyn Gang?" a boy with a green bandanna said.

"Yes."

"I know him," he said, "but it's a long time since I've seen him."

Before he could say anything more, the boys' attention was drawn away by the approach of a tall, lanky youth of fourteen or fifteen. They broke into a chant.

"Mosquito-Mosquito-Mosquito . . ."

"We're in luck, Inspector," Patience said. "This is Mosquito—he's in the Brooklyn Gang."

A smile broke out on Mosquito's small, tight face as he joined his friends.

"*Ei,* Mosquito!" Patience exclaimed. "Won't you ever stop growing? Look, even your trousers are already too short."

He laughed, shaking hands with her, and then with Dawson after a moment's hesitation. She beckoned to Mosquito to come with them over to the side where there was less video noise.

"How are you, Mosquito?" Patience asked, seriously now.

"Please, I'm fine."

"When was the last time you saw Ebenezer?"

He frowned, worried. "He didn't come back last night. We looked for him everywhere, but we didn't find him."

Patience rested her hand on his shoulder and squeezed it. "I don't like to bring bad news to you, Mosquito. I'm sorry, eh? Ebenezer was killed last night. I'm sorry, Mosquito."

"You say what?" He took a step back. "He was killed?"

"Yes," she said. "They found him in Jamestown."

"Oh." Mosquito nodded. For the moment, he didn't appear to be completely absorbing it. The full impact would take effect later.

"What time were you expecting Eben last night?" Dawson asked gently.

The boy shrugged. Dawson realized it might be difficult to get information from him right now. The news had thrown his mind into turmoil.

All of a sudden Mosquito looked up at Dawson and then at Patience. Something had struck him.

"Is he a policeman?" He was referring to Dawson as if Dawson wasn't present.

"Yes, Mosquito. He's just trying to find out what happened to Eben," she explained.

Dawson wasn't prepared for what happened next. Mosquito turned and bolted, gangly legs moving with astonishing speed. Dawson took off after him and followed as the boy took a sharp right down a row of shacks and past a group of butchers waving flies away from their fresh, red meat. He was sure Mosquito was headed to the south side of the market, where he could disappear in the maze of streets, but he ran into an obstacle before he could make it. A crowd was gathered around a fast-talking card trickster. Scrambling to make a path through, Mosquito lost his lead, and Dawson caught up with him as the con artist's audience yelled insults at Mosquito for upsetting their gathering.

Dawson grabbed the boy's arm and led him to an alley nearby.

"Why are you running?" Dawson demanded, breathing as hard as Mosquito was.

The boy kept his head down and turned away. He was trembling and pouring with sweat.

"Sit down for a moment," Dawson said quietly.

Mosquito sat. Dawson squatted on his haunches next to him.

"*Wote Twi?*"

The boy nodded, so Dawson continued to speak it.

"Why did you run away?"

"Please, I thought you were going to arrest me."

"Did you do something wrong?"

"Please, no."

"Then what are you running away for?"

Mosquito had no answer.

"Ebenezer was your good friend?" Dawson asked.

"Yes, please."

"I'm very sorry, eh?"

Mosquito was silent, head bowed.

"When was the last time you saw him?" Dawson asked.

"Yesterday morning. When I came back to the base in the night, he wasn't there. I asked Issa where he was, but he didn't know."

"Who's Issa?"

"The leader of our gang."

"When was the last time Issa or the other boys saw Ebenezer?"

"Ebenezer was the first watchman. They saw him before they slept."

"Watchman?"

"We have to be on guard, otherwise someone will come and try to steal our money."

"What did you do when you saw Ebenezer was gone?"

"We went to look for him. We were calling his name, but he didn't come."

"Do you know anyone who would want to kill Ebenezer?"

"Please, no."

"Do you know Tedamm?"

"Ah. Everybody knows Tedamm."

"Did Ebenezer fear him?"

"Not at all. Ebenezer didn't fear anyone."

"Where can I find Tedamm?"

Mosquito shook his head. Dawson wasn't going to get an answer on that one. He stood up and reached his hand out. Mosquito took it and got to his feet.

"Oh, my goodness."

They turned at the sound of Patience's voice as she came around the corner and joined them in the alley. She was completely out of breath.

"I was trying to run after you," she managed to say, "but I'm even more out of shape than I thought."

Dawson smiled. "Catch your breath."

But Patience wasn't going to wait. "Ah, Mosquito, but why did you run like that? Didn't I tell you never to run away from a policeman?"

"Yes, please, ma'am."

"But you forgot? You're growing so fast your brain is left behind?"

Mosquito grinned sheepishly.

"Will Issa be at your base right now?" Dawson asked him.

"*Mepaakyɛw, dabi.* Unless this evening."

"We can go with him to the base so you can see where they stay," Patience suggested to Dawson. "Maybe you can come back this evening to talk to them."

"Good idea. Come on, Mosquito, let's go. This time, we can walk."

24

Mosquito showed Dawson his base on Knutsford Avenue. By day, the stores were open and the street was bustling with traffic and pedestrians. It was hard to imagine that at night the area would become one big open bedroom for hundreds of homeless youth.

After leaving Patience and Mosquito, Dawson called Chikata to let him know what had happened and that he wanted them both to visit Issa's base that night.

"I'll make sure we have a driver," Chikata said.

Meanwhile, Dawson owed his brother a visit and thought this was a good time to get one in. For years as a paraplegic, Cairo had lived with their father, Jacob, who had taken care of him. Now Cairo was married to Audrey, a gem of a woman who loved him dearly. Together they owned a craft shop in Osu just off the bustling tourist trap Oxford Street. Cairo had started off small, selling his handmade traditional masks from home. He still made masks himself, but now he had to contract out to keep up with demand. He had done well for himself. Above all, Dawson was glad Cairo no longer lived with Papa. It meant being able to visit his brother without having to deal with the father Dawson felt so uncomfortable around. Papa had never shown any affection to him when he was a child, let alone now that he was an adult. What Dawson did remember were beatings and harsh words.

Cairo would probably be at work for another hour or so. Dawson turned off Oxford onto Third Kuku Crest, where he found a parking spot near the shop with the bright green canopy bearing its name, Ultimate Craft.

With outside temperatures past the century mark, the air-conditioned interior of the shop felt like paradise. Dawson loved the fresh smell of carved wood, new pottery, and crisply folded fabrics. Georgina, Cairo's assistant, was at the counter helping a customer. She greeted Dawson with a smile and told him Cairo was in his office.

He went through to the back, poked his head in the open door, and found his brother at his desk rapidly punching numbers into a calculator. Over the years Cairo had put on weight. His face was rounder, but he was still handsome, sporting a goatee that looked good on him.

"Counting your millions?" Dawson said.

Cairo looked up and laughed. "I wish it was so. Come in, you rascal."

They hugged each other. Dawson pulled up a chair. "How are things?"

"Could be better. Tourism is down. It's killing us."

Dawson nodded. "I can imagine. Where's Audrey?"

"She went to Tema to take care of some imports. How are you doing?"

"I'm all right."

"Oh, I'm glad you dropped by. I want to show you something new. Let's go to the front."

Cairo effortlessly swiveled his ultralight wheelchair and wheeled himself out ahead of Dawson.

"Take a look at this," Cairo said, handing Dawson a small attractive box.

"Wisdom cookies," Dawson read off the top. "What's that?"

"Our own twist on fortune cookies. Instead of something that predicts what's going to happen to you, these contain Ghanaian proverbs imparting wisdom."

"That's a clever idea. Who came up with it?"

"My brilliant wife. Try one."

The cookies were flat but bowed in shape. Dawson snapped one open and read the strip of paper on the inside. *Sankofa: It is not taboo to go back and fetch what you forgot.* The classic proverb.

Dawson popped the cookie in his mouth. It was crisp and crunchy. "Mm, delicious. Selling well?"

"Like beer at a bar. Perfect gifts for the tourists. Along with Ghanaian chocolate, of course."

"I'll take a box of the cookies home. Where do you get the proverbs from, by the way?"

"Right here," Cairo said, wheeling over to the small selection of books. He took one down called *Three Thousand Six Hundred Ghanaian Proverbs.*

"Three thousand six hundred?" Dawson said in surprise as he leafed through. "Are there even that many in English?"

"That's what I wondered myself," Cairo said, with a chuckle.

After sending Georgina home, Cairo closed the shop. He and Dawson sat talking for almost an hour about family and politics. Dawson had never seen his brother happier.

When it was time to go, he offered Cairo a lift home, which

was little more than a mile away. On the way there, Cairo phoned Audrey to let her know that she needn't pick him up from the shop.

Dawson unloaded the wheelchair and brought it around to the passenger side. Cairo expertly transferred himself out of the car.

"Take care," Dawson said.

"You too. My love to Christine and Hosiah."

Smiling, Dawson watched his brother roll away to his front door with impressive speed.

Christine was in the kitchen making dinner when Dawson got home. He presented her with his gift from the shop.

"Wisdom cookies!" she exclaimed. "Now why didn't I think of that?"

"My thought exactly," Dawson said, peering into the pot of simmering stew. "Mm, smells fantastic. Where's Hosiah?"

"Sulking in his room."

"Sulking? About what?"

"He announced today that he wanted pizza. I told him it's too salty."

Dawson frowned. "Pizza? Where has he been eating pizza?"

Christine hesitated. "Um . . ."

"Um, what?" He looked at her quizzically. "Oh, wait a minute. I bet you I know what's going on."

"Darko . . ."

But he was already out of the kitchen on the way to Hosiah's bedroom. The boy was lying in bed with his face pressed into his pillow. Dawson sat next to him and shook him gently.

"Hey, what's wrong with you?"

Hosiah whined.

"That's not an answer. Get your head out of the pillow, turn over, and talk to me."

Hosiah did as he was told, pouting.

"What's the matter?" Dawson asked.

"I want pizza." He pronounced it *pee-za*.

"What did Mammy tell you about pizza?"

"It has too much salt."

"Right. And what does salt do to you?"

"Makes my heart sick."

"Correct. You want to go to the hospital again?"

"No," Hosiah said miserably. "But . . ."

"But what?"

Hosiah stammered out an incoherent sentence with incomprehensible reasoning.

"Have you been eating pizza somewhere?" Dawson asked.

Hosiah was evasive. "I had some once."

"What do you mean you had some 'once'? Where and when?"

"At Frankie's at the Accra Mall."

"Granny took you there?"

Hosiah nodded.

"Aha," Dawson said triumphantly.

Back in the kitchen, he stood in the doorway with folded arms. "Good try, Christine."

She was practically squirming. "Sorry, Dark."

"Okay, that's that. Hosiah doesn't go to your mother's ever again."

"Dark—"

"Dark, nothing. I gave her another chance. Does she ever do anything right?"

"That isn't fair," Christine said sharply. "Look, it's partly our fault. We didn't really talk to her about the salt."

"No," Dawson said, shaking his head. "Oh, no. We're not taking the blame for this. She was well aware that salt is a problem for Hosiah, and she goes and chooses one of the *worst* foods for salt content. Good Lord, what is wrong with that woman?"

"But she probably doesn't know there's that much salt in pizza," Christine tried.

"Oh, please, Christine."

She sighed in exasperation, pouring the stew into a dish with a plop. Dawson called out to Hosiah and told him to wash his hands for dinner. The boy appeared in the kitchen a few minutes later with an aggrieved look.

"But why can't they take the salt out of the pizza?" he said as he sat at the table.

"Oh," Dawson said in surprise. He looked at Christine. "He does have a point. Couldn't we make a pizza ourselves with fresh tomatoes and no salt added?"

"I haven't a clue how to make it," she said.

"But how hard could it be?" Dawson said. "It's just dough and tomato and cheese, isn't it? I know cheese is expensive, but we could just use less of it."

"*Yay!*" Hosiah cheered. "Our own pizza! Let's make it now."

"We don't have the ingredients yet, silly," Dawson said, grinning. "We'll do it tomorrow."

Hosiah jumped off his chair and did a victory dance while chanting, "Pee-*za*, pee-*za*, pee-*za*!"

25

At the pit latrine near the railway station, Tedamm paid his twenty-pesewa fee, took the few sheets of wiping paper the custodian handed him, entered, took care of business, and emerged in under seven minutes feeling a trifle lighter.

He joined his boys Antwi and Ofosu waiting for him around the corner. They began their prowl, up to mischief of any kind—a small boy to beat up, a girl to harass or have sex with, someone to steal from. It was only nine o'clock at night. There was still plenty of time and a good selection of innocent people to pick from.

First they walked along Okai Kwei Road and then up Kwame Nkrumah Avenue to the CMB area, where there were a lot of girls to look at. From there, they went searching for their *akpeteshie* supplier on Tudu Road, where the pavement was already filling up with rows of homeless people for the night.

Watching commercial trucks loading and unloading merchandise, Tedamm and his boys shared the akpeteshie they had just bought. Bitter and powerful, it shot to their brains like the flame of a blowtorch.

"*Chaley,* they say somebody killed Ebenezer," Antwi said. "Did you hear that?"

"Yes, I heard," Ofosu said. "Maybe he annoyed somebody." Giggling, he looked pointedly at Tedamm, who stared back at him for a moment before delivering a resounding slap to the side of his head. Ofosu jumped back, clutching his face and squealing like a wounded piglet.

"Don't talk shit," Tedamm snapped.

Something caught his attention up the street. "There's that girl Comfort I told you about," he said, pointing with his chin. She was walking toward them, but then she crossed the road. "Let's go and get her."

They caught up with her, surrounding her like a pack of dogs. Tedamm told her he loved her beautiful copper color and her big buttocks. She laughed and tossed her head. Tedamm put his arm around her, and they all walked along Tudu Road together. "Have some akpeteshie," Tedamm said. "Come on, it's good for you."

She took a sip and spat it out. The three boys laughed at her.

"Take some more," Tedamm said, bringing the bottle to her lips. Some of it ran down her chin.

"I know somewhere we can go," Tedamm said, winking at his boys.

He took Comfort's hand as Antwi and Ofosu followed behind them. Someone was walking straight toward them. In the poor light of the street, it took Tedamm a moment to realize it was Issa. He kept coming without moving aside to give them any space to go by. He locked eyes with Tedamm as they got closer. They stopped two meters apart. Issa glanced at Ofosu, Antwi, and Comfort before coming back to Tedamm.

"So now you are happy that Ebenezer is dead."

"What are you talking about?" Tedamm said.

"You killed him because he wouldn't let you have his territory."

"*Kwasea*," Tedamm said. "Don't waste my time."

"You wait. You'll be sorry."

Issa kept his eyes on Tedamm as he went around him. As Issa walked away, Tedamm laughed at him, calling out insults until he was out of sight.

"Come on," he said to the others. "Let's go."

He turned up a narrow alley between Jabs Electric and the Ghana Commercial Bank building. On the other side, there was a short, unpaved road with a Vodafone kiosk and a brick wall at the end of it in a cul-de-sac. Apart from faint light from the ATM, it was pitch dark.

Antwi sat on a concrete block, and Ofosu knelt while Tedamm sat with his back against the wall with Comfort reclining against him. He fed her more akpeteshie. The drunker she got, the more he was able to expose her breasts and fondle them. He waited until Comfort became completely incoherent. They stretched her out on the ground, pulling up her skirt and tearing her flimsy underwear. Antwi and Ofosu held Comfort's legs apart. More than ready, Tedamm lowered his trousers to his thighs. She let out a shriek as he forced his way like a battering ram. He pressed his hand hard over her mouth and face. Her nose began to bleed all over his hand as she struggled. Tedamm felt a rush of excitement. Each thrust knocked the breath out of her.

They heard the sound of a car's tires as it turned into the cul-de-sac, and then headlights appeared.

"Someone coming!" Antwi said.

"*Hold her!*" Tedamm gasped. He couldn't stop now. The lava had begun to flow. Antwi bolted. Ofosu followed. The volcano erupted.

Breathing hard, Tedamm yanked up his trousers. He swung around. The car was stationary, the beams of the headlights trained on him. Blinded, Tedamm couldn't make out what kind of vehicle it was, but it wasn't a small car, for sure. The door opened, and someone, a man, stepped out and stood in front of the left headlight.

"Who are you?" Tedamm shouted.

The man, his face in shadow, didn't move. Tedamm, suddenly afraid, turned and fled.

26

A little past ten o'clock, Dawson and Chikata found Mosquito hanging around the outside of the railway station.

"How are you?" Dawson asked him. The boy looked nervous.

"I'm fine. Let's go to my base."

They crossed Kwame Nkrumah Avenue and walked along Knutsford Avenue. People were still awake, but many were already asleep on the pavement.

"Here is our place," Mosquito said, as they got to about the middle of Knutsford. On the veranda in front of the store, there were a couple cardboard mats. Only two members of the gang were back for the night: Issa, the leader, and Mawusi, who was sleeping. Dawson and Chikata shook hands with Issa, who was visibly uneasy.

"Is he all right?" Dawson asked, indicating Mawusi.

"He's sick," Issa said. "Fever."

Ironically, Mawusi meant "in God's hands," Dawson remembered from school. He was struck by how small the boy was.

"How old is he?"

"Thirteen," Issa said.

He looked more like ten.

"Maybe tomorrow I'll get some medicine from a pharmacy," Issa said lamely.

"Do you know about the clinic at the Street Children of Accra Refuge?" Dawson asked him.

"Eben told me something about it, but I've never been there before."

"You should take Mawusi there," Dawson said. He gave Issa one of Patience's cards.

Issa examined it for a moment. "Thank you."

"Not at all. I'm very sorry about Ebenezer."

Issa looked away, his gaze morose.

"Ebenezer was watchman from what time to what time?" Dawson asked.

"From nine to midnight," Issa said.

"And Mosquito came back at what time?"

"Almost ten-thirty."

"And Ebenezer was gone by then."

"Yes, please."

"And then you went to search for him?"

"First, Mosquito went to that side," Issa said, pointing to the east end of Knutsford. "When he came back, then the two of us went together to the other side."

"Let's take a look," Dawson said.

Issa led the way. Mosquito stayed behind to watch Mawusi. Dawson glanced back and saw the older boy covering the sick one with a cardboard mat.

There was an old bola truck at the end of the street parked

parallel to Kojo Thompson Road. Standing there rusting into oblivion, it reminded Dawson of the railway car at the station.

They went around the perimeter of the truck, carefully searching the ground with their flashlights. They looked inside the rear loader and poked around in the bola with a stick they got off the ground. Dawson wasn't expecting to find anything special, and they didn't.

"Let's go to the other end of Knutsford now," he said.

There was a pharmacy called A-Plax at Knutsford's western end, about a dozen street children sleeping on its veranda. Behind that was the dark hulk of the UTC building. Turning right took them up to Derby Avenue, Commercial Street, Kimberly Avenue, and Station Road, all of which ran parallel to Knutsford in that order going north. They had one feature in common: With little or no street lighting, they were very dark, particularly at their far ends. Ebenezer could easily have been attacked here or snatched away. Dead this morning in Jamestown, about two miles away, he had to have been moved and then killed or killed and then moved. There was a third possibility: killed *while* being moved.

Dawson was thinking about this as they stood at the side of Nkrumah Avenue. It was deadly quiet in the city now.

"Issa, we're also looking for Tedamm," Dawson said. "Have you seen him?"

"Yes, I saw him this night with his boys."

"Which boys are you talking about?"

"Antwi Boasiako and Michael Ofosu. They always follow him around."

"Where did you see them?"

"At Tudu Road. They were with some girl."

"Ebenezer had a quarrel with Tedamm, not so?"

Issa nodded, bitterness twisting his features. "He was trying to take Eben's spot. Eben wouldn't give him way. That's why Tedamm killed him."

Dawson was startled. "What? How do you know?"

"I just know."

"A feeling in your bones."

Issa nodded.

"How did Tedamm kill Eben?" Dawson asked. "And how did he get him to Jamestown?"

"I'm sure he came with his ruffian friends and put Eben by force inside a car, then they drove him to Jamestown and killed him there."

"Is there someone else who maybe wanted to kill Eben?"

Issa sucked his teeth and shook his head. "No one, except Tedamm. Everybody liked Eben."

"Do you know one Musa Zakari?" Dawson asked.

"No. Who is he?"

"They found him dead in the lagoon about two weeks ago."

"I heard something about it, but I didn't know him."

Dawson suddenly thought of Sly. He asked Issa if he knew a boy by that name. Again, no luck.

A scream rang out and whipped their heads around. It came from the general direction of the railway station. And a second one, now more like a woman keening.

"Let's go," Dawson said to Chikata.

They began to run.

27

Inside the railway station courtyard where Dawson had been just hours before, a crowd had gathered to stare at something going on in the garbage dump abutting the wall. There was some light coming over from Nkrumah Avenue but not much. Dawson and Chikata went around the crowd, skipping across the gutter and running up to the rear section of the trash pile, where a fat man was shining a flashlight on the body of a partially disrobed woman.

"Police," Dawson said. "Get back, please."

They did. Dawson and Chikata crouched on either side of the woman. With their flashlights trained on her, they saw she was young, probably in her midteens. She was lying on her stomach. Her buttocks were like enormous melons, but her limbs seemed collapsed and crumpled, like those of a squashed insect. *Dumped, like trash,* was Dawson's first thought. He was faintly aware of someone crying in the background.

"Blood," Chikata said, pointing.

Her disheveled blouse was soaked with it, and more so on the right. Dawson touched her. She wasn't cold. She wasn't warm either. She was tepid. *Tepid.* He'd never used that word for the temperature of a human being. That was for bathwater or a beverage.

Her head was turned in Dawson's direction. He shined his flashlight in her face. Her eyes were open, but her pupils didn't react and the corneas were already turning opaque. There wasn't a pulse.

"Dead," Dawson said. "See if you can get Bright and the crew."

"I'm on it," Chikata said, phone already out.

Dawson looked up at the fat man.

"Did you find her?"

"No, massa." He pointed his beam about ten meters away, where a young man was comforting a weeping woman. "That woman over there."

"Do you have a mobile?" Dawson asked.

"Yes, massa."

"Give Detective Sergeant Chikata your number in case we need to get in touch with you. Stand to one side, please—over there—but do not leave, understand?"

"Yes, massa."

"I can't reach CSU," Chikata said.

"Why not?"

"No network coverage."

"No network coverage in the center of Accra? Ewurade." Dawson pulled out his own phone, and handed it to Chikata. "Try mine."

He went over to the crying woman and the guy with her, who told Dawson his name was Patrick. The woman, Faiza, was his friend. She was eighteen or nineteen and pregnant, her belly stretching out her T-shirt.

"Are you okay?" Dawson said.

She moaned but didn't really answer.

"What happened?" Dawson asked.

Patrick spoke to her in Hausa. She babbled something incoherent in reply.

"She was coming to throw something away and she fell over the body," Patrick translated.

"We heard a scream," Dawson said. "Was that Faiza?"

"Yes, we all heard it too and came running."

"Does she know the dead girl?"

"No. She's just shocked, that's why she's crying."

"I understand. Did she see or hear anyone else around here?"

Patrick asked her and translated her reply to Dawson.

"No, she didn't see anyone. And she says she begs you, don't take her to jail."

"I'm not taking her to jail," Dawson said. He looked around. *How did the dead girl get here?* Was she carried through the entrance? Or from the station?

Chikata walked up, handing Dawson back his phone. "Bright says they're on another case in Mataheko."

"How long before they get here?" Dawson asked.

"At least one hour."

Dawson grunted. That really meant considerably more than one hour.

Chikata was staring at the body. "Is it the same killer, Dawson?"

"If that's a stab wound to the right side of her back, then I think it is." He glanced at the spectators. Some were dispersing while a fresh bunch was arriving to take a look. "I need you to question people who live in and around the station—ask them if they saw anything suspicious this evening. We want to know how this girl got here."

"I'll try my best, Dawson." As he walked away, Chikata added over his shoulder, "But you know how Accra people are—they don't talk to policemen."

"Have some faith," Dawson called back. Chikata's question was echoing in his mind. *Is it the same killer?* He made a call. As it rang, he prayed there'd be an answer. There was.

"Dr. Botswe? Inspector Dawson here."

"How are you, Inspector?"

"I'm well, but there's been another murder."

"Really. Where?"

"Inside the railway station courtyard. We're waiting for the CSU to arrive. Can you come to the crime scene? I would like your opinion."

"I'll be there as soon as possible, Inspector. I'm not too far away."

"Thank you very much, sir."

The crime scene team had still not arrived. The corpse, now covered by a length of cloth someone had produced, was getting colder and stiffer.

"Inspector?"

Dawson turned at Allen Botswe's voice.

"Thank you for coming, Doctor. You got here very quickly."

"I was close by on Graphic Road."

"Are you ready to take a look at the body?"

"Yes, I am."

Dawson pulled aside the cloth. "Her blouse is full of blood," he said. "Looks like it's a stab wound to the back, but I don't want to disturb her clothes until CSU gets photos."

With a small grunt, Botswe crouched next to the body. "If it is indeed that—a stab in the back—then it resembles Musa Zakari's."

"There's something you don't know," Dawson said. "This is the second case since Musa's."

"*Second?*"

"Yesterday we found a young male teenager murdered in the same way, dumped in a muddy ditch in Jamestown. And his neck was broken with his head twisted around one hundred and eighty degrees."

"Goodness."

"Again, my question is whether these could be ritual killings."

"Were there any other mutilations of the teenager? Eyes, genitals?"

"No."

"What about his background?"

"He was a shoeshine boy living on the streets."

Botswe was nodding. "These are not ritual killings. This is a serial offender with motivations completely different from those of the ritual killer. You can see what his signature is— single stab wound to the back with an additional mutilation, and then throwing the body in a distasteful place: the dirty lagoon, the muddy ditch, and now the garbage dump. His M.O. is to prey on these street youth. I have no doubt that we'll find this girl to be in that category."

"I'm still not sure about the signature. Why chop off Musa's fingers but not do something similar to Ebenezer?"

"Evidently that macabre twisting of the head *is* similar in the mind of the offender."

"Wait," Dawson said, snapping his fingers. "Dr. Botswe, you said the killer does what? *Throws* the body in a distasteful place."

"Yes, that's right. What is it, Inspector?"

Dawson sprang to his feet. "I'm a fool," he said. "The killer didn't drag the body here. He *threw* it."

Dawson turned, leapt across the gutter, and ran out the railway station's entrance. Now on the outside of the wall running along Nkrumah Avenue's sidewalk, he turned left and trotted up about thirty meters to four concrete blocks piled on top of one another next to the wall. Stepping up on them brought Dawson's shoulders past the top of the wall. He could easily see everything on the other side. The garbage dump was right below him.

Botswe looked up as Dawson's head appeared, and the light of realization dawned on his face.

Dawson returned to him at the crime scene. "You get me now?"

"Yes, I believe I do, Inspector."

"Here is my theory," Dawson said. "Level with the garbage dump on the pavement the other side of the wall, there's a stack of concrete blocks. The sidewalk is wide enough to accommodate any size vehicle, even up to an SUV. The killer drives up with the dead body in the boot or whatever. He mounts the sidewalk with the vehicle, backing it up to the concrete blocks. He stands on those while dragging the dead body out of the boot, then tosses the body over the wall."

As they were talking, CSU arrived. There were four of them, including Bright.

"We meet again," Dawson said.

"And in the same kind of place," Bright observed. "Smelly and dirty."

"Aptly put," Botswe said. "Part and parcel of the signature."

Bright looked at him, wondering who he was. Dawson introduced them.

Chikata came up. "Dawson, Issa is with a friend who says he might know the victim."

"Good," Dawson said. "Let's go and talk to him."

Dawson followed Chikata to where Issa and his friend stood next to the gutter.

"Hi, Issa," Dawson said. "What's happening?"

"This is Jonathan," Issa said, indicating the boy beside him. "He says maybe he knows the dead girl."

Jonathan looked to be sixteen or so. He had a lazy eye. "I heard someone say her name is Comfort," he said, "and I know a girl called Comfort."

"Who is that someone?" Dawson asked.

"I don't know the man," Jonathan said. "He was here earlier, but he's gone now. I heard him telling people that he recognized that girl and that her name is Comfort and that she's a head porter at Agbogbloshie Market."

"What did this man look like?"

"Tall," Jonathan said, lifting his right hand high above his head. "And thin like he hasn't eaten for two months."

"How old?"

"Maybe . . . thirty? I don't know. He looks old."

"Was he wearing some colorful clothes?" Issa said.

"Eh-heh, yes," Jonathan said. "Some crazy orange and purple clothes."

"Then that must be Flash," Issa said. "The prostitutes at Timber Market pay him to use a tent belonging to Tedamm."

Tedamm. Again.

"And you think you might know the same Comfort this guy Flash was talking about?" Dawson asked Jonathan.

"I know one Comfort Mahama who is a *kayayo* at Agbogbloshie Market."

"Are you willing to look at the body and identify her if possible?"

Jonathan looked nervously at Issa, who said to Dawson, "Please, can I go with him? He's afraid."

"Sure."

The three of them walked over to where the girl lay under the sheet.

Dawson looked at Jonathan. "Ready?"

Issa put his arm around his friend's shoulders. Jonathan swallowed and nodded.

Dawson uncovered the girl's head, shining his flashlight on her.

"Yes," Jonathan said tightly. "It's her."

"You're sure?" Dawson said.

"Please, yes, I'm sure."

Issa drew in his breath sharply, looking at Dawson in surprise.

"What's wrong?" Dawson said.

"Please, she's the same girl I saw with Tedamm and his boys tonight."

28

Chikata stood slightly behind Dawson in the morgue at the autopsy table as Dr. Biney looked over Comfort's body. It was his first autopsy of the morning.

"Age sixteen to seventeen," Biney said. "There's a penetrating knife wound to the back on the right side, identical to the two previous cases we've seen."

"Any mutilations like Musa's?" Dawson asked.

"Yes, there are."

George, the venerable morgue attendant, turned the corpse over.

"Here are those mutilations, Inspector," Dr. Biney said. "Deep wounds to both knees inflicted well beyond the joint capsule, followed by excision of both patellae. In other words, wholesale removal of the kneecaps. Almost as if he scooped them out."

"Like the amputation of Musa's fingers."

"Yes, but there's something else. I see signs she was raped."

"*Raped,*" Dawson said, startled. "Oh. Now I'm confused."

"Why?" Chikata asked.

"Rape says sexual homicide," Dawson said, "and that's not what the other two were."

"Maybe Dr. Botswe can shed some light on this?" Biney suggested.

"I agree," Dawson said. "I had him come to the crime scene, so I'll go back and tell him about this rape thing."

"Were there any helpful leads at all at the scene?"

"We're looking for two people who may be involved," Dawson said, "and they appear to know each other—the ubiquitous Tedamm and a new character known as Flash. We searched for them last night but came up short."

Dawson glanced at his detective sergeant, whose fine forehead had begun to bead with sweat. He didn't look too good.

"What's wrong with you, Chikata?"

"I feel somehow hot."

"That's because you're getting faint," Biney said. "You'd better go outside for some fresh air."

Chikata walked out quickly.

"Good call, Inspector," Biney said, with a smile. "This place can get to you after a while. Another few seconds he would have been on the floor."

"He's on the squeamish side," Dawson said, with a tint of disdain.

"Low threshold, I call it," Biney said. "What's next in your investigation?"

"We have to find Tedamm and Flash. If you don't mind, I'll leave you to do the rest of the post without me."

"Of course. I'll call you later with the full report."

As Dawson got to the door, he hesitated. For several days now, he had been turning something over in his mind, something he had been planning. The only question was, When was the right moment?

"Something else, Inspector?" Biney said.

Now was the time.

"Doctor, I wanted to discuss something with you, if you wouldn't mind," Dawson said falteringly. "It has nothing to do with any of the cases."

"But of course. Let me get off all this garb and we can talk in the office."

They went back together to a bare, echoing room and sat side by side at the table where the pathologists usually wrote up their final reports.

"How can I help, Inspector?"

"I know I mentioned my son, Hosiah, to you when we first met," Dawson started. "What I didn't tell you at the time is that he has a ventricular septal defect."

"I'm sorry to hear that. Is he doing all right?"

"I'm afraid not. He's slowly getting worse, in spite of his medicines and salt restriction. He needs the surgery, but we're up against a sum of money we simply can't afford, and what we have in savings is still meager compared to the amount we need. We made an appeal to Korle Bu for financial clemency, but that was turned down. We didn't qualify for a personal bank loan either."

"The Ghana Police Service can't help?"

"They can reimburse us. However we have to pay for the operation first. I'm not asking you for money, Dr. Biney—I wouldn't do that. I'm just hoping you might have a suggestion as to what my wife and I can do at this point."

"It's a dire situation for you," Biney said sympathetically. "If I were a cardiac surgeon, I would perform the operation myself and not charge you one pesewa. Alas, I'm not that. But there still might be some way I can help. I know the director of the Cardiothoracic Center, Dr. Solomon Gyan. Let me talk to him about it and see if we can work something out."

"Thank you so much, Doctor," Dawson said, brightening. This sounded promising.

"Of course I can't guarantee anything," Biney cautioned hastily, "and it may take me a little time. Give me a few weeks to work on it. Dr. Gyan is constantly out of town."

"Thank you, Doctor," Dawson said again. "This means a lot to me."

"Don't mention it at all, Inspector. This is what friendship is all about." With a twinkle in his eye, Biney added, "So when I show up at CID with a sticky problem, I'm marching straight to your office."

The two men laughed together.

His heart uplifted, Dawson joined Chikata outside and they returned to the railway station to ask around for Tedamm. The name was from the northern regions, so they thought one of the kayaye might know him. But no one had seen him around.

"All right, then," Dawson said, "let's go to the Timber Market to look for this Flash guy," Dawson said.

Wednesday morning traffic was predictably heavy along High Street. Dawson sat in front next to Sergeant Baidoo. Chikata was in the backseat.

"Wow," he muttered, swiveling around to look at a pretty woman walking by.

"Chikata, when are you going to settle down and get married?" Dawson asked.

He laughed. "I don't know. Soon."

"Are you dating anyone?"

"There are two women I like," Chikata said. "I can't decide between the two of them."

"Maybe it's neither, then. One of them should stand out."

"Maybe so." Chikata smiled. "Ei, Dawson! You surprised me. You never asked me anything like that before."

"Just interested in your well-being."

Out of the corner of his eye, he saw Chikata staring at him.

"What, you think I have no heart or something?" Dawson said.

"Oh, no, Dawson, I would never think such a thing."

"*Omale,*" Dawson retorted, Ga for "you're lying."

They burst out laughing in unison.

At the Timber Market, they went past buyers and sellers haggling over rows of stacked planks and logs. Wood wasn't all there was. There was a fetish stall with herbs, animal skins, and scary looking skulls. Kayaye walked by with skyscraper head loads, and a young man with a lightweight mike and speaker system slung over his shoulder was going through the market broadcasting a get-tested-for-HIV campaign.

Dawson and Chikata split up but kept within visual distance of each other. If one of them ran into Tedamm, the other should be close by to help.

Dawson caught up with a kayayo and walked alongside her. She was much shorter than he, but the sacks of flour on her head towered over him.

"How are you?" he asked her.

"Fine." She moved her eyes, not her head, to look at him.

"I'm Darko. What's your name?"

"Amariya."

"Beautiful name. From where?"

"Northern Region. Walewale."

"You like Accra?"

"Life is too hard." Amariya went one way to avoid an oncoming cart. Dawson went the other. They reunited on the other side. "But in Walewale I can't make money to support my children, so I have to stay here."

"I'm looking for someone."

"Who?"

"His name is Tedamm."

"Hmm. That man." She wrinkled her nose.

"Have you seen him?"

"I saw him last week."

"What about a man called Flash?"

"Him, I know where he is." She pointed ahead and to the right. "Turn there, walk all the way to the end where there's no more traders, and you'll find him. Don't tell him I showed you the way."

"I won't." Dawson tucked a cedi bill in the fold of the cloth around her waist. "Take care of your children."

She smiled. "Thank you."

"Not at all. Be careful."

Dawson joined Chikata again. "Let's go and get Flash."

29

They followed the kayayo's directions, walking until the heavily commercial section of the market fell behind them. They saw a few girls loitering. Dawson picked one out and beckoned to her. She was about sixteen, as bony and hungry as a stray cat. She approached them a little warily. Maybe she had caught a whiff of policeman.

In Twi, Dawson asked her how much. *"Sɛn?"*

She wasn't sure if he meant both him and Chikata. *"Mmienu?"*

"Only me, not him."

"Four cedis."

"What's your name?"

"Thelma."

"Is Flash there?"

"Yes, please."

"Okay, let's go."

"Follow us," Dawson said to Chikata, "but stay out of sight."

They rounded a corner. There, standing in front of a makeshift tent in a cul-de-sac, was Flash in a crimson shirt and bright green-striped pants. He gave Dawson the up-and-down.

"Who are you?" Flash said, his voice like a frog's croak.

"What do you care who I am? I just want to have sex with this girl and go."

Flash grunted, his eyes darting past Dawson's shoulder to check that there was no one else. Like a policeman, for instance. He held out his hand to Thelma, who was about to give him the fee when Dawson stopped her. He took out his badge, showing it to Flash. "Police. You're under—"

Flash made a run for it, but he didn't get far. Chikata appeared seemingly out of nowhere, grabbed him, and swept his feet from under him. Flash went down in a cloud of dust. He coughed and spluttered as Chikata cuffed him.

Dawson turned to Thelma, who was trembling in fear of arrest.

"Listen to me," Dawson said. "Life as an ashawo is dangerous. These men have diseases that can kill you. Be a porter, or a sweeper, or sell on the street, but not this."

"Please, I do all those things already," Thelma said sadly. "Not enough pay."

"Do you have children?"

"No, please."

"But you want some, not so?"

"Yes, please."

"Then don't do this. If you die, how will you have children? Do you understand?"

"Yes, please."

Dawson took one of Genevieve's cards from his wallet. "Go to this place. They can help you. And I don't want to see you here anymore. Hear?"

She walked away quickly, giving Chikata and Flash a wide berth. Dawson watched her leave and suddenly felt hopeless. *Such a hero, aren't you.* As if he was making the slightest difference to what this girl would do with her life. In a week, she'd be back.

He grabbed a plastic chair that had been perched to one side of the tent. He plunked it down next to Flash, who was still on the ground with Chikata standing over him.

"Mr. Flash, I'm Detective Inspector Dawson. Please get up and have a seat."

Chikata helped him up into the chair.

"We have a few questions for you," Dawson said.

"I haven't done anything," Flash said wildly, his eyes bobbing and jerking.

"Then what were you doing last night at the railway station where Comfort Mahama was killed?"

"I wasn't at any railway station and I don't know any Comfort."

"People saw you there, my friend, so don't lie to me," Dawson snapped. "Let me tell you something, Mr. Flash. For every lie you tell, I'll give you five years in jail. You've just told me two lies, so you already have ten years. Next lie, fifteen."

"You can't do that," Flash challenged nervously.

"Oh, yes, he can," Chikata said without missing a beat.

"You want to spend ten years in jail or not?" Dawson said.

Flash swallowed. "No."

"Then tell us the truth," Dawson said, noticing a small crowd of spectators beginning to collect. "If you tell the truth, I'll let you go. Agreed?"

Flash nodded resentfully.

"Good," Dawson said. "So, asking the question again, what were you doing last night at the railway?"

"I live around CMB. I was walking home with my friends when I heard that woman scream. When I went there, one man was shining his light on her and I saw it was Comfort."

"How did you know Comfort?"

"Ashawo."

"She used your tent?"

"Yes."

"Did she ever cheat you or try to cheat you out of money?"

"No. These girls can't cheat me. I'm too smart for them."

"Where were you between seven and ten o'clock last night?"

"Heh?"

"Between seven and ten o'clock last night, where were you?"

"With my friends. We went to a chop bar in Ussher Town."

"What's the name of the chop bar?"

"Jesus Is Coming."

"When will that happen?"

"Eh?"

"Never mind. Maybe you'll get it later. Where is Ted-amm?"

Flash was thrown off by the sudden change in direction.

"We know you know him," Dawson jumped in. "You pay him out of the money you collect at the tent."

"Eh-heh."

"So where is he?"

"I don't know."

Dawson lifted the hem of Flash's shirt and snapped his mobile off his belt, thumbing through the address book until he came to "Tedamm." He dialed the number. Once it started ringing, he held it to Flash's ear. "Ask him where he is, but don't say anything about us."

Dawson brought his ear close to the phone. Tedamm came on the line.

"Yes, Flash?"

"Where are you right now?" Flash asked in Hausa.

"Jamestown. Looking for that boy who hasn't paid me. What are you doing?"

"Nothing. I call you later."

Dawson pocketed the phone.

"Ho!" Flash cried. "My phone!"

"You won't need it where you're going. We're taking you to the station."

Flash looked as if he was going to cry. "Oh, Inspector, abeg you. Mepaakyεw, you said you would let me go if I tell the truth."

Dawson raised his eyebrows. "I never said that. Did I say that, Chikata?"

"I never heard you say that, sir."

They escorted a protesting Flash along what turned out to be his walk of shame. Men, women, and children jeered at him as he went by, even if they had no idea who he was or what he had done. The fact that he was in handcuffs was enough reason to join in the fun.

Dawson booked Flash into Korle Bu Police Station. Then Sergeant Baidoo drove Dawson and Chikata toward Korle Lagoon, where Tedamm had said he was.

Chikata texted him, *whre r u?*

"Let's hope he responds," Chikata said. "If he isn't in the habit of texting Flash, he might get suspicious."

The phone buzzed ten minutes later with the reply *nr fi stn.*

"Dawson, he's near the fire station."

"That must mean the one at Jamestown," Dawson said.

They were only minutes from the fire station, which was on the north side of Cleland Road, where Jamestown trailed off. On the south side were the beach, the fishing harbor, the slave-era James Fort, and the Accra Lighthouse.

Baidoo pulled over onto the pavement opposite the fire station. Dawson and Chikata got out, heading toward the unoccupied expanse of land between the station, the edge of the lagoon to its west, and the beginning of Agbogbloshie to its north. A developer's dream was that expensive chalets would one day populate the banks of a crystal clear lagoon. Until then, the Accra Metropolitan Assembly deemed the area off-limits for any new construction. A few unauthorized buildings on the edge of the property had been shut down and condemned, including one warehouse belonging to Woodcrest Services, a gypsum board and acoustic tiling company. When the demolition would actually take place, Dawson thought every time he went past the warehouse, was anyone's guess. It was like the bola truck on Kojo Thompson Road, the old railway car, or the UTC building— all doing nothing except deteriorating with time and the elements.

"What's going on up there?" Chikata said.

Two hundred meters to their north, about a dozen boys stood in a circle watching something. Dawson and Chikata faintly heard someone screaming. They broke into a run. Closer, they saw a muscular, shirtless young man kicking a boy on the ground. Rolled in a ball, skinny, and probably no more than about thirteen, he was crying out as he clutched his head, trying to shield himself.

A boy in the crowd shouted, "Tedamm, beat him well!" and a couple others guffawed.

So this is the infamous Tedamm.

Each time Tedamm drew his foot back, he shouted, "You think you can trick me? Eh? You think I don't know you're trying to cheat me?"

He kicked the boy again, this time in the head. The boy appeared to lose consciousness. Something expanded in Dawson's chest, like a parachute opening. The old, terrible rage came out of hibernation. He changed direction in an instant, circled around, and came up behind Tedamm so quickly that few people saw his approach. Left forearm behind Tedamm's head, right arm across the front of Tedamm's throat, hand anchored to his left shoulder. Dawson did it very quickly and tightened the noose.

Tedamm was a mass of muscle. He pushed back, kicked his legs in the air, and twisted his body, throwing Dawson off balance. They went to the ground together, Tedamm on top, faceup. He tried to writhe out of Dawson's grip, but it was steady and deadly. After seven seconds, Tedamm went limp. *Five seconds more will kill him.*

Dawson didn't release.

Let him go.

Dawson didn't release. Time seemed to stop. His hearing deadened and his surroundings darkened.

Suddenly he realized Chikata was screaming at him. Dawson looked up at his sergeant's terrified face. He released his hold. Chikata pulled Tedamm off. Dawson got to his knees. Tedamm didn't move.

Chikata's mouth was open in shock. "Dawson," he whispered. "What are you doing?"

Dawson slapped Tedamm's face. His eyes fluttered open. He tried to sit up.

"Stay where you are," Dawson said, pushing him back down. To Chikata he said, "Check if the boy is okay."

Chikata went to attend to him. Dawson rolled Tedamm over and cuffed him, leaving him facedown. The audience was stunned and silent. They had just witnessed the felling of the most powerful tree in the forest.

30

Dawson and Chikata reported their progress to Chief Superintendent Lartey. Tedamm was ready for interview in the assistant superintendent's room.

As they left Lartey's office, Chikata said, "Dawson, at the lagoon today I was really scared."

"Of what?"

"I thought you had killed Tedamm. That choke hold is dangerous."

"I admit maybe I went a little too far," Dawson said, "but look at what he was doing to that kid." He paused for a moment. "Not that I'm recommending you ever use a choke hold on anyone."

Chikata nodded. "Yes, I know."

"Get a shirt for Tedamm before we begin."

Chikata trotted downstairs, returning with a shirt from the so-called Lost and Found. It was really suspects' abandoned clothing.

As they went in to talk to Tedamm, Dawson threw the shirt on the table at which Tedamm was sitting.

"Put this on," Dawson said. "We don't need to see your chest."

Tedamm would have sneered, but a sneer was on his face already. He didn't put the shirt on.

Dawson took the only other chair in the room. He set it down with a bang opposite Tedamm. Chikata stood between Tedamm and the door with a clipboard and paper.

Dawson dropped a folder on the table and sat down. "I said, put the shirt on."

Tedamm picked it up and threw it over his head in one smooth motion. Not bad for a guy who rarely wore a shirt.

"How are you, Mr. Tedamm?" Dawson asked.

No answer. Tedamm kept his head angled downward, but his eyes were turned up at Dawson like nuggets of red-hot charcoal.

Dawson recited the standard police advisory statement. Nothing worse than an arrestee getting off on a technicality.

"What is your full name?" Dawson asked.

He waited a moment for Tedamm to speak. The man kept his clap shut. Dawson stood up abruptly, the legs of his chair squeaking on the floor.

"Lock him up," he said to Chikata with a dismissive wave. "I don't have time for this. We'll come back sometime tomorrow and see if he's ready to talk to us."

He started toward the door.

"Kareem Tedamm." It came out like the growl of a bush cat.

Dawson returned and sat down again. "Why were you beating that boy?"

"He was supposed to pay me, but he wouldn't," Tedamm said. His voice had lost the growl. Now it was surprisingly soft.

"Pay you for what?"

"I found him his job at Makola Market, so he has to pay me."

"Every week?"

"Yes."

"So everyone you find a job has to pay you like that?"

"Of course. That's how it is."

"So you make a lot of money."

"Not as much as you."

"And you also beat up a lot of people, not so?"

"Do you even know how the life is in the streets?" Tedamm challenged. "You have to fight to be on top, and when you get on top, you have to fight to stay there. People fear me—I *make* them fear me, you hear?"

"You're a bully," Dawson said. "That's all you are. And behind every bully is a coward. If that boy dies from your kicking him in the head, you'll be charged with murder."

Tedamm's eyes met Dawson's unflinchingly.

"Ebenezer Sarpong," Dawson said. "Did you know him?"

Tedamm shook his head.

"Yes, you did," Dawson said. "You told him he would be sorry if he didn't leave his shoeshine corner in Lartebiokorshie, but he didn't do as you told him."

"And so what?"

Dawson slid one of Ebenezer's autopsy photographs from the folder to Tedamm's side of the table. "And so this."

Tedamm's gaze flicked down for a moment, and then back up.

"Do you know something about that?" Dawson asked.

"I know he's dead, that's all."

"Not just dead. Murdered."

"So what are you asking me for?"

"Where were you on Monday night between nine o'clock and midnight?"

"With my friends in Agbogbloshie."

"What are the names of your friends?"

"Antwi and Ofosu."

The same names as the two people Issa had told Dawson always followed Tedamm around.

"What about after midnight?" Dawson asked.

"We slept at Agbogbloshie."

"Did you see Ebenezer Sarpong at any time on Monday night?"

"No." He blinked.

"You're lying, Tedamm. I want to warn you about something. There's a lie detector in this room. No, don't look up at the wall. It's not there. It's right here." Dawson V-pointed to his eyes. "And in here." He pistol-pointed to his temple. "So, one more time. Did you see Ebenezer on Monday night?"

"I saw him when he was coming back to his base. I greeted him. That's all."

"Did you argue with him?"

"No. About what?"

"I'm asking you."

"I don't waste my time with small boys like Ebenezer. He's dead, and so what? Sorry, but I'm not going to cry for him."

Dawson brought out a photo of Comfort and put it in front of Tedamm. "Do you know her?"

Tedamm looked down for only a second. "No."

"More lies. You've already forgotten what I said. We know you were with her last night. Someone saw you with her. You, Antwi, and Ofosu. All three of you were with her."

Tedamm looked at Dawson dispassionately. "It's a lie. I wasn't with her."

"Look at the picture carefully." Dawson brought it closer to Tedamm's face. He drew his head back. "Here's another one. This is how they found her. Comfort Mahama was her name. Is this what you did to her? Threw her away like rubbish?"

Tedamm turned his head away.

"We know she was raped, Tedamm. Did you do that to her?"

"I didn't do anything."

A faint sheen of sweat showed at the top of his forehead like light drizzle on asphalt.

"Why can't you look at it, Tedamm? You raped her, didn't you? Your boys Antwi and Ofosu held her down while you did it. And then you killed her."

"No, I didn't."

"Didn't what? Rape her or kill her?"

"None of them." Tedamm's voice strengthened. His eyes narrowed. "So, why don't you beat me now, Mr. Inspector Man? I know about you. You caught one friend of mine two years ago. The one you said raped a girl. And you beat him well, remember?"

Chikata's head popped up like a jack-in-the-box.

Dawson was flabbergasted. Tedamm was absolutely correct. In a fit of temper that rarely troubled Dawson nowadays, he had repeatedly hit a rapist in the face after the man declared that his victims deserved what they had got.

"You broke his nose," Tedamm continued. "You say behind every bully is a coward. So who is the coward here, apart from me?" Tedamm symbolically pointed his index finger to his right eye. "You see now?"

And Dawson did see something. Stains underneath Tedamm's fingernails.

"Tell me about Comfort, Tedamm."

"Tell me why you beat my friend when he didn't do anything."

"Just because the court didn't find him guilty doesn't mean he didn't do it."

"But why did you beat him? You made him bleed all over his face, Inspector Dawson. Why?"

A smile played at the corners of Tedamm's lips as he locked eyes with Dawson. "When somebody says the word *rape,* you become like a madman."

Dawson's phone rang. He kept his gaze steady on Tedamm as he answered. "Hello?"

"Biney here."

"Yes, Doc?"

"We have semen suitable for DNA testing."

Outstanding. "And we have a suspect," Dawson said.

"Excellent. Get me swabs and a blood sample."

"We will. Thank you, Doctor."

Dawson pocketed his phone. Tedamm was looking amused, but something about Dawson's face made his smile fade.

"You're going back to your cell now. Cuff him, Chikata."

Tedamm leapt up. *"I didn't do anything!"*

Chikata tackled him, thrusting him flat on the table, wrestling to get his wrists behind his back.

Dawson leaned on Tedamm's shoulders to hold him still.

"Don't fight. It's two against one, and more outside the room."

They guided their prisoner to a corner to face the wall. He stood breathing heavily, his torso heaving.

"Get someone here from Korle Bu to swab his cheek and his fingernails," Dawson told Chikata. "We need blood too."

He moved closer to Tedamm, speaking softly. "We're going to find your friend Antwi. We'll see if you were telling the truth."

Tedamm shrugged his muscle-knotted shoulders.

"Oh, you don't care, eh?" Dawson said. "When we find out whose sperm is inside Comfort and whose blood is under your fingernails, we'll see if you still don't care. And then we'll see if you don't care after you've been in prison so long you forget what the sky looks like."

Tedamm turned his head and spat on the floor.

Dawson went back to Chief Superintendent Lartey's office.

"We want to find this boy Antwi as soon as possible, sir. I need people."

"How many?" Lartey asked, like a suspicious parent.

"At least six."

"What, you think yours is the only case in town? We have other priorities besides your case, you know."

"I understand, sir, and I don't know what these other priorities are that you talk about, but—"

"Let me give you just one example," Lartey interrupted, his voice sharp as a straight blade. "The VP of Ghana Petroleum was murdered early this morning in his house in Airport Residential. Shot execution style. Did you know about that?"

"Oh," Dawson said. "No, I didn't."

"I've got an internationally connected oil executive dead, and you've got these nameless prostitutes and good-for-nothing street people. Who do you think wins?"

"It's murder either way, sir," Dawson said. "Prostitute or oil exec, dead is dead."

Lartey closed his eyes for a long-suffering moment. "Four constables, Dawson. That's all you get. And you'll need to fill out an official request for them."

31

Localized scleroderma. That was what Austin Ansah had. It caused the strange deformity called *en coup de sabre* that ran from his scalp into his forehead like an oblique lightning bolt. It could, and most probably would, become worse.

As he read through a paper written by researchers from UNICEF, he rubbed his fingertips across the irregular depression in his brow, an unconscious habit.

"I imagine you must be used to it by now," a stupid woman had once said to him.

"So is an amputee," Austin had retorted. "That doesn't mean he wouldn't like his leg back."

He was thirty-eight. Women were not attracted to him. He knew that. In fact, they were repulsed. They looked away when they saw him. If they were in a group, they would whisper to one another, *What's wrong with his forehead?* At wedding receptions, the single women wouldn't dance with him even if he asked, which he no longer did. He had some male friends. They invited him places sometimes—whenever they felt sorry for him.

Austin had been working on his thesis, "Social Structures Among Migrant Groups of Accra," for three years. He had begun to take notice of migrant girls the way an ornithologist realizes the beauty of the birds he studies. A year ago while he was in the field one night at the Nkrumah Circle, a street girl had walked up to him and propositioned *him*. Taken completely by surprise, Austin had stammered his refusal. The girl went away, but her image and her voice never left him. It was as if he had been given an analgesic for pain but not quite enough. He had tasted a tiny bit. He craved much more.

So he went back. That first time, he was shaking with excitement and fear. He didn't find the girl who had originally set fire to his kindling, but the one he chose was just as young. Fifteen. When he had done the deed, he felt revolted. He threw up and vowed never to do it again. But it was like heroin. He was hooked. He went back again and again. Each time, he had the same reaction: disgust and loathing.

Austin looked around his cramped lodgings, a rented room in Ussher Town. Papers and books were piled wherever there was any space. He got up, paced a few steps, sat down again to make some desultory notes on his yellow pad. He rested his head on his desk for a moment, closing his eyes, gritting his teeth, trying to quench the urges. It was twelve-fifteen in the morning. Accra was silent, but that was when the city beckoned Austin most. The tumult of the daytime pushed him away, but at night, the city became seductive and sensual.

He stood up quickly, threw on a shirt, and left the room.

I promise. This will be the last time.

32

Dawson had got home late that night. Christine was in bed waiting for him. He lay across the bed with his head in her lap.

"Do you want something to eat?" she asked.

"I'm too tired to eat."

"You should eat. You're a scarecrow. Get up and take a shower while I make something. Dark, wake up."

"There must be a better way to make a living," he muttered.

Dawson drove Hosiah to school the next morning.

"Bye, Daddy!" the boy said, about to bolt out of the car.

Dawson pulled him right back. "Aren't you forgetting something?"

"Oh, yah." He kissed his father on the cheek. "Bye."

Before pulling away, Dawson watched his son disappear into the school grounds.

He got to work at eight-fifteen. There was a surprise waiting for him. Leaning against the wall outside the detectives' room, journalist's pad in hand, was Wisdom Asamoah.

"Morning, Wisdom," Dawson said evenly.

"Good morning, Inspector Dawson," Wisdom said, following him into the clamor of the office.

"How can I help you?"

"You're not going to at least offer me a seat?" Wisdom said, taking Chikata's chair.

Dawson sat opposite him. "What can I do for you, Wisdom?"

"I need to know a little about these murders. The girl at the railway trash dump is number three?"

"What girl?"

"I think you know exactly who I'm talking about, Inspector. Her name is Comfort Mahama. She was found dead Tuesday night."

"How do you know about her?"

"My sources. I'm reliably told that she's number three in the series. Musa Zakari, Ebenezer Sarpong, and now Comfort Mahama. You've arrested Kareem Tedamm. Is he the alleged serial killer?"

"Serial killer! Who says there's a serial killer?"

"Ah, come on, Inspector. Three young people killed in the same way with bizarre removal of body parts? It has to be the same offender. I know a little about these things, you know. Signature and M.O. and all that stuff. Remember? *Forensic Files?*"

"Oh, yes. How did I forget that? And you have an informant at the Police Hospital Mortuary, do you?"

"Not necessarily. Tell me what's going on, Dawson."

"Here's my official statement, Wisdom. You can quote me. Are you ready?"

Wisdom uncapped his pen, positioning it over his pad. "Go ahead."

"We've made an arrest in connection with the murder of a young woman by the name of Comfort Mahama, found dead on Tuesday night on the railway station premises."

"The person you've arrested in that regard is Kareem Tedamm."

"Yes, but he has not yet been charged with the murder."

"You have to do that soon then, don't you? If he is, will he be additionally charged with the murders of Zakari and Sarpong?"

"We haven't made a connection between those cases and Comfort's."

"But you're trying to make it?"

"Only if there's one to be made."

"But am I correct that the M.O. and signature in all the cases are identical?"

"There is some resemblance."

Wisdom smiled slyly. "You are very slippery, Inspector."

"You mean cautious."

"Is that all you have for me?"

"Yes, sir."

"Is it true that Comfort Mahama was an ashawo?"

"I have work to do, Wisdom."

He stood up. "Thank you, Inspector. It's always a pleasure."

Dawson had sent Chikata out early that morning with the four loaned constables to look for Antwi. He called the detective sergeant to see if he'd made any progress.

"Can't find him," Chikata said.

"Keep looking. We'll get him. Good job, Chikata."

"Thank you." He sounded pleased.

Dawson sat thinking for a moment, tapping his fingers on the table. Where would Antwi take refuge? That's when it occurred to Dawson that he wasn't making use of a good resource.

33

When Dawson got to SCOAR, he knocked first on Genevieve's door. With no reply, he went on to Socrate's office. He
wasn't there either.

Dawson went to the building's rear entrance. He opened
the door onto the courtyard. Groups of boys were playing basketball and soccer in the hot morning sun. Space was limited,
but they were doing fine. To the side, Socrate was taking photographs of them. Dawson watched him for a moment before
walking up.

"Morning, Socrate."

"Morning." He didn't really look at Dawson.

"Quite a crowd you have back here," Dawson said.

"They do their exercise here. Work out all their frustra-
tions."

"And the pictures?"

"What pictures?"

"You're taking photographs."

"Oh. For the website. I have to update it."

Dawson noticed the *have to.*

"How do you feel about these kids, Socrate?"

Socrate gave Dawson a long, detached stare. His eyes seemed empty and sightless. Dawson felt the hair on his neck rise.

Socrate turned away to take another photo. *Did he not hear the question?*

"Is Genevieve in today?" Dawson asked, hopeful for an answer this time.

"Mrs. Kusi is in a meeting. She'll be finished soon. Let's go back inside, Inspector."

Dawson followed, noticing Socrate's slumped shoulders. The man walked as if it was a chore. In the office, he sat at the computer quietly uploading the images from his camera.

"I'm looking for a boy called Antwi Boasiako," Dawson said.

"The one who hangs around with Kareem Tedamm?"

"That's him. Does he come here to the center?"

"In and out."

"But not here at the moment?"

"I don't think so, but let me just check the Refuge Room." Socrate leaned over to the second computer monitor on his desk. "No, he's not there."

Interested, Dawson came around to Socrate's side of the desk. "You have surveillance cameras?"

"Just for the entrance and the Refuge Room," Socrate said. "Mrs. Kusi can access them too."

The images were of medium quality at fifteen frames per second, which made them slightly jerky, but they were adequate to keep an eye on what was going on.

"Who set up this system?"

"I did," Socrate said, sounding a little insulted.

"Oh, sorry," Dawson said. "Very well done. There must be nothing electronic you don't know."

That seemed to reverse the affront somewhat. Socrate smiled his sour smile.

"I'll see if Genevieve is back in her office," he said and buzzed her.

"Yes, Socrate?"

"Inspector Dawson is here to see you."

"By all means have him come to the office then."

Minutes after Dawson had left, Socrate glanced at his surveillance monitor and saw Antwi coming into the building, turning left to go upstairs. Socrate got up and followed him, catching up with him before he got to the Refuge Room.

"Yes, Mr. Socrate?"

"Come with me, Antwi. I want to talk to you."

The boy followed him. Socrate stopped short of the woodshop, turning instead to a rarely used exit.

There was a veranda outside. Socrate leaned against the balcony, facing Antwi. "What have you done wrong?"

"Please, nothing."

"Then why is a policeman looking for you?"

Antwi jumped. "Policeman? *Where?*"

"He's downstairs talking to Madam Genevieve. Are you in any trouble?"

"Please, no," the boy said. But he was jittery.

"All right, I believe you," Socrate said. "I can help you. You can hide in the storeroom we have up here. When the policeman leaves, I come back and get you."

Antwi became suddenly wary. "The storeroom? Mepaakyɛw, I don't want to go in there."

"What's wrong with the storeroom?"

"Let me climb over the balcony, rather?" Antwi suggested.

"Foolish boy. And break your leg? Come on, before the policeman finds you."

Socrate led the way around the corner to the storeroom, undid the padlock, and opened the door. Antwi gaped. The "room" was tiny, not bigger than a cupboard, really. There were brooms and mops, disinfectant liquid, and stacked gallon containers of water in case the water supply got cut, which happened often enough.

"How can I go in there?" he gasped.

"Oh, you can go in for sure," Socrate said. "You are slim, so you can fit."

"Please . . ."

"Get inside."

There was a violent struggle as Socrate forced him in.

When Socrate shut the storeroom door on him, Antwi was squeezed in between it and the gallon containers. He could barely breathe. He heard the padlock click shut. It was pitch black except for a sliver of light at the bottom of the door. He tried to shift position, but it was impossible. Antwi began to feel his throat closing up. He couldn't get any air. Panic gripped him. *Let me out. Please.* He screamed Socrate's name. Then he just screamed.

34

There was soft jazz playing in Genevieve's office when Dawson came in. He looked up at the two speakers mounted high on the wall facing her desk.

"Very nice, I must say."

"The genius of Socrate," Genevieve said. She looked stunning in an olive business suit. "He threw it in along with the surveillance system."

"Yes, he showed it off to me. Impressive."

"His brother owns an electronics store on Oxford Street, so we got it all for cheap."

"Why the surveillance? I'm just curious."

"We need to know who is going in and out of the center, for one, and there's the occasional theft. As for the Refuge Room, there can't be someone in there supervising the kids every single minute, so we need another way to keep an eye on them."

"I understand."

A framed painting on her wall had caught Dawson's attention. "You didn't have that when I was here last."

"It's by Wiz Kudowor. *Urban Profiles.*" Genevieve walked up to it. "I got it as a gift. Beautiful, isn't it?"

Dawson joined her next to the piece. "It certainly is."

"Wiz is internationally known."

"I know. Congratulations. His work sells for a pretty penny."

She was between Dawson and the wall. He was still concentrating on the painting when she turned to face him.

"Thin, but strong," she said.

"Pardon?"

"You look thin, but up close I realize how strong you are."

"Mm-hm. Kind of like bamboo."

"Yes. Very attractive."

"I agree. It's my favorite kind of wood."

She laughed. "I meant you." Her eyes raked his torso and his slim, taut hips. "Being a policeman is such a dangerous job. Do you have any intriguing scars?"

"None that I can show you." Dawson said. "My wife doesn't like other women looking at my scars."

"I see." Disappointment came over her features like a pall. "Happily married, then?"

"Very. You're not?"

"Married, just not happily." Her pretty eyes moistened up. "Were it not for the kids, I would leave. Do you have children?"

"One boy. Seven."

"What's his name?"

"Hosiah."

"Nice. So musical. You must love him very much."

"I would kill or die for him," Dawson said, stepping away from her.

"I'm looking for an Antwi Boasiako. Socrate says he's been here before, but that he's not here today."

Her eyes lingered on him for a moment before she answered. "Is he in trouble?"

"He might be. But more important, he could have some information for me."

"I see. I don't know if and when he'll return to SCOAR. But if he does, I can let you know."

"Thank you. I appreciate that."

There was a knock on the door. Genevieve opened it to find a girl of about ten.

"Mepaakyɛw, madam," she said, "Mr. Socrate said I should call you and the policeman because he has found Antwi Boasiako hiding."

35

Dawson and Genevieve ran up the stairs, following the girl out to the veranda. Socrate was standing in front of the open storeroom. Antwi was sitting on the ground before him with his head down and his arms wrapped around himself.

"Inspector, I believe this is the boy you're searching for," Socrate said. "I came up here to get something from the store-room and found him hiding inside."

"Antwi!" Genevieve exclaimed. "Why are you hiding?"

"Apparently he found out the police were looking for him and so he ran up here to conceal himself," Socrate said.

Exchanging glances with Dawson, Genevieve kneeled next to the boy and lifted his face. "Antwi, what is going on?" And then she saw that he had fresh abrasions on his forehead. "Oh, what happened to your face?"

He sniffed and wiped his runny nose with the back of his hand.

"I saw that too," Socrate said. "I think he hurt himself in

the storeroom. There isn't much space in there. Antwi, did you hit yourself on the forehead when you were inside?"

Antwi gave Socrate a look laced with pure hatred.

Dawson moved closer to the storeroom and peered inside. True, there wasn't much in the way of space.

"You were hiding from me?" Dawson asked Antwi.

The boy sniffed again, wiped his nose, but wouldn't answer.

"Do you need to question him?" Genevieve asked Dawson quietly.

"At CID, not here."

"Can we take care of his forehead first, Inspector?" Socrate asked. "I think Nurse has come in."

"Yes, of course."

"He did it," Antwi said suddenly.

"Who?" Dawson said. "What?"

The boy's head was bent. He spoke to the ground. "Mr. Socrate did it. He told me to hide from you. He put me inside there. And he closed the door and locked it. I couldn't breathe."

Socrate's mouth dropped. "Ho, Antwi!" He looked at Dawson and then at Genevieve, stunned. "I can't even believe he's telling such a lie."

"Antwi," Genevieve said sorrowfully and with heavy rebuke. "What is one of the five rules we teach here? No lying. Not so?" Shaking her head, she stood up. "All right, let's go and see Nurse. Then you're going with Inspector Dawson. Oh, Antwi, you've made us sad today."

Sitting at Dawson's desk, Antwi looked like a little, trapped animal. He was dusty and ragged. The SCOAR nurse had bandaged his forehead.

The room was noisy, detectives taking and making reports and coming and going and sometimes almost colliding in the doorway. Dawson gave Antwi a bag of water from his desk. The boy tore a corner of the plastic off with his teeth and thirstily gulped the water down to the last drop. His hand was shaking.

Dawson sat down opposite him, speaking in Twi. "Are you okay now?"

He nodded. "Yes, please."

Chikata perched on the edge of the table next to him.

"What happened, Antwi?" Dawson asked.

"Please, I was going to the Refuge Room." He had a boy-man's voice—on the verge of breaking. "Mr. Socrate came and called me and told me some policeman was looking for me. He said he was going to help me, that I should hide until the policeman goes away."

"Ei, small boy," Chikata warned. "Don't come here and tell lies, you hear?"

"Please, I'm not telling you any lie. I didn't want to go inside that room because it's too small, but Mr. Socrate made me go inside by force. Then he lied to you and told you I was the one rather who went to hide there."

Dawson was studying Antwi. His eyes were direct, his voice rock steady. He was telling the truth.

"Please, maybe you don't know how he is, that Mr. Socrate," Antwi continued. "He hates all of us who come to SCOAR. The only person in the world he doesn't hate is Madam Genevieve. And as for her, she would be a head porter for his shit if he told her to do that. She doesn't know how mad he really is."

"Why do you say he's mad?" Dawson asked.

"Some boys, they used to tell me about a storeroom, that Mr. Socrate always used to lock them in that storeroom. They said it was at the top of the building, but me, I never went to see it. One time too, he took one of the boys and put electric shocks on his body with some kind of machine."

Dawson and Chikata exchanged surprised glances.

"Why didn't you report all this to Madam Genevieve?" Dawson asked.

"Please, because we fear," Antwi said, turning his palms up. "We fear too much. Mr. Socrate tells us if we say anything to her, he will sack us from SCOAR, or he tells us he would report us to the police. When we go to SCOAR, we feel somehow happy and free, so if Mr. Socrate tells us we will never come back if we say anything bad about him, do you think we will say anything bad? Of course not. Look at us. We don't have anything. We don't have money, we don't have house to live. Some of us don't even have shoes."

Antwi sighed, deflated and despondent.

"How old are you?" Dawson asked him.

"Please, fifteen and a half."

"And you've been in Accra how long?"

"Three years."

"Why did you come?"

"To make money."

"Where are your mother and father?"

"My mother, she died. My father, I don't know where he is. After my mother died, he went away and left me and my brothers with my grandmother and my grandfather. Then my grandfather too, he left."

"Where did he go?"

"Please, I don't know."

"So your grandmother was taking care of you."

"Yes, please, but when I was about to go to junior secondary school, she got sick, so she couldn't work. She told me to work on the farm to get money instead of going to school." Antwi sucked his teeth three times in a row, shaking his head.

"But the farm too, you can't make any money. So, no money, no school, no nothing."

"What happened to your grandmother?"

"Please, she died."

"Sorry."

"After that, I came to Accra."

"Do you like living here?"

"I make more money than in my village, so I'm happy like that. But life is hard too. At least in my village I know no one would hit me on my head and steal everything from me."

"Did Tedamm help you get a job when you first came to Accra?"

"Yes, please."

"Do you give him part of the money you make?"

"I used to. Not anymore. But if he needs something, I bring it to him."

"Like what?"

"Akpeteshie, food, anything. He likes to eat rice and *shito* all the time." Antwi snorted in momentary amusement but grew quickly serious. "Please, Mr. Dawson, somebody told me you took Tedamm to jail yesterday. Is it true?"

"Yes. He's still in jail. What about girls? You bring them to Tedamm?"

"Please, no one has to bring girls to him. They just come like water."

"Did Comfort Mahama come to him?"

Antwi started visibly. His voice dropped in pitch and volume, dry as a tree's fallen leaves. "Please, who is Comfort?"

"You know who she is. You, Ofosu, and Tedamm were with her on Tuesday night."

Antwi's eyes darted back and forth.

"Someone saw you with her," Dawson pressed. "What were you doing with her? What happened?"

"Please, nothing."

"Where were you going with her?"

"Please, we were just talking."

"What did Tedamm do to her?"

Antwi bravely met his gaze. "He didn't do anything."

Dawson got up and walked to the door, hands thrust in his pockets, head down. Antwi's eyes followed him there and back as he returned.

Dawson stopped at his side, resting a hand on his shoulder. "If you don't help me and tell me what happened, they will send you to jail and I won't be able to stop them. You want to meet Tedamm in jail?"

Antwi was chewing his bottom lip as if it were food, blinking rapidly to stop tears. He sniffed.

"Tedamm doesn't care about you," Dawson said. "He never cared about you. If you died today, he would forget about you by tomorrow."

Antwi began to cry, trying to wipe the tears away like a dog pawing for a bone.

"What did Tedamm do to Comfort?" Dawson asked gently.

"Please, we were drinking akpeteshie with her at Tudu Road. Then Tedamm was touching her . . ." Antwi circled his hand over his chest.

"Breasts."

"Yes. And then he told us to take off her clothes and then . . . then me and Ofosu held her and Tedamm started to fock her by force."

"You did it too?"

Antwi shook his head. "Please, no. I ran away. Ofosu too."

"You left Tedamm with Comfort?"

"Yes."

"Did you come back?"

"Please, no, I didn't."

"Did you see Comfort again that night?"

"No, I never saw her again, please."

"What about Tedamm?"

"I was hiding from him because I knew he would beat me for leaving him like that."

"Why did you run away and leave Tedamm?"

"Someone was coming."

"Who?"

"In a car. It stopped and shined the lights on us. I thought it was the police, so I ran away."

"You didn't see who was in the car?"

"Please, no, because the light was in our eyes."

"Could you tell what kind of car it was?"

"No, please."

"I see." Dawson paused. "You know Comfort was killed on Tuesday night, don't you?"

"Please, yes, I know." He looked down.

"Did you kill her?"

"Please, no."

"But what you did was still wrong," Dawson said. "You helped Tedamm rape Comfort. That's wrong. Never forget that, understand?"

Antwi's chin was quivering. New tears began. "Please, yes," he whispered.

"Do you think Tedamm killed Comfort?"

Antwi rested his forehead in his palm. "I don't know, I don't know. I just wish I never met him. Don't let him go. Please, don't let him go."

"I won't," Dawson said. "And what about you? What are you going to do with your life?"

Antwi was downcast. "I don't know. Me and Ofosu, we want to do something together to become better and leave this shit life. Ofosu is the only one I trust."

"He's your best friend?"

"In all the world."

Dawson smiled. "What about school? You said you were about to enter junior secondary before you came to Accra. Why don't you let SCOAR help you?"

Antwi shook his head so hard it might have come off. "Please, if Socrate is there, I'll never go back."

"I'm going to do something about that," Dawson said.

Antwi gave him a quizzical smile.

"I would like to meet Ofosu," Dawson said. "Do you know where he is?"

"Sometimes we used to go to Kaneshie Market together," Antwi said. "Maybe he's there now."

Kaneshie Market is massive. Dawson and Antwi went to several areas where street kids hung around and where Ofosu might be found, like the video game kiosks. These key spots all had nicknames like Frytol, Roadside, Gold Store. Their last stop, called Dora, was where Ofosu was. He was joking around with three boys his age, while two others were washing a black Altima under the watchful eye of its owner.

When Ofosu saw Antwi approaching, a smile burst on his face and he broke away from the others and came to meet his friend. Ofosu, a year or two younger than Antwi, was wearing a faded orange T-shirt and jeans. With a heart-shaped face, he had some of the most beautiful features Dawson had ever seen on a boy.

"Ei, Antwi!" Ofosu exclaimed. "Where have you been?"

Speaking in Twi, they playfully jostled each other and held hands for a moment. Ofosu was easily the more effervescent of the two, constantly smiling and laughing about something.

"This is my friend Dawson," Antwi told him. "Chaley, he beat Tedamm, oh!"

"Serious?" Ofosu looked at Dawson in admiration. "Where is Tedamm now?"

"In jail," Dawson said.

Ofosu and Antwi looked at each other with eyes shining, as though they had secretly wanted this for a long time.

"Dawson works at CID," Antwi said. "When something bad happens, then he investigates."

"Not policeman?"

"Ah, chaley, no. This one, they call it 'detective.' Better than policeman. He wants to know about what happened that night we were with Comfort."

Ofosu nodded, looking uncomfortable.

"But he already knows everything," Antwi warned him. "Tedamm told him, and me too, I told him. So when he asks you some question, don't tell any lie. He'll catch you at once."

Dawson looked at Antwi with new respect. The boy was doing a masterful job.

Antwi gave Ofosu another good-natured shove and then left him alone with Dawson to join his other friends.

"Ofosu, ɛte sɛn?"

"Mepaakyɛw, ɛyɛ."

"You're happy Tedamm is in jail?"

"Oh, yes."

"Did he rape that girl Comfort?"

"Yes, please."

"What about you? Did you rape her too?"

"No, please."

"You know what is rape?"

"Please, yes, I know."

"What is it?"

"Please, when the man make sex on the woman by force."

"Yes. Is it wrong?"

"Yes, please."

"You know it's wrong, but you and Antwi helped Tedamm do it."

"Because we fear him."

"Listen to me. I said, you know it's wrong, but you helped Tedamm do it."

Ofosu bowed his head.

"So that means you did wrong too," Dawson said.

"Please. Yes."

"Did Tedamm kill Comfort?"

"Maybe, but I don't know."

"When you ran away with Antwi, did you go back to Tedamm?"

"No, please."

"Did you see Comfort again?"

"No, please."

"Do you know anyone who wanted to kill her?"

"No, please. Not at all."

"What about Ebenezer Sarpong? Do you think Tedamm killed him?"

"Please, I don't know."

Ofosu was beginning to squirm visibly with discomfort.

"Okay," Dawson said. "That's all. Be good. You and Antwi should try to go to school, you know?"

"Yes, please." He smiled, showing all his flawless teeth. "I want to do that."

Dawson walked with Ofosu to the rest of the group. They launched into boisterous teasing and joking around, occasionally punching one another to peals of mirth. Dawson turned away with a smile. *Boys will be boys. And it takes them such a long time to grow up.*

36

In the evening when Dawson came home, a flour-dusted, spatula-wielding Hosiah greeted him excitedly.

"Daddy, we're making pizza!"

"So I see." Dawson swept his son up onto one shoulder. "And looks like you were rolling around in the pizza dough. Are you going to be *in* the pizza?"

"No, Daddy!" Hosiah giggled. "How could I be in the pizza?"

"I don't know, but if I find a foot in there, I'm not eating it."

Hosiah went weak with hysterics. Dawson carried him into the kitchen, where there were two surprises waiting. The first was a pleasant one—Cairo and Audrey.

Dawson rumpled Cairo's hair. He hugged Audrey. "It's so nice to see you again."

She was sweet, with dimples and a smile that had hooked Cairo and reeled him in the first instant he laid eyes on her.

Christine, who was at the side counter rolling out pizza dough, said, "Dark, Mama brought you something you really like."

That was the other surprise, much less pleasing: Christine's mother, Gifty. She was sitting at the table with her legs demurely crossed.

"Really," Dawson said. "What would that be?"

As always, Gifty was beautifully turned out, this time in a glamorous short bob hairstyle from her vast collection of wigs, a slim-fitted turquoise top, black slacks, and stilettos to match the blouse. Ironically, her stylishness made it easier for Dawson to dislike her. Almost to his regret, though, his wife was physically very much her mother's daughter. The older and the younger, each of them was lovely, but there the similarity ended.

Gifty stood up. "Come, my dear. I'll show you."

My dear? Dawson winced. He followed her out of the kitchen.

"There you are," she said triumphantly with a dramatic sweep of the hand.

Arranged on the sideboard to form the letters *DD* were sixteen bottles of Malta.

"Oh, wow," Dawson said.

"Do you like it?"

"A supply of Malta? What could I possibly not like about that? Thank you, Mama. It's very good of you."

"You're welcome, Darko. It's my peace offering. Look, I'm so sorry I took Hosiah to eat pizza. I shouldn't have done that. It won't happen again, I promise."

Dawson kissed her on the cheek. "All is forgiven, Mama. I realize you didn't mean any harm."

Hosiah came in and tugged at Dawson's trousers. "Daddy,

Mammy says come and grate the cheese because we're going to start baking the pizza."

Hours later, a contented, pizza-filled Hosiah was fast asleep, there had been a power failure, and Dawson, drowsy and spent, was sprawled naked and sweating on the bed in the dark beside an equally naked Christine.

"Hmm," she murmured.

"What?"

"You're amazing. You used so much energy you cut the electricity."

He laughed languidly. "You must have put something in that delicious pizza. Christine's Aphrodisiac Pizza. If you open a shop with that name, the place would be mobbed."

"I could offer special Ghanaian toppings."

"Kenkey pieces for the Ga consumers," Dawson contributed.

Christine snorted. "Miniature fufu balls."

"Tatale."

"Fried yam."

They went on suggesting the most outlandish toppings possible, laughing until the pain in their sides stopped them.

First thing in the morning, Dawson, showered and fresh, went to SCOAR and found Socrate in his office.

"How are you, Inspector? Please, have a seat."

"Thank you. How are you?"

"I'm fine. Can I help you with something?"

"I have a question for you." Dawson eyed Socrate long enough for him to start to get uncomfortable. "Yesterday, who was really responsible for Antwi being in the storeroom?"

Socrate frowned. "I don't get you."

"I don't think it's physically possible for somebody to fit in there and pull the door closed."

"Is your question to me which of his friends might have helped him hide and then closed the door on him?"

"No, that's not exactly my question."

"Oh, all right." Socrate laughed. "Then I don't know how I can be of any help to you."

"Did you know Antwi had never seen this storeroom himself, and he only had a vague idea where it is? So I was trying to put myself in his shoes. Would I really run to the storeroom to hide, not having seen it or been there before, or would I take my chances and try to escape the building without Inspector Dawson spotting me? You know what I mean? Getting out of the building, if I can, is a much better option than hiding *in* the building."

"I would think so, but, well . . . kids. They are what they are. And these ones in particular? Many of them are born liars, thieves, and tricksters. Antwi is one of them. There isn't an honest bone in his body."

"Did you ever feel the need to apply corrections to these children? Physical punishments?"

"We try to impart moral behavior to them every day, Inspector, but physical punishment is not part of our methods."

"You've never beaten any of the children?"

Socrate shook his head hard. "We never do that."

"I meant *you* in particular."

"What are you implying?"

"There are some stories about you. Forcibly locking the kids up in the storeroom. Applying electric shocks . . ."

Socrate lifted his massive frame from his chair and leaned across his desk. "Inspector, I beg you. Do not come in here to make disgusting accusations about me to my face. For you to take the word of this . . . this worthless Antwi over mine is just insulting."

"Worthless?" Dawson asked in surprise.

"*Yes,* he's worthless!" Socrate's face contorted with sudden fury. "Compared to me, to Genevieve, to everyone who spends precious time slaving over kids like Antwi with nothing to show for all that work, *yes,* he's worthless. Do you understand me, Inspector? This is Ghana, the real world. What we put on our website and in those brochures with those stupid pictures of smiling children we so sweetly call success stories is far from the reality. These aren't street children we're dealing with, Inspector Dawson, these are street *vermin.*"

Socrate sat down as abruptly as he had stood up. His face was streaming with sweat, and there were broad rings of perspiration in his armpits that had not been there just a minute ago. He rested his forehead against his palms, chest heaving with wheezing breaths, as if he had just completed a sprint.

Dawson was speechless.

"Socra?"

He lifted his head as Genevieve came in.

"Socra, are you all right? What's going on?" She came to his side, squeezing his shoulder and rubbing his neck. She lowered her voice so it became silky and soothing. "Slow down your breathing, Socra . . . slow . . . slower . . . that's right, you know how to do this . . . you're doing fine . . . that's better."

"I'm okay," he said in a strangled voice. "Sorry. I'll just go outside for a while."

He stood, almost upsetting his chair, then left the office with shoulders hunched over.

Genevieve stared at Dawson. For the first time, he saw hostility. He turned his palms up and lifted his shoulders.

"Don't even ask me what happened, because I don't know. I thought we were just talking—"

"About what?"

"The episode with Antwi."

"Why are you bringing that up again, Inspector Dawson?" she said coldly. "Why? Please. Let it rest. It's over and done with."

"But maybe not. There are accusations against Socrate."

"What accusations? What are you talking about?"

"Locking kids up in the storeroom, torturing them with electric shocks."

"Torturing! Inspector, please. You heard this from Antwi?"

"Yes."

"And you don't think Antwi's making this kind of stuff up? You don't see how that would serve his own interests?"

"Why should he make this up? What does he have to gain from it? I don't know about your employee Socrate. There's something loose somewhere."

"He can be a little highly strung and emotional."

"A little?"

She gave him a look that could have withered a plant.

"All right, okay," he said, standing up. "I'll go."

At the door, he turned. "Has your organization always been called SCOAR?"

"In the beginning, when I took it over, it was something else. I renamed it."

"By that time, had Socrate already come onboard?"

"Yes. Why?"

"He must have been something special to you."

"He helped me get this place off the ground, Dawson. It was a mess, and I'm grateful to him for all his help in turning it into a success."

"Which is why you can't ask him to leave. Puts you in a tough position. After all, this place bears his name."

"What do you mean?"

"Socra. It's an anagram of SCOAR."

Genevieve smiled slightly. "You are very clever."

"Thank you," he said.

She didn't escort him out.

Once Genevieve had left for the evening, Socrate was alone and SCOAR was as quiet as a library. This was his favorite time. Just him and his computers—especially on a Friday night like this. He would work on the website, answer emails, and surf the Internet. If this were all he had to do all day long, he would be happy.

First he had to attend to the Gennie-cam, as he called it. He had a key to her office, just as she did to his. They trusted each other completely. In the corner of the room left of the doorway, Socrate stood on a chair and took down one of the pair of miniature speakers. He snapped open its gray foam grille and removed the spy cam secured inside with putty.

Socrate waited as the data was uploading to his computer. He had set up the sound system for Genevieve a year ago. It was great for jazz, which Genevieve loved to listen to if she worked late. The idea for the spy cam began to haunt Socrate months later. The thought came out of nowhere, pounced, and would not let go. On the first few nights that he watched the days' recordings of Genevieve in her office, his entire body burned with the excitement that every taboo engenders.

Now, as he searched through the week's surveillance, he dreaded proving himself right that Inspector Dawson had designs on Genevieve. He had not liked the man from the very start, and after today's events, he positively despised him.

He found the spot he was looking for . . . Dawson going

into the office with Genevieve. As he watched them standing together by the painting, Socrate felt the suffocation returning. He concentrated on imagining Genevieve's voice. *Slow down your breathing . . . slow . . . slower . . . that's right. You're doing fine.*

PART THREE

37

Dawson turned over in bed and gazed at the ceiling splashed with Saturday morning sunlight. A little over two weeks had passed since Tedamm's arrest. DNA analysis showed a match with the semen inside Comfort. It was her blood under his fingernails. Ofosu's account of the rape had corresponded to Antwi's. It was a strong case. Tedamm had been charged with rape and first-degree murder. He denied both, claiming Comfort had been actively soliciting sex, which had therefore been consensual. The blood under his fingernails, he said, was from her nosebleed, but he had not murdered her. He was sticking to that. Neither would he confess to the murders of Musa and Ebenezer. The autopsy had confirmed that Comfort had had a nosebleed, but that little island of truth did not exonerate Tedamm.

As for Flash, that sliver of scum, his alibi in Comfort's case had checked out, including his drinking session with his friends at the Jesus Is Coming chop bar. Still, he was in jail for the prostitution racket. Tedamm would get bundled into that charge as well. So, although Dawson wasn't completely satisfied about the way everything had turned out, there was at least something to be happy about.

Hosiah came in, jumped on the bed, and snuggled into a spot between his mother and his father.

"How are you, champ?" Dawson asked him, kissing the top of his head.

"Fine."

"Fine, what?"

"Fine, thank you."

"That's better. Did you sleep well?"

"Yes, thank you. Daddy, look." Hosiah held up his most recent toy creation, a turbo sports car.

Dawson examined it. "Nice!" he said. "How fast can it go?"

"One hundred and fifty."

Dawson smiled. "That's fast."

Making appropriate *zoom-zoom* noises, Hosiah pushed his car along an imaginary road on Dawson's chest and up his chin.

"Hey!" Dawson said in mock protest. "Where you think you're going?"

Hosiah giggled. "Driving up a mountain. The Daddy Mountain."

No longer did he and Dawson have playful wrestling matches on a Saturday morning like this. Dawson missed the tussles. He knew his son did too, but there was nothing they could do about it. Hosiah could not sustain that level of exertion anymore. Sometimes when Dawson looked at him, he had to swallow down the knot in his throat and blink away the pricking tears. His son was dwindling before his eyes.

Before breakfast, Christine came and stood in the doorway. "You have a visitor, Dark."

"Who?"

"Surprise," she said mischievously.

She moved to one side and brought someone else into view.

Dawson leapt to his feet, flabbergasted to see his old mentor standing there. "My God! *Armah!*"

They laughed as they embraced.

"How are you, Darko?"

"What a surprise! Welcome, welcome. I didn't even hear you arrive."

"I smuggled him in," Christine said. "I spotted him out of the kitchen window as he was walking up."

Daniel Armah, in his early sixties, friend, father figure, and mentor, was shorter than Dawson. His hair was speckled with gray, his face wide and welcoming. His eyes held deep thought and a twinkle of humor that often caught people by surprise.

"It's so good to see you, Armah. You're looking well."

"You too, Darko."

"Please, come and have a seat. Would you like anything? We're about to have breakfast, if you'd like to join us."

"I would love to. Thank you."

Christine went about finishing up breakfast while Dawson and Armah talked.

"So what brings you to town?" Dawson asked.

"My cousin is ill," Armah explained. "His wife asked me to come down and see him. He's not doing well, and she's afraid he may not last long."

"I'm sorry to hear that. How long will you be in Accra?"

"It depends on how my cousin does."

"I understand."

Washed and dressed, Hosiah came marching into the sitting room.

"Look who's here, Hosiah," Dawson said.

"Uncle Daniel!"

Armah hugged him. "How are you, Hosiah? My goodness, you're growing tall!"

Hosiah beamed. "Daddy says I'll be taller than him when I grow up."

Armah laughed. "I don't doubt it."

After breakfast, Christine took Hosiah with her to run weekend errands. Dawson sat with Armah in the small backyard.

"I was closely following your case in the papers," Armah said.

"It must be providence that brought you here," Dawson said, "because I had been thinking about calling to talk to you about it. I wish I could feel completely happy with the result, but I'm not."

"What's troubling you?"

"Well, Tedamm is a rapist and a bully, no doubt, and maybe even a murderer, but in locking him up I have the same feeling you get when you put a piece of equipment together and there are nuts and bolts left over. For instance, a boy called Antwi, who was a witness to the rape, told me that, on the night Comfort was found dead, someone drove up in a vehicle while Tedamm was in the act. Thinking it was the police, Antwi and his friend Ofosu ran off, leaving Tedamm. We still don't know who this person in the car was. Could it have been him who killed Comfort after Tedamm had left her? It's a missing piece, and it bothers me."

"Of course, the car could be a red herring."

"True, but here's another thing. We know Tedamm and Ebenezer were enemies because of turf battles, so there could be motive there. Maybe there was also a turf battle with Musa that Tedamm doesn't want to admit to, but a turf battle with Comfort? That's unlikely. And again, Comfort's murder looked like a sexual homicide because of the rape, but that doesn't fit with the motive of the other two murders."

"Yes, I see what you mean."

"What do you think I should do? I feel like I've achieved something but not *the* thing."

"Are you still working full-time on the case?"

Dawson shook his head. "With all this excitement over Ghana's new oil industry, practically everyone is focused on the murder of this Ghana Petroleum exec. Lartey's asked me to help as well. Look, as he put it himself, poor people, prostitutes, and street children versus oil executive. Who wins?"

"What about Professor Botswe? He's quite sure this is serial murder?"

"Yes."

"Are you?"

"I have to say yes. That identical signature in all three cases is hard to ignore. Identical with only one exception."

"What is that?"

"The killer took body parts from Comfort and Musa as trophies, but he didn't do the same with Ebenezer."

"So we have no explanation for that either."

"No. Can you make any sense of any of this?"

Armah reflected a moment. "I think you have Tedamm in prison for rape just as he deserves. I also think you and Dr. Botswe are right—there's a serial killer—it's just not Tedamm. We're looking for someone who deals regularly with street

children. That gives him the opportunity. I believe it's someone with a truck, SUV, or large car, because these victims appear to have been *brought* to the places they were found, not
murdered on the spot."

Dawson nodded but sighed in frustration.

"I haven't been a lot of help, I know," Armah said. "A couple months ago I was having a small medical problem—
nothing serious, it turns out, but at first the doctor couldn't
figure it out. He said something very interesting to me. He
said, 'Sometimes you just have to let the disease declare itself.'
And as blithe as that might sound, I think that's what happens
with murder cases too."

Dawson winced. "In other words, I just have to wait
awhile."

"Yes," Armah said. "Particularly in this case. Something is
going to happen."

They chatted a little longer, moving on to happier topics.
Too soon, it was time for Armah to take his leave. Dawson saw
him off in a cab, waiting for it to be completely swallowed up
by Accra traffic before he turned back to the house.

Next, Dawson had a debt of gratitude to pay off. He went
across the street to Awo's and bought some tilapia and *banku*.
That was the easy part. The hard part was finding Jason Allotey, the Korle Bu technician who had processed Musa's
tooth DNA results in record time. He lived in Chorkor,
but the directions to his house were as confusing as a rat's
maze.

After some patient hunting, Dawson found it. It was a tiny
place with corrugated metal roofing. Jason was relaxing outside with his wife and children. He was thrilled to see Dawson
and overjoyed by the gift. With ceremonial flare, Jason introduced the members of his immediate family and several of the

extended relations. Custom demanded that Dawson sit and chat and have something to drink. When it seemed he had spent enough time, he made a gracious exit and went home, where Hosiah was eagerly anticipating their outing to the Silverbird Cinema at the Accra Mall.

38

Akosua Prempeh was a child *on* the street, not *of* the street. She had a home to go to, but her new stepfather, who had beaten her up three days ago, had told her to stay away unless she could bring back money.

"Useless girl," he had called her as he threw her out. "Kwasea."

The little bit of money she had made today was gone. Not because she had spent it, but because it had been stolen from her. Two men had roughed her up, searched her, and taken her money. On top of that, they tried to rape her. Another man who had been coming along raised the alarm and Akosua escaped.

Now she was wandering around Nkrumah Circle unsure what to do. It looked as if she would have to stay out tonight and get some kind of job in the morning. Had Musa been alive, she could have gone to him. They had killed the boy she loved with all her heart. Musa had once said to her, "Never,

never sell your body." She had promised him it was something she would never do.

But that was then.

Right now, it was a different story. She was hungry and tired. She wanted to sleep in her own bed, even if it was just a folded-over cloth. She was lonesome. The bustle of people around her didn't make her feel any better. Tears pricked her eyes, but she pulled herself together. For a while, she sat and watched the goings-on at the circle.

Accra was a late-night city in only a few places. The Vienna City nightclub was the hub that kept Nkrumah Circle alive and crowded well into the early morning. Powerful music from inside the club spilled out to the sidewalk café, where people-watching patrons sat sipping cocktails. Just south of the circle, Nkrumah Avenue was jammed with shiny sedans and SUVs, their drivers looking for sex and drugs. "Enjoyment people," Akosua called them. Prostitutes worked the club both inside and out. Taxis lined either side of the street waiting for passengers returning home or ashawos leaving with their customers. The taxis would take them to nearby lodges with names like California Inn and Beverly Hills Hotel. They accepted prostitutes and their clientele and made good money off them.

Akosua got up, walking past a tro-tro driver's mate calling out his destination in a monotonous singsong. Mobile Fan Milk vendors were selling hot chocolate and coffee from the insulated containers attached to the fronts of their bicycles. In the midst of all this noise, a truck pusher slept peacefully on his cart next to a wall marked POST NO BILL.

A group of ashawos hung out at the corner of Nkrumah Avenue and Kente Street. They wore blouses and skirts that barely contained their big breasts and buttocks. They had bright makeup, wigs, false eyelashes, and heavy mascara. Ako-sua felt shabby in comparison. Three ashawos were having a squabble about something with a tall, slender male prostitute in a black see-through shirt, but the rest of them were flagging down cars and negotiating prices with drivers who had pulled over.

Akosua went on to a smaller street called Kente Link. She was faintly aware of the crunch of tires on gravel not too far away from her. At first she paid no attention. A horn sounded. Not impatiently—just a quick *pim-pim* to get her to look.

The man in the car waved. Akosua pointed questioningly at herself to be sure he really wanted her. He nodded and beckoned to her. *Come.*

What did he want? She wasn't dressed anything like an ashawo.

For safety, she stayed on the passenger side.

He spoke to her in Ga, checking first that she understood.

"What's wrong?" he said. "Are you sad?"

She shook her head.

"Yes, you are." He smiled sympathetically. "I can tell."

There was almost no street lighting, but she thought she saw a scar on the man's forehead.

"You have no money," he said. "You are hungry."

She nodded.

"I can help you with some money if you help me too." He took out a five-cedi bill and waved it.

Akosua swallowed hard. The temptation was powerful.

He smiled. There was something about his smile Akosua didn't like. It gave her goose bumps. She backed away. He watched her like a thirsty man. She turned and walked off. Seconds later, she heard the tires spinning as they tried to gain traction in the dirt. For a panicky moment, she thought he might be coming after her, but when she whirled around to look, she saw the man driving away in a furious cloud of dust.

Relieved, Akosua walked farther along Kente Link. Many people slept at the storefronts along this street, some in pairs or groups. All ages, from babies to grown men and women. Akosua chose a spot and sat down with her back against a wall. She would half sleep, half stay awake. She was scared that if she lay down and went into deep slumber, she might be attacked and raped.

She dozed off but started awake again after a while, she wasn't sure how long. A car was parked at the end of the street, lights on, engine running. It was one of those really beautiful cars she saw when she sold water to drivers on Liberation Road, silver and shiny. Through the partly open door of the driver's side, Akosua caught sight of the dashboard lights twinkling like different colored stars.

But there was no one in the car. Akosua's gaze moved to the sidewalk not far away. Underneath a storefront canopy, a man was kneeling beside a street boy, talking softly to him. She couldn't hear what they were saying. It was too dark to make them out clearly, but after a few minutes, they both got up to go to the car. The boy was maybe fourteen or fifteen. The man opened the passenger door for him, and then he came back around to the driver's side, got in, and shut the door. The car pulled smoothly and silently away.

Akosua reflected on it. *Hmm, so this is Ghana now.* Nothing was a surprise anymore. The driver of the car must have a liking for boys. But not nice, clean boys with fine clothes. He liked raw, dirty boys fresh from the street.

39

Five-thirty the next morning, Sunday, Dawson woke with a start, swung his legs out of bed, and got to his feet.

Something's happened.

Another nightmare—Armah trying in vain to drive away vultures pecking at Comfort's corpse awash in blood. Dawson's heart was pounding as if it was banging its way out of his chest. But there was something else too—not just the nightmare. *What's happened?* He looked at the phone on the nightstand. It rang.

Chikata.

"Morning, Dawson. I'm sorry to—"

Dawson cut him short. "Where's the body?"

"Novotel Lorry Park."

On the way out, Dawson called Dr. Biney and asked if he would come to the crime scene.

"Of course," Biney said. "I'll be there as soon as possible."

The lorry park had borrowed its name from the Novotel

Hotel a couple hundred meters away on the other side of Independence Avenue. The place was already bustling by the time Dawson arrived at six-thirty. Passengers were lining up for transportation to different parts of the city and country. Hanging off the sides of tro-tros departing in plumes of dust, drivers' mates made last calls for one more passenger to squeeze into a space that did not really exist. Carrier boys and kayaye made mad dashes after every arriving tro-tro or bus, hoping to get a job.

Where there was transportation, there was commerce. Vendors, both mobile and stationary, traded inside the park and out. Dawson dodged two truck pushers and their cart as he made his way to the Independence Avenue side of the park.

He found Chikata with Bright and his crew in front of the public latrine, which was painted brown and yellow underneath the dust that coated it. TOILET 20P was scrawled on the side in fading letters. It was the pit latrine type, the very lowest in the hierarchy of public toilets and supposedly banned by the Accra Metropolitan Assembly.

"Where's the body?" Dawson asked, looking around.

"In there," Chikata said, making a face. "Young male."

"*Inside* the latrine?"

"Yessah."

"Ewurade," Dawson said.

"Bright went in," Chikata said, "but he couldn't take it for very long. It really stinks in there."

"Who found the body?"

"Early morning, someone went inside to do his business, and when he got to the last stall, he saw the body," Chikata said. "Came running out, shouting."

"What about the latrine custodian?" Dawson asked.

"Gone. We heard he went inside to look, turned right around, and left without saying one word."

Dawson shook his head in disbelief. "The very man in charge of taking care of the place has abandoned it. Jesus."

They had an audience—a few who had been wanting to use the facilities but had been turned away, to their annoyance, others who had heard a rumor about a dead person in the latrine, and the rest who had nothing better to do than hang around. But in general, Novotel Lorry Park was a busy place with people who had things to do and places to go.

"How were you notified?" Dawson asked Chikata.

"Someone made an anonymous call to the Kinbu Police Station early this morning that there was a dead person in the latrine. A sergeant took the call, and I suppose he couldn't be bothered, so he tells one of the constables to come and look around the alleged area. The constable gets here, sees the body and calls the sergeant, who tells the station inspector, who tells the sergeant to handle it; the sergeant tells the constable to make a report and have the body taken to the mortuary. Constable wasn't sure what to do, so he called CID, and they called me."

"Where is the constable?"

"I questioned him and sent him home. What he said was straightforward, but if you want to talk to him, I have his mobile number."

"What about the station inspector and sergeant? Do you have their names? Both of them need to be reported."

"Yes, I have their names. I'll let you handle the reporting, if you wouldn't mind."

"Of course. I'll take care of it." Dawson turned to Bright. "Do you have some gloves to spare, sir? I'm going in."

Bright handed him a pair. "Mask?"

"No, thank you. I don't think it would help much."

The look on Bright's face said something like *Best of luck*.

Dawson went in, switching on his flashlight. It was as dark

as a dungeon. The six open stalls of about three-by-four feet had soiled, filthy walls that Dawson didn't dare touch. The stench was thick and impenetrable. It had no boundary beyond which you could pull in a little fresh air. It made you reel as if you had been bludgeoned. It coated your skin and your mucous membranes, and clogged your windpipe.

Dawson clenched his teeth. *Good sanitation and clean toilets are human rights, surely.* He followed the beam of his flashlight. One, two, three, four, five stalls. And then, number six. The body sat upright against the back wall, legs splayed on either side of the squatting hole. For a second, Dawson's mind reacted mildly, as if avoiding any emotion. The victim was a young teenage male, barefoot. He had on an orange T-shirt and jeans, which coincidentally was the same outfit Dawson remembered Ofosu had been wearing over two weeks ago.

Heart pounding, Dawson trained his flashlight beam on the victim's face, that same beautiful, heart-shaped face and those finely sculptured cheekbones. His almond eyes were open and looking at Dawson. His mouth was open too, but his tongue was cut out.

Ofosu.

Dawson turned his head to one side as he heard a strange noise—a strangled cry, a cough, and a violent choking, retching sound. He realized it was coming from his own throat.

He was about to vomit.

No, don't throw up. Don't.

It passed. Dawson bent forward slightly, resting his hands on his knees. He felt dizzy. At first he thought he was only hyperventilating, but in fact he was weeping.

"Dawson?" It was Bright at the entrance of the latrine, shining his flashlight down. "Are you okay?"

He hastily straightened up. "I'm fine, sir. Thank you, sir."

"Dr. Biney has just arrived. He'll be joining you shortly."

Minutes later, gloved, masked, and gowned, Biney entered the latrine with his black forensics bag in one hand, flashlight in the other.

"I got here as soon as I could, Inspector," he said as he came up.

"Thank you for coming, Doctor. I'm glad to see you."

"What do we have?"

Dawson shined his flashlight.

"My God," Biney whispered. "Good Lord."

"I know him," Dawson said. "His name is Ofosu; he's a street boy I spoke to about two weeks ago."

"And for talking to you his tongue was cut out? Is that what this is all about?"

Dawson didn't have an answer.

Biney got closer to Ofosu, touching his head in his uniquely intimate way. He gently lifted the eyelids. He shined a flashlight into the mouth.

"The tongue was lifted and sliced right out. I don't think I've ever seen anything quite as cold-blooded."

"But there's not much bleeding from his mouth," Dawson observed.

"Yes, good point. Likely done postmortem."

Biney attempted to raise one of Ofosu's arms from his side. It did not give an inch.

"Still very rigid," he said. "Time of death, since I know you'll ask, has to be a broad range, I'm afraid, Inspector. Taking into consideration warm temperatures and his lean body, I'd say within the last eight hours, most likely between midnight and three or four in the morning."

He tugged at Ofosu and pulled him away from the wall. The body stayed eerily sitting up in exactly the same posture. Biney shined his flashlight down Ofosu's back.

"This is a bad angle to look at it," he said, "but he does have a stab wound on the right. Undoubtedly there'll be internal hemorrhage at autopsy. Here, I'll move out so you can take a look. There isn't room for three."

Biney and Dawson switched places.

"Same thing as the others," Dawson said. "The killer's back. He couldn't stay quiet very long."

40

At the morgue, before Dr. Biney covered Ofosu's body with a clean sheet, he shut the eyes fully and "broke" the rigor mortis of the jaw muscles, allowing the mouth to close. Then Dawson brought Antwi in. The boy stood at the side of the table and stared at Ofosu for a long time. He looked up at Dawson.

"Can I touch him?"

Dawson glanced at Dr. Biney, who nodded.

Antwi touched Ofosu's face with a light, brushing stroke.

"He's very cold."

"Yes," Dawson said.

As he gazed at his dead friend, a smile flitted across Antwi's face as though a pleasant memory had come briefly to mind, but then powerful grief returned. He cried with his eyes open. His body shook until it became weak and began to sway. Dawson put his arms around the boy, picked him up, and carried him out of the room.

Staring blankly into the distance, Antwi leaned against the flame tree outside the mortuary building. Dr. Biney saw Dawson off at the door.

"It's sad, isn't it, Inspector?" he said.

"Yes, it is. And very hard for him. He and Ofosu were very close."

"How are *you* doing?"

Dawson gazed at the ground without seeing, his jaw working. "There's a cold, heavy anger inside here." He thumped his chest twice. "Murder is murder, but out of the four victims, Ofosu is the only one I had met, and he was also the youngest. My own son will be his age before too long." He looked up at Dr. Biney. "What is the hatred, the fury, that drives a man to kill that way?"

Biney nodded, there to listen, not to talk.

"I'll get him, though," Dawson said. "He believes he's invincible, but he's not. I *will* get him."

Dawson sat beside Sergeant Baidoo as they drove Antwi back to Kaneshie Market. The boy was very quiet in the backseat.

Dawson called Chief Supol Lartey.

"There's just been another murder, sir. A teenager found in a public latrine. It appears to be the same signature as the other three. I just wanted to let you know."

Silence.

"Sir?"

"Yes, I'm here. So Tedamm is not our man."

"Except for the rape."

Heavy sigh. "All right. I want to meet with you and Philip at eight sharp tomorrow morning. Present everything you've got to me."

"Yes, sir."

Ending the call, Dawson glanced back at Antwi. He was staring out the window.

"I don't want you to be by yourself at any time," Dawson said. "I want you to stay with someone I trust. Do you know Issa?"

"I know him."

"What if I ask him to let you stay with his gang?"

"He doesn't like me."

"Did he tell you that?"

"Please, no, but I know it already."

"You don't like him either?"

Antwi shrugged.

"He's a good person," Dawson pressed. "If I talk to him, he'll be your friend."

Antwi looked doubtful.

"Let's branch to the UTC area before we go to Kaneshie," Dawson said to Baidoo.

They didn't find Issa there, but someone said they'd seen him up at the CMB building earlier in the morning. It wasn't far, so Dawson and Antwi left Baidoo and the car parked in the Ghana Commercial Bank lot and walked up the hill past the railway station to CMB. It was going on eleven in the morning. The sun shone fiercely down on churchgoers in their Sunday best, including men who must have been pouring with sweat inside their dark suits.

Antwi spotted Issa first. He was taking a rest, sitting on his cart, which was loaded with strips of scrap metal. Dawson and Antwi went up to him.

"How are you, Issa?" Dawson asked.

"I'm fine."

They shook hands.

"You know Antwi?" Dawson said.

Issa gave the boy something of a glance. "Yes, I know him."

"His friend Ofosu was killed early this morning."

Issa's eyebrows went up. Cautious concern. "What happened?"

"Someone found him dead in the Novotel Park latrine. Let me talk to you for a moment."

Dawson took Issa a few meters away, dropping his voice. "He's feeling very bad because of Ofosu's death, the same way you felt the day when Ebenezer was found. You get me."

Issa nodded.

"I know he and Ofosu used to follow Tedamm around," Dawson continued. "Tedamm was Ebenezer's enemy, and yours too, but it was Tedamm who was running the show. Antwi and Ofosu were just small boys to him. If they ever disobeyed him, he beat them."

"Yes."

"So now Ofosu is dead and Antwi is by himself. I don't want him to be alone right now. I want him to be with someone, and it's you I trust most. You hear what I'm saying."

"Yes, please."

"You'll do it for me?"

"For you, yes."

"Thank you." Dawson shook his hand. "I want Antwi to be at your base at night, not somewhere out there by himself. The man who killed Ebenezer and Comfort and Ofosu might come after Antwi."

"I won't let anything happen to Antwi," Issa said. "Maybe I failed Ebenezer, but I won't fail Antwi. And if I catch the one who killed Ebenezer, I will kill him myself."

"No, don't do that," Dawson said. "Because I want him first. Rather, you hold him for me and *I'll* come and kill him."

They laughed.

Dawson called to Antwi. "Come and talk to your new older brother."

41

Dawson left Issa and Antwi after the rules had been laid down. Antwi was to leave Issa's base no earlier than five-thirty in the morning and be back not later than eight at night. No exceptions. During the night, he wasn't allowed to go anywhere by himself, including the latrine. He was to wake Issa up to accompany him.

Dawson called Chikata. "How are things?"

"I'm just finishing my report. Do you need anything from me, Dawson?"

"No, that's all for today. Chikata, thank you, eh? You've done well."

"Thank you, Dawson, sir."

"We'll meet at CID tomorrow morning at seven to talk."

"Sure, no problem." Before they ended the call, Chikata added, "Oh, I've been meaning to ask you how Hosiah is doing these days with the heart problem."

Dawson was surprised, pleasantly. Chikata had never asked him this before. "He's holding on," he said, "but he needs the operation. We're hoping for the best."

"Okay, I pray for him, then."

"Thank you, Chikata. Enjoy your Sunday."

It was just after noon now, so Christine would be out of church and Hosiah out of Sunday school. Dawson got her on the first ring. She told him some church friends had invited them to lunch.

"I have one more person to see," Dawson said. "I'll call you after that."

"Okay."

Next, Dawson dialed Dr. Botswe's number, wondering what the professor's Sunday schedule was like and whether he went to church. Compared to most other Ghanaians, Dawson was quite "religionless." Some might have insisted he was Godless as well, but on that point he was still undecided. What he did know was that it would be over his dead body that his hard-earned money would go to a rich pastor in one of the so-called charismatic churches like Assemblies of God or Lighthouse Chapel International. Dawson regarded them with deep suspicion. Were they servants of God or Bible-wielding con men?

Botswe answered his phone. "Good afternoon, Inspector Dawson. Good to hear from you again. How are you?"

"I'm okay, Dr. Botswe, but there's been another murder."

"Really."

"Yes—early this morning. I'd like to come by and discuss it with you, if I may."

"By all means. I'm at home all afternoon."

"I'll be there soon."

Botswe's gate was open when Dawson drove up, but he parked outside on the street. As he walked in, a smiling Obi came forward to greet him. He was in a blindingly white shirt, dark blue tie, and perfectly pressed navy blue trousers. It was a transformation.

"I almost didn't recognize you," Dawson said. "You are sharp!"

"Thank you," Obi said. "You are welcome. How are you?"

"Very well, thank you. And yourself?"

"I am blessed and full of joy for the Lord, sir."

"Oh, very good. Off to church then?"

"Yes, please—to give praises to the Almighty and ask for His guidance in all I do. Let me take you inside to the doctor."

He escorted Dawson into the house, which, again, was unapologetically cooled. Dawson wondered idly how much Botswe paid for his electricity.

"Good afternoon, Inspector Dawson," the professor said, appearing from his study.

"Afternoon, Dr. Botswe."

"Please, do you need anything else?" Obi asked Botswe.

"No, thank you, Obi. Have a nice time in church."

"Yes, please. Thank you, sir. Good-bye, Inspector."

"Come into my study," Botswe said to Dawson. "Would you like some Malta?"

"I never refuse that offer."

Botswe smiled. "Make yourself comfortable while I get you some. The staff is all off on Sundays. After all, they have their lives too."

Dawson almost said, *really?* but thought better of it. As Botswe went for the refreshments, Dawson noticed a new painting on the far wall. *Wiz Kudowor.* When Botswe came back with a tray of Malta and some Club beer for himself, he found Dawson in front of the painting.

"Admiring the Wiz?" he said.

"Yes. Spectacular."

"That one's called *Groom Awaits the Bride*."

"I haven't seen this one before," Dawson said. "Genevieve Kusi has another of his pieces in her office."

Botswe's eyes skidded, like a car losing its grip on the road for a second.

"Do you know Genevieve?" Dawson asked.

"Yes, I do. She's a tremendous resource, and she and her institution do excellent work in this city. They've picked up a couple of national and international awards, you know. Please, Inspector Dawson, do have a seat and help yourself to your Malta. I trust it's cold enough."

They sat with a side table between them. Dawson closed his eyes momentarily as he took the first sip.

Botswe chuckled. "That good?"

"I think it's a sickness," Dawson said, looking at the bottle as though it might reveal something new. "Well, you tell me. You're a psychologist. Is this a terrible addiction?"

"Oh, that everyone should have such a harmless addiction! So, tell me about this new murder."

"A boy of about thirteen to fourteen, name of Ofosu, who along with another boy, Antwi, used to follow around a brute called Tedamm. But Ofosu was, and Antwi is, basically decent."

"Tedamm is the one I read about in the papers who was charged with the rape and murder of Comfort?"

"Yes, him. Ofosu was stabbed sometime last night between midnight and four. I'll show you the pictures I took with my phone. Most of the signature is the same as the other three, but this is the first one in which the body has been placed inside a building. Does that mean anything special?"

Dawson brought out his camera and toggled to the right spot in the picture gallery. He handed it to Botswe. "I took six photos."

The professor began to look at them.

"Sorry about their small size," Dawson said.

"Would it help to upload them to my PC?" Botswe asked cautiously.

"I wish I could, Dr. Botswe, but police regulations prohibit that."

"Of course. I understand." He smiled. "You have remarkable integrity. I'm not sure that another person in your position would take so much care."

Dawson said nothing to that. Botswe went from one image to the next and back again. He returned the camera to Dawson. "Same signature, same killer."

"Even though this body's dumped indoors instead of out?"

"Indoors, outdoors—it doesn't matter to the killer. What he's expressing is that these people's lives are worthless to him. They might as well be rubbish or refuse. That's why he chooses the filth of Korle Lagoon for Musa, the muddy ditch for Ebenezer, a rubbish dump in Comfort's case, and now the latrine for Ofosu."

"By 'these people's lives' you mean street children."

"Yes."

"He hates them."

"Or what they represent in *his* mind. He could be a messianic killer on an apocalyptic mission to rid us of this scourge, as he sees it, of street children."

"That would mean a psychotic person, surely?"

"In the sense of distorted reality, certainly, but not in the true wider sense of psychosis. These aren't really psychotic killings because they are too organized and too planned. Psychotic killings are disorganized, often opportunistic, spur of the moment. This isn't what this fellow is doing."

"Perhaps he was once traumatized as a street child himself. Maybe he's trying to kill that part of them that's in him."

"Ah, indeed, perhaps so. Have you thought of psychology as a career, Inspector?"

Dawson laughed. "With all due respect, no. Back to this killer, I still don't understand why he takes these body parts away. You've said these aren't ritual killings, and I'm willing to agree, but fingers, kneecaps, and now a tongue? He cut out Ofosu's *tongue,* for goodness' sake."

Botswe nodded. "Your point is well taken. I feel comfortable in saying that he is taking trophies, which serial killers often do, and that he is escalating. This last murder was more intense—the setting, the trophy taking, everything."

"Like he's taunting us with Ofosu's murder."

"He is almost certainly following you closely through newspaper reports and such. He might interject himself into the case, and he might find ways to view his work a second or third time. And, Inspector, if you don't stop him, he will most certainly kill again."

42

Dawson spent some time with Christine and Hosiah. To their disappointment, he had to leave them after a while, on a mission to the area bounded by Tudu Road, Kantamanto Market, Knutsford Avenue, and Kojo Thompson Road.

It was almost eight. Many of the kids had returned for the night. Dawson found Issa, Mosquito, and little Mawusi, who had recovered from his malaria bout, but Antwi hadn't arrived yet.

Dawson stayed calm outwardly. Inside, he was getting nervous.

"Oh, here he comes," Issa said finally, and Dawson turned to see Antwi running like a schoolboy late for class, breathing heavily as he came up.

"Antwi, you're late," Dawson said.

"Please, I'm sorry. I was at Kantamanto. I found some work there."

"Don't be late again."

"Yes, please."

"I need all of you to help me," Dawson said. He paired Issa with Antwi, and Mosquito with Mawusi.

"Go around and fetch everyone to come to your base," Dawson instructed. "I want to talk to them."

It took about thirty minutes to get them all together—scores of kids of all ages from six up. Dawson felt like a politician, father, headmaster, and policeman. Like all children, they took a little while to settle down, but once they did, they listened to what Dawson had to tell them about how to avoid becoming a victim, and how to turn a hunter into the hunted.

Dawson was exhausted when he got back home. Christine was in the sitting room watching TV. Dawson took a shower to wash the day's dirt away. The water pressure was low, but it did the job. He kissed Hosiah, already fast asleep in his room, and then crawled into bed. For a moment he thought of the kids he had talked to tonight. They slept on the hard pavement every night. Hosiah slept in a comfortable bed.

He was faintly aware of Christine slipping into bed beside him. Later, he saw Issa and Antwi walk into the bedroom. An invisible force held Dawson down, preventing him from moving. Issa drew a knife, holding it high in readiness to strike. Mosquito came in pushing a cart. Issa brought the knife down slowly. Dawson struggled to get up but couldn't. The knife plunged into Antwi's back. Warm blood spilled across Dawson's face.

Chest tight, he shot up in bed, groped for the lamp, but knocked it over instead. Christine's light came on. He looked at her but saw her only indistinctly.

"I've sent Antwi straight into the arms of the killer," Dawson said. "Issa will kill him. I have to go and get him before it's too late."

He started to get up, but she held him back.

"Dark, stop. It's a nightmare. It's not happening."

"What?"

He stared at her for a moment, then he groaned and fell back.

"Relax, relax," she whispered, cradling his head.

"It can't be Issa, can it?" Dawson muttered.

"In the morning, things will look different by the light of day," she said confidently.

He sighed. "I want some Malta. With a scoop of ice cream in it. Do we have any ice cream?"

"A little. I don't know why I spoil you like this."

43

Monday morning, the *Graphic*'s headline was SERIAL KILLER STALKS ACCRA. The corresponding photo was the Novotel Lorry Park latrine, which would undoubtedly become a new Accra landmark. Lartey was reading the article when Dawson came into his office.

"If we let the press take control of this," the chief supol said, "they'll cause all kinds of panic and hysteria among the public. We have to wrestle the control back from them."

"How should we do that, sir?"

"We'll talk about that in a little while. Right now, I want you to summarize everything we know about the case." Lartey checked his watch. "We'll wait a few minutes for Philip."

Just as he said that, Chikata hurried in, mumbling an apology. "Have a seat, Philip," Lartey said. "Go ahead, Dawson."

Dawson took his position in front of Lartey's giant wall map of the Accra metropolitan area. Using an erasable marker on the map's coated surface, he circled the sites of the four murders: Musa, dead in the Korle Lagoon, Ebenezer in a muddy ditch in Jamestown, Comfort at the rubbish dump at the railway station, and finally Ofosu in the Novotel latrine.

"With Musa's murder," Dawson said, "I thought it might be a ritual killing because his fingers had been cut off, but Dr. Allen Botswe didn't think so. When Comfort's murder occurred, we became certain that there was one killer responsible for all three—hers, Ebenezer's before her, and Musa's before Ebenezer. The M.O. of targeting street people and the signature of striking them down with a single deep and fatal stab to the back, along with an additional mutilation, is consistent throughout. Musa's and Ebenezer's locations are only a kilometer apart or so, and both are south of Comfort's and Ofosu's."

He connected his four points on the map with lines.

"The area is within Accra Central and is approximately the shape of a parallelogram. There are at least a couple possibilities. One, the killer lives within the perimeter of the parallelogram and murders his victims there. Two, he chooses victims *outside* the parallelogram but chooses to dump them within it."

"What is special about the parallelogram area?" Lartey asked.

"Excellent question, sir. Very likely it has special significance to the killer because it includes major areas where poor children of, or *on,* the street live—Jamestown, Agbogbloshie, the railway station, CMB, Tudu, and so on. In other words, these are the places that set him alight and get his motor running, that stimulate him to kill.

"At any rate, we believe he is highly mobile with a pickup truck, a van, or a large car with enough room in the boot to hide a body—because as far as we can tell, the four victims were not killed where they were found, they were transported."

"How did you come to that conclusion?" Lartey asked.

"A couple reasons," Dawson said. "The first is that at the spots the victims were dumped, there hasn't been the amount and severity of bleeding one might expect from their stab wounds, suggesting that most of the hemorrhage occurred prior and elsewhere. Second, part of the killer's signature is to dump his victims in specific places that convey filth—rubbish dump, gutter, latrine, and so on. It would be difficult to choose victims who are at those locations at exactly the right moment. He kills them and *then* he places them where he wants."

"Has a specific truck or van been detected that's common to the murder sites?"

"No, but Antwi and his late friend Ofosu reported a vehicle a short time before we believe Comfort was killed. However, they couldn't make out the vehicle or the driver."

"That could be something," Lartey said. "Or not. All right, so what are you going to do about finding this killer?"

"We need to concentrate on people and places that have contact with street children. We already know one place, SCOAR, but there are other organizations in Accra that advocate for the kids. We need to go in and look around and talk to people. We'll focus on employees who live within our parallelogram, and employees who have left the organizations or been sacked for some infraction, like abuse of the children."

"What else are you planning?"

"I had an idea when Dr. Botswe told me that the killer might try to involve or inject himself into the investigation. I was trying to think of something that would engage him, make him come forward in some way."

Chikata snapped his fingers. "What about call-in radio programs? People love them. He might be tempted to call a station so he can be on air."

Lartey beamed at his nephew. "*Brilliant,* Philip. You could get that set up with Joy FM and Bola Ray."

"Sure."

"How would that work?" Dawson asked. "He'd call in to the station and then what?"

"The number would show on the studio screen, and then we can have the phone company either trace the call or check phone records."

Dawson was doubtful. "Are you sure the caller's number shows on the studio screen? I don't think so. The call screener doesn't need your number when you call the studio, she just needs to know from where you're calling."

"Maybe you're right," Chikata conceded. "Still, they could trace the call for us."

Dawson shook his head. "How? The phone companies haven't started registering people to their phone numbers."

"I thought they had."

"They're supposed to be doing it soon," Dawson said, "but they haven't yet. Think about it. You just walk into a phone store and buy a SIM card, which has your new phone number on it. The store gives you a receipt that may or may not have your name on it, but they don't connect that SIM card phone number to your name in a computer system, or any system, for that matter. Some people even have more than one SIM card, or lend SIM cards to their friends. So how can anyone be reliably traced?"

"I still think there's a way," Chikata insisted.

"I'll bet you lunch at Papaye's," Dawson said.

"Okay, look," Lartey interrupted impatiently, "just find out if it's possible, one of you, would you? I'm not going to sit here and listen to you argue all day about phones."

"I need something else, sir," Dawson said boldly.

Lartey's brow clouded like a darkening sky. "What exactly do you mean?"

"I need people. Nighttime surveillance for the whole parallelogram area."

Lartey looked about as happy as a child swallowing bitter medicine.

"You're always asking for things, Dawson," he complained. "All right, I'll see what I can do."

44

Later that morning, Lartey granted Dawson four detective constables for his surveillance plan, *for one week only, understood?*

Dawson spent part of the morning briefing the constables on their positions, what they were looking for, and what to do in different situations. *Any vehicle slowly circling these areas should arouse suspicion and should be watched. A car whose driver picks up a street child should be followed and assistance called for if necessary.*

While Chikata was off calling the phone companies, Dawson went to SCOAR.

Genevieve was out for the moment, to Dawson's relief. He didn't want to have to navigate around her guardedness.

He found Patience in the staff room.

"I know you've probably seen and heard the bad news about Ofosu's death," he said to her as he took the seat she offered him.

"It's terrible what's going on, Inspector," she said. "I work every day with these boys and girls. I call them my children. Yes, there are problems, and no, they are not all angels, but I do love them."

"To your knowledge, did Ofosu ever come to the center?"

"Not that I know, but you should check with Socrate, and also check the other street children centers in Accra. There's the Catholic Street Child Refuge, CSCR, for instance. They're much larger than we are."

"That's my next stop today," Dawson said. "I also wanted to let you know, Patience, that last night I spoke to a bunch of the street kids from around the railway station about how to look out for themselves and each other, what suspicious signs to watch for, and so on. Issa is going to be my main contact person."

Patience beamed. "Thank you for doing that, Inspector. You may not realize how much a gesture like that means to the kids, especially coming from a policeman. They are so used to being vilified. Are you sure you don't want to be a social worker?"

"Funny you should say that. Someone recently asked me about becoming a psychologist. I had a question for you that maybe you can help me with. Do you mind if I close the door?"

"No, of course not."

The door shut, Dawson continued. "I wanted to ask you about Socrate."

Dawson saw a brief flicker of discomfort flash across Patience's face. "Mm-hm? What did you need to know?"

"What's your opinion of him?"

"Well, you know, he does a very good job at what he does—electronic stuff, the computer, and so on, and he really helps us to raise money."

"Have you had any complaints about him from the children?"

"What kinds of complaints?"

"Abuse or maltreatment."

She shifted in her chair. "Did you hear something like that?"

"Yes. From Antwi."

"I see. In that case, you should bring that up to Genevieve. I'm very sorry I can't help you much with this kind of thing. It's really the boss's area."

"Thank you, Patience."

He could tell that she knew something. Either she had been afraid to bring it to Genevieve's attention or she had brought it up and been shot down.

Dawson made his way to CSCR in Accra New Town. The director, Sister Sylvia Kwapong, was a gracious, gray-haired woman who took no offense at Dawson's inquiries, providing him with detailed information on all past and present employees. Nothing really stood out about any of them, but Dawson took away a list just the same.

As he was leaving, he thought of something.

"Sister, do you know a nine-year-old boy called Sly?"

Dawson gave her Sly's description, relating how they had met. She searched her mind for a moment and shook her head. "No, I'm afraid no one comes to mind. If I come across him or anyone who knows of him, I'll be sure to give you a call."

"Please do."

"I can tell you're very worried about him," Sister Sylvia said gently.

"Yes, I am."

"I will pray that you find him safe and sound, Inspector. The good Lord will answer my prayers."

"Thank you, Sister."

Dawson left her with his card. He headed home. Accra New Town was adjacent to Nima, where Daramani lived. For a moment, Dawson wondered how his "friend" was doing. For the first time in many months, Dawson felt a craving for wee return like a conniving ex-lover. It seized him, pulled him into its bosom, and planted an openmouthed kiss. Dawson fought to pull away, but he felt himself weakening.

The phone rang, and he jumped. *Thank God.* It was a welcome rescue from temptation.

It was Chikata on the line. "Okay, seems we were both kind of wrong and kind of right," he said. "Tigo phone says they can't link a phone number to a particular person for the same reasons you were giving, but one of the engineers told me they could possibly help in another way. He said if the radio station can split the broadcast feed and send one portion to the phone company, they could try locating the caller with their Global Positioning System. But the process might take a few minutes and the caller has to stay on the line long enough."

"I see," Dawson said. "It's worth a try."

"So who is buying at Papaye's?"

"I'll buy, of course. The superior officer always buys."

45

Genevieve had left the office earlier that day for the first day of a weeklong seminar at the Accra International Conference Center. She was to make a presentation the following morning, Tuesday. It was as she drove home that she remembered she had left her thumb drive in the office. She debated picking it up early in the morning before going to the seminar, but she knew morning traffic would make that risky. Annoyed with herself, she turned off on the next street and headed back to SCOAR.

Everyone had left for the day, the center was quiet. Socrate had the place to himself. He listened to Joy FM on the Internet while he updated the website and surfed around the Internet for pleasure. He went to Genevieve's office to get the spy cam. He removed it, resting the speaker on the corner of his desk as he began the upload to his computer. While that was taking place, he went to the toilet.

Genevieve let herself in the side door. Down the corridor, the lights were on in her office as well as Socrate's, two doors down. She popped her head in hers, but he wasn't there, nor was he in his own office.

"Socra?" she called out.

Suddenly alarm flared in her mind. Was it Socrate in the building or someone else?

"Socra?"

She looked behind her and down the corridor again. No one.

On his desk was a small, partially dismantled speaker, which looked just like the one in her office. Puzzled, Genevieve went back to check and, indeed, only the speaker's mounting bracket was in place. The speaker *had* been taken down. In Socrate's office again, she peered at the speaker, whose front grille had been removed. Right beside the bass unit was a space lined by putty.

Something else was on the desk: a miniature camera. Connected to Socrate's PC by a USB cable, it was tiny. Genevieve's eyes darted between it and the speaker. She picked up the camera and pressed it into the putty. She was right. It fit snugly and firmly.

Her heart pounding, a sickening feeling in the pit of her stomach, she circled the desk. She looked at the monitor screen. A pop-up window asked whether to save or launch the download. Genevieve's hand hovered over the Enter key for a moment. She hit it. The surveillance image started. She saw herself in her office. She gasped and staggered back.

Socrate was at the door. "Genevieve. What are you doing here?"

"What am *I* doing here? No, the question is what are *you* doing here, Socra? What is this?"

He came into the room slowly, his eyes blinking rapidly. He already knew what Genevieve had seen. He stood next to her, staring blankly at the screen.

"You're *spying* on me?" she said, her voice up one octave.

"I wouldn't call it spying," he said dully.

"What would you call it? Oh, Ewurade, Ewurade." She took another step back, suddenly feeling suffocated. She could not control her breathing. She felt like she was about to faint.

"*Why?* What is this for, Socrate? Are you selling information to someone?"

He shook his head. "No."

"Then what? How long have you been doing this?"

Socrate kept his head down. "I started a few months after I set up the sound system."

"Oh!" she cried. "Oh, Socrate, no."

"I'm sorry," he mumbled.

"Is this why you stay late? So you can *watch* me? Watch your day's *film* of me?"

He nodded. Genevieve shuddered, wanting to get out of her own skin as though it had been coated with filth.

"Why, Socra?"

"You don't understand," he said.

"No, I don't."

"I care a lot about you."

"And this is how you show it?"

"I know things aren't going so well with you and your husband—"

"That's my business, not yours—"

"There are too many men who want you. I need to keep an eye on them."

"Socra, I can take care of myself."

"Yes, but it's always good to have a guardian angel. Someone to watch over you."

"Watch over me?" she said, bewildered.

"Yes. For instance, I know Inspector Dawson wants to have an affair with you. Be very careful of that man."

"Socra, the man is happily settled down with a wife and a seven-year-old boy."

"If it were not for you," Socrate said, looking wistfully at her, "I would never stay in this job. You think I care about these worthless children? You think I really enjoy going around town taking pictures of them as if they were movie stars? I do it all for *you*, Gennie. That's all. Just for you."

Worthless children. The words stung her like a whip on wet skin. Tears poured down her cheeks.

"Gennie, please . . ."

He came toward her.

She put a palm up to stop him. "No, no. You stay away from me. Stay away."

Socrate stopped where he was.

"It's true then," Genevieve said. "What Inspector Darko said is true. You *did* lock Antwi in that storeroom."

"He's a nasty little liar, that boy."

"And the stories of your torturing them—those must be true as well. Oh, my Jesus Christ."

She put her face in her hands.

"So now you trust Darko's word more than mine? Does that mean you like him more than me?"

Genevieve was agape. "Socra, what fantasy world are you living in? This isn't about a contest between you and Dawson. It's about what you've done. You've betrayed my trust and that of the children. You've abused them. But why do you detest them so much?" Her eyes widened as something hit her. "Those four murdered street kids . . ." She stopped and drew in her breath.

He looked away. "I didn't kill them."

They said nothing for several minutes.

"I'm sorry, Socra," she said.

He nodded. "I know. I have to leave."

He picked up his satchel, opened it to show Genevieve that he wasn't stealing anything from SCOAR, slung it over his shoulder, and slowly walked out with his head down.

46

In the morning, Socrate woke with a heavy heart. He had a relentless headache and no appetite. The vision of Genevieve's pained expression kept coming back to haunt him.

He sat on the edge of his bed in his underwear with his head bowed. The radio was on in the background. He paid little attention until he heard something that made him sit up. It was a promo announcement for Bola Ray's *Drive Time* show that evening. Detective Inspector Darko Dawson would be on with Dr. Allen Botswe discussing serial killers.

Beautiful, Socrate thought. He sprang up with renewed vigor. Before this evening, he had a lot of work to do and some electronic gadgetry to design. This was where his genius came in. He would need a throwaway phone and a voice disguiser.

Dawson met with the surveillance officers who had been on duty overnight. They had little to report. No suspicious vehicles had been spotted cruising. The clusters of sleeping street kids had been quiet. But Detective Constable Juliet Quaynor brought up an interesting point.

"Since Comfort was a prostitute," she said, "should we also be watching places like Nkrumah Circle, or even Danquah Circle, where many of these ashawos loiter?"

"I see what you're saying," Dawson said, "and it's a good thought. But that assumes the killer is specifically targeting ashawos, and we don't think that's the case. He's after street teenagers, and although some of them hang around the circles, we just don't have enough people to cover those areas in addition to the key spots we're already targeting."

As the officers left the room, Dawson made a mental note that Quaynor should be watched as a detective with great potential.

In Joy FM's purple and white four-story building in Kokomlemle, Dawson sat in the studio with Bola Ray and Allen Botswe. Like all FM stations in Accra, there wasn't a separate control room, so the Joy engineer was stationed in the studio itself while Chikata and Carlos, the Tigo phone technician, stayed in the adjoining all-purpose greenroom visible from the studio through a glass window.

After the intro music, Bola Ray, with his round face, trademark glasses, and broad, easy smile, pulled the mike closer to his mouth and began the segment.

"First on this evening, we've got a very interesting show," he said. "Dr. Allen Botswe, the renowned University of Ghana professor and criminal psychologist, is here with us to talk about a serial killer roaming the streets of Accra. Some in the press have even dubbed him the Latrine Killer because he murdered one of his victims in a latrine. To give us the perspective of the law enforcement side, we have Detective Inspector Darko Dawson in the studio as well."

As the discussion proceeded, the calls began to come in fast and furiously, handled in his usual deft fashion by Bola.

"Salifu from Koforidua," he said, looking at his console, "you're on the air, go ahead."

"I want to ask the doctor and the inspector who are talking about this thing, how are you so sure that it is one person alone who is committing these terrible killings?"

"It's because of the signature, as we call it," Botswe said. "Although we can't reveal details, we see a unique pattern to the murders that could not have been so exactly duplicated by more than one person."

"Inspector Dawson, do you have anything to add to that?" Bola said.

"Dr. Botswe is correct. It's what we see in the characteristics of the murders that leads us to conclude that there's a single perpetrator."

"Erica is calling from Labone. You're on air."

"So does it mean that this man, the Latrine Killer, will only kill certain types of people like these street children? In other words, should I worry about my teenage girl who is well taken care of and is nothing like a street child?"

"I don't think you need worry about this particular offender, the Latrine Killer as you call him," Botswe said, "but you should continue to exercise the sensible precautions that all parents should take to protect their children."

"Next we have Samson in Central Accra."

"Good evening, gentlemen. How are you?"

The voice made Dawson sit up straight. It sounded like an empty oil drum rumbling down an echoing cobblestone alley.

"Doing well, thank you," Bola said. "Go ahead."

"The perpetrator will not necessarily confine himself to these street children, as you call them."

Dawson signaled to both Carlos and the Joy FM tech that he wanted this one tracked. The tech went to work on a row of switches. Outside, Carlos was on his mobile to another engineer at Tigo HQ.

On a scrap of paper, Dawson scribbled "keep him on air as long as you can" and slid it in front of Bola. He nodded.

"That's interesting, Samson," Bola said. "How do you know what the perpetrator will do?"

"Because I'm him. *I* am the perpetrator, and I know what I'm planning."

That stopped even the irrepressible Bola for a second. He glanced at Botswe and Dawson, who signaled him to keep on going.

"If that's the case," Bola said, "why call in to Joy FM?"

"I want to deliver a message to the inspector."

"Yes, Samson?" Dawson said. "What's the message?"

"Be careful."

"Meaning what?"

"While you're trying to find out what happened to those other youngsters I murdered, look out for your own seven-year-old boy."

Dawson felt goose bumps rise. "If you're really the killer, Samson," he said, "give me a secret sign that you know how those kids died."

"You mean what I did to them? Let's just say it was intimate contact. I must be going, because I'm sure you're busy trying to find my global position."

"Samson, this is Dr. Botswe. If I may ask—"

"Oh, looks like we've lost Samson," Bola said.

Dawson snatched off his headphones and dashed next-door to the greenroom. "Did you get it?"

Carlos was on his feet, phone to ear.

"I think they've got it. Hol' on, hol' on, it's coming."

"Please, Jesus, hurry up," Dawson said. "Let's get going while we're waiting for it."

He, Chikata, and Carlos made for the stairs.

"Here it is," Carlos said as the information was relayed in text form on his mobile. "Three fifty-three Faanofa Street, Kokomlemle. *What?*"

"Shit," Chikata said. "That's the building next door."

Dawson felt a thrill surge through him. "God," he said. "We've got him."

Bright lights illuminated the front of 353 Faanofa, which was a shop called Come Closer Fashions.

"I'll go inside while you check the back," Dawson said to Chikata.

The detective sergeant veered off to the alley while Dawson went inside the small, air-conditioned shop. Hip-hop music pounded as a chick in a condom-tight black-and-white outfit and stilettos sorted clothes on a rack.

"Hello," she said, chewing gum and smiling. "Can I help you?"

"Was there a man in here a few minutes ago making a phone call?"

She raised her eyebrows and shook her head. "No."

Dawson charged out, annoyed with himself. Why would the caller go *inside* where he would be seen?

Vaulting over the railing at one side of the shop, Dawson landed at a run toward the rear of the building. At that moment, Chikata was coming in the opposite direction with something in a clear plastic bag. Carlos was right behind him. Dawson knew at once from the looks on their faces that the mission had failed.

"We missed him, boss," Chikata said, fuming. "*Shit!* He left this for us taped to the wall back there."

He handed the bag to Dawson. It was a cheap plastic phone, the kind Dawson had bought for Akosua. On the screen, there was a smiley face and a text message underneath it: *You came fashionably close, but not close enough.*

"You get it?" Chikata asked.

"Yes, I get it, thank you, Chikata," Dawson said, his jaw grinding in anger. He wanted to smash the phone into a thousand pieces. "Come Closer Fashions. I get it."

47

The program segment over, Botswe was waiting for them in the downstairs lobby.

"Any luck?" he asked.

"No." Dawson handed the joke phone to Botswe.

"Oh," he said, reading the text. "Good gracious."

"Is that the killer or just a prankster?" Dawson asked him. "What's your opinion?"

"Could be both, really. Some of them are that way. But even if he's the true killer, he doesn't have designs on your son. He's just trying to scare you."

"Are you sure?"

"I'm positive. He doesn't have any interest in the kind of boy you have in the age-group he is. He targets teenagers. Killers are remarkably predictable, and he would not switch gears at this point."

"I was afraid he might be escalating," Dawson said.

"Even if he was," Botswe said, "it would never involve a boy like your son."

Christine was up watching a TV movie as Dawson came in. He flopped down beside her with a sigh.

"Bad day," she said.

He nodded.

"I heard the broadcast," she said.

"Scared you?"

"Um, yes, a little."

"I don't blame you."

"You don't sound very concerned."

"Christine, of course I'm concerned. I'm just tired. Tired, confused, depressed, all of it."

"Sorry."

He shook his head. "It's okay. Look, Dr. Botswe thinks it's someone playing a prank, and I think I know who it is, although I'll probably never prove it."

"Who?"

"Someone called Socrate who works at SCOAR. He's the kind of crazy, immature person who would do this."

"Okay, but whoever it is, are you certain this is an empty threat?"

Dawson sighed. "Okay, let's think about this logically. Even if this *were* a true threat, how would anyone get hold of Hosiah? He's not out on the street without us, he's safe in the house when he's at home, and at school he's supervised. Even when he goes to play with his friends there's an adult around."

"It isn't very reassuring if you're out as late as you were tonight. It's true the house is well barricaded and I'm not going to open the door to just anyone, but still."

Dawson chewed on the inside of his cheek. In a way, she had a point.

"Let's do this, then," he said. "Some of the constables do watchmen jobs on the side to make a little extra money. I'll get a couple of them over on late nights. Would that make you feel better?"

"Yes, it would."

Dawson woke at two-fifteen in the morning thinking he had heard a noise in the backyard. He looked out the window but saw nothing. He slipped on his sandals and headed outside, pausing on the way to check that Hosiah was peacefully sleeping. He walked around the perimeter of the house. All was quiet. When he got back in bed, he told himself he was being paranoid.

In the morning, he called up P.C. Gyamfi to ask if he was on duty that night.

"No, Dawson, sir," Gyamfi said. "I'm off."

"I have to be away from home on a surveillance job for several hours tonight," Dawson said. "Can you watch my house from eight at night until about three in the morning? I'll pay you."

"Thank you, sah! I would be happy to do that for you. Is there something I should know?"

Dawson explained about the on-air threat that had been made Tuesday night.

"Yes, of course, Dawson, sah," Gyamfi said. "No problem. I will take care of it. Anytime you need me and I'm free, I can help you."

"Thank you, Gyamfi."

At dinner, Dawson told Christine and Hosiah that he would very likely be out late at night, but that Constable Gyamfi would be watching the house in his absence.

"My relief is supposed to come in at two in the morning," he said, "so I'll be back home soon after that."

"Who are you going to catch tonight?" Hosiah asked, dexterously spooning up his rice and stew.

"Good question," Dawson said. "That's what I don't know."

Chikata was to watch the perimeter of Kantamanto Market, the railway station, and Kwame Nkrumah Avenue as far up as CMB. Kantamanto itself was shut down at night, so he was spared the impossible task of monitoring the interior of the market itself.

Dawson would take Kinbu Road and points south, which included Issa's base. Quaynor and two other constables would cover the rest of the areas within the parallelogram. The fourth constable was Chikata's driver, while Baidoo was Dawson's. All were to keep in close touch with Dawson. He badly wanted the killer to show himself tonight.

Dawson called Chikata. "All clear?"

"Everything's quiet."

And that's how it remained for another two hours. At 1:06, as Dawson was making a pass south on Kojo Thompson, Chikata called.

"Dawson, an adult male walking near Liberty House on Okai Kwei Road before it intersects with another street—I'm not sure what it's called."

"Commercial," Dawson prompted. He knew his streets cold.

"Okay, yes. He looks suspicious. Too dark to see his face well, but he's about five-ten, well built . . . Oh, wait. He's disappeared."

"Try following him. Be careful. I'm coming over."

Dawson sprinted west on Kimberly Avenue the five hundred meters to Okai Kwei and Commercial. When he got there, he didn't see Chikata at first. He turned down an alley where empty market tables were stacked upside down for the night. He jumped as a shadow appeared out of yet another alley. It was Chikata.

"I lost him, Dawson," he said.

"Did he see you?"

"I don't think so."

Dawson saw a movement in his peripheral vision and swung the beam of his flashlight around to find a boy of about twelve standing a few meters away.

"What are you looking for?" Dawson asked.

"My friend."

Dawson went up to him.

"What's your name?"

"Labram."

"Who's your friend?"

"Hassan. I saw a man talking to him. He went with the man."

"Which way?"

Labram pointed south toward the UTC building.

"Did you see what the man looked like?"

The boy shook his head.

"As tall as me?"

"I don't think so."

"Okay, let's walk that way."

They went quickly. Except for Dawson's and Chikata's flashlights, it was pitch dark. They whirled around as an engine started up. A hundred meters away, a large, silver car was pulling out of a small side street off Commercial. They shined their flashlights, but the car moved off too quickly for them to see who was in it. It made a left on Kwame Nkrumah and sped north.

"Get your driver and the other constables," Dawson said to Chikata. "I'll take Baidoo, and you follow us."

He took off for Baidoo's parking spot. The sergeant must have figured out he was needed because he was already pulling up to Dawson in the Tata jeep.

Dawson hopped in. "Did you see the vehicle?"

"Silver Benz," Baidoo said, bumping over the avenue divider to get to the opposite side. There were no cars on the streets now, so it was easy to keep the taillights of the Benz in view.

Dawson called Chikata. "He's going on Tudu toward Novotel," he told him.

"Coming that way now."

"I'll stay on the line until you catch up with us. Baidoo, move up a little bit so we can see the license plate—not too close, though."

As they neared the car, Dawson's blood ran cold. "Oh, Jesus."

"What's wrong?"

"I know the owner of the car."

"Who is it?"

"Dr. Allen Botswe."

48

Dr. Botswe's silver Benz swung into his driveway. Less than a minute later, the two police Tata jeeps went by, pulling over just a few meters up. Dawson jumped out, and Chikata, Quaynor, and the other constables came up behind him as he hid near the wall and watched the Benz being parked. The driver got out. It was Obi. He opened the passenger door to let Hassan out. The boy looked about the same age as Labram.

As Obi and Hassan reached the front of the house, the door opened and Dawson caught a glimpse of Botswe as he let them in.

"Okay," Dawson said. "Let's go."

He ran up to the door and rang the bell. As soon as Obi opened up, Dawson pushed past him. The others followed. Genevieve Kusi, standing in the foyer with Botswe, Obi, and Hassan, let out a startled cry.

"Everyone stay where you are," Dawson said.

"What's going on?" Botswe spluttered.

"Quaynor, take care of the boy."

She sidled up to Hassan, took his hand, and escorted him outside.

"What are you *doing* here?" Botswe shouted.

"Would you come with us to the station, please, Doctor?"

"What for? Are you arresting me?"

"No, but I do need to ask you some questions. I would like Genevieve and Obi to accompany us as well. If there's any attempt by any of you to resist, you will be handcuffed. Is that understood?"

It was going to be a long night. Botswe, Genevieve, and Obi were transported to the Legon Police Station and separated. Fortunately there was one office and two small rooms available to confine them.

Dawson would take on Botswe first. He briefed Chikata on how to interview Genevieve and the key information he wanted out of her.

"You're okay with me interviewing her by myself?" Chikata asked.

"Yes, I trust you."

"Thank you, Dawson."

Dawson went into Botswe's room and shut the door behind him. A ceiling fan was circulating the warm, oppressive air.

"So, Dr. Botswe. We meet again under rather different circumstances."

Botswe, who had been seated in front of the table in the center of the room, shot to his feet, tipping the chair over. "This is an outrage, Inspector!" he shouted.

"Doctor," Dawson said softly, "please sit down so we can talk in the proper fashion."

His chest heaving with anger, Botswe righted his chair and took his seat again.

"Thank you very much, sir," Dawson said, now sitting

down himself on the other side of the table. "Certain areas of Central Accra have been under surveillance in regard to the recent killings of street youngsters. This evening, we observed your vehicle taking a boy away from the UTC area. In view of recent events, which you're well aware of, I'm obligated to question you."

Botswe looked incredulous. "That's all this is about?" he cried. "Why didn't you simply ask? There is a perfectly harmless explanation for this, Inspector."

"I'm listening."

"Look, for about a year now, I have been interviewing street children about their experiences in the city, some of it for an article I'm writing for the *Ghana Journal of Psychology* on coping mechanisms of street kids."

"Does this have something to do with the paper Austin Ansah is writing? He says he was a student of yours."

"Austin is an excellent Ph.D. candidate. He and I have collaborated on papers before, although we're not doing that right now. He gets some of his ideas and techniques from me."

"Go on."

"So I've been interviewing these kids. Sometimes they're random picks from the street, sometimes Genevieve suggests children at SCOAR. But there are a couple problems in regard to SCOAR. First, it's a somewhat contrived environment, whereas I prefer the rawness of the street. Second, about six months ago, I began to feel that I was using these kids as a resource without giving them anything in return. So I decided that, whomever I interviewed, I would give them a treat.

"So the way I do it is I send Obi out to discreetly pick up a child or two from the street, bring him or her here in the Benz or the Infiniti. We feed them, allow them to have a refreshing shower, then I interview them, and they sleep overnight in the guest rooms. In the morning, Obi returns them to the street."

Dawson's lip curled. "It seems almost cruel. You give them a sip of water and then pour the rest away."

"Not at all. If you could see the looks on their faces, Inspector, and see just how grateful they are that someone has paid attention to them, pampered them. It's an experience of a lifetime. And I always tell them, all this comes with hard work and education, and I encourage them to go into educational programs like that offered by SCOAR and other organizations."

Dawson stared at Botswe. "This is one of the strangest things I've ever heard."

"Because you're cynical, like most of the rest of the world, Inspector. You don't believe that people who have a lot can extend a little kindness to those who have nothing. Are you telling me you've never done anything like this before?"

Dawson suddenly thought of Sly and how he had hoped to get the boy in school. But that was different, wasn't it? School would presumably get the boy ahead in life. How would wining and dining him in a fancy house for one night help?

"How many children have you given this treat, as you call it?" Dawson asked.

"Some twenty-odd."

"Where were you the night of Saturday, fifth June, Doctor?"

"Fifth June?" Botswe thought for a moment. "Oh, I was in Kumasi visiting my sister for the weekend. Is that the date of Musa Zakari's death?"

"You have a good memory. What time did you arrive in Kumasi?"

"Saturday afternoon around three or so."

"Who can confirm your whereabouts on that date at that time?"

"Well, my sister Eloise, of course. And Austin Ansah can help confirm it as well."

"Why, did he go with you?"

"No, but he babysat the house that weekend. I gave Obi the weekend off, and I prefer not to leave the house unoccupied. We've had burglary attempts before."

"Austin is an ex-student of yours and he babysits your house? Seems a little bit unusual. Is there another connection between the two of you?"

Botswe's eyes flickered. "Just because I'm well off doesn't mean I'm not kind."

"Separate matter," Dawson said steadily. "This is something else. I believe the connection is Genevieve."

"Well, he's her brother. Otherwise I don't get your meaning, Inspector."

"I'm guessing that you and Genevieve have a relationship that is more than professional."

"How did you come to that absurd conclusion?"

"One, she's at your house in the small hours of the morning. Two, she told me the painting by Wiz Kudowor that hangs in her office was a gift. His works run in the thousands of dollars, so someone well off must have given it to her."

"And I'm the only well-off person in the country?" Botswe said with a smile.

"No, but you too have a painting by Wiz in your home. It just seems too coincidental to be really coincidental, if you see what I mean."

"Okay, you're right." Botswe closed his eyes for a moment. "Please. I don't want this to get out, Inspector. For her sake."

"I understand. Can I ask you where you were on the night of Monday, twenty-first June? That was the date we first met. The following morning, the body of Ebenezer was found."

"Do you mind if I look at my calendar?"

"Go ahead."

Botswe checked his phone. "Oh dear," he said, looking sheepish.

Dawson almost smiled. "You were with Genevieve?"

"Yes."

"All right. I'll check with her if that's accurate. What about the following night?"

"Em, I had a dinner party. I can give you names for the guests as well."

"How late were they there?"

"Most were gone by midnight, but a couple of my very close friends stayed over for a couple hours—you know, brandy and cigars. That was the night Comfort was murdered?"

"Correct."

"I hate to say this, Inspector, but you're wasting your time with me. I am not the murderer you're looking for."

"I'll decide that. Your alibis have to be checked. I need the phone numbers for your sister Eloise and for all the guests you had on Tuesday, twenty-second June."

"Yes, I can supply them to you if you would give me something to jot them down."

Dawson stood up. "Would you please wait here?"

Outside the interview rooms, Dawson met with Chikata. "What did you get out of Genevieve?"

"She thinks the world of Botswe," Chikata said. "Tries to help him in whatever he does."

"How are her alibis?"

"Solid if they check out. Only one date she wasn't able to recall."

"Let me guess. Twenty-first June."

"How did you know?" Chikata's face lit up with the realization. "Oh, now I get it. Are you going to interview her too?"

"I doubt it, but leave her where she is for now. I'm going in to Obi. Get the numbers from Botswe and start calling. Yes, that's right, wake all of them up."

Obi was pacing the floor anxiously. He heaved a sigh of relief as Dawson entered.

"Please, is everything all right with the doctor?"

"Have a seat, Obi."

He did, fidgeting. "Please, he's done nothing wrong."

"It amazes me how you're so worried about him and not yourself," Dawson said, taking a seat. "In total, how many street children have you picked up to transport to Dr. Botswe's house?"

"Twenty-two."

"So you bring them to the house at night and take them back in the morning?"

"Yes, please, Inspector. I do what the doctor asks me to. He tells me I must find a street boy or girl, or at most two, but I have to find those who are alone, or separated from the rest. I can't go and pick one out of a crowd. If I do, they will fight."

"How do you feel about doing this for the doctor?"

"Dr. Botswe is like . . . how can I say this? Like a saint. He should be called Saint Allen. He shows so much kindness to these children. Even after some of them tried to steal from his house."

"When was that?"

"One time in April, I caught one of them trying to steal a valuable crystal."

"You were angry?"

"Please, Inspector, they have nothing, these children. How can they not be tempted? But I serve the doctor. I'm devoted to him alone. Him and the Lord."

"You stay in the servants' quarters at all times?"

"When the doctor has dinner parties, or if he needs me early in the morning, then I don't go home."

"Where do you live?"

"In Madina, please."

"When was Dr. Botswe's last dinner party?"

"Twenty-second June."

"And you waited for all the guests to leave?"

"Yes, around two o'clock, and then I cleaned everything after that."

"What time did the doctor go to bed?"

"I said good night to him about three in the morning."

"That's very late."

"He doesn't sleep well. Since the wife died, you see. Sometimes he stays up for hours listening to his music. I go to bed only when he tells me he doesn't need me for anything more."

"I see. You're one of the most devoted people I've ever met."

"Thank you, Inspector. I just try my best."

"Wait for me here."

"Yes, please."

Dawson went outside, where Chikata was making phone calls. "I got hold of the sister, Eloise," he told Dawson. "She wasn't happy about hearing from me at this time of the night, but she confirmed Botswe's Kumasi visit. I got one confirmation on the dinner party."

"Thank you, Chikata. That's probably enough for the night. We'll follow up with the rest later on."

Dawson returned to Obi. "You're free to go," he told him.

"That's all?" Obi was surprised. "Is everything okay?"

"Everything is fine. A constable will drive you back home with the doctor and Mrs. Kusi."

Obi's eyes dropped.

Dawson nodded. "It's okay. The secret is safe."

49

The *Daily Graphic* reported that Detective Inspector Dawson of CID had led a raid of world-renowned Professor Allen Botswe's home and "arrested" the criminal psychologist for possible child abduction. The professor was later released when it was discovered that his only crime had been an "act of pure compassion and humanitarianism."

On Joy FM's *Super Morning Show*, Kojo Oppong-Nkrumah and his sidekick dissected the newspaper stories and pointed out the irony that D.I. Dawson and Dr. Botswe had been on the *Drive Time* show *together* only two days before. What was this detective inspector *thinking*?

Dawson got to work in a foul mood that wasn't improved by practically everyone talking about him. He was the overnight sensation in all the wrong ways. Chikata didn't dare say a word when Dawson walked into the office like an ogre. They both knew that at nine o'clock sharp Dawson would be summoned to Lartey's office.

"What happened?" the chief supol demanded.

Dawson was able to tell him only a portion of the story. Lartey cut him short as he snatched a copy of the *Graphic* from his desk. He held it up to Dawson's face.

"Have you read this?"

"I glanced at it."

"*Glanced.* Well, I suggest you read it to see just how much of a *fool* you look."

"It's the press, sir. That's what they do."

"Oh, now it's the press's fault? D.I. Dawson, competence is our responsibility and *in*competence our burden."

"Nothing incompetent about this, sir. Just because Botswe has social status doesn't mean he doesn't get investigated. Taking a child off the street and bundling him into a car does not look aboveboard to me."

"But it turned out it *was,* and the sad thing is that you could have figured it all out with just a few minutes' chat with Dr. Botswe *at his house.* You did not have to arrest the man, not to mention the other two."

"I didn't arrest him, sir."

"It amounted to the same thing, especially in the public's view."

"He came voluntarily."

"Just barely. You threatened to handcuff him first. Don't think I don't know every single detail of what happened, Dawson. Botswe called me himself early this morning."

"Did he really."

"Oh yes. He said you were arrogant, cocky, and insolent. And I believe him because that's exactly what's on display right now. What happens to you, Dawson? You're going along nice and steady with the investigation progressing smoothly, and then it's as though someone turns a switch and you go off the rails and everything is out of control. Why is that?"

"I don't know how to answer that. I'm sorry you feel everything is out of control."

"I do, Dawson. And if you had a little humility, you would see it yourself. Have you checked Dr. Botswe's alibis?"

"I have," Dawson said soberly. "He's telling the truth. He was in Kumasi at the time Musa Zakari was killed. He was also holding a dinner party the night Comfort was murdered."

"Exactly correct."

"You looked into it yourself, sir?"

"Of *course* I did, Dawson. When he called me, I asked him for the details of his alibi and then I did my own little bit of detecting—probably even faster than you did. I didn't get to be chief superintendent of police by being an idiot, you know."

"I didn't mean to imply that."

Lartey sighed. "This is what you're going to do. You're to issue a public apology to Dr. Botswe and his guest and staff member through the press. That's number one. Number two, you will visit Dr. Botswe and personally apologize for maltreating and disrespecting him. Three, you will from now on report to me every single morning what your plans are for each day before you embark upon them. Understood?"

"Yes, sir. Is there anything else?"

Lartey pointed a finger at him. "You're lucky that practically everybody is tied up with the Ghana Petroleum affair, otherwise I might have removed you from this case. So be thankful."

"Yes, indeed," Dawson said, standing up. "Every day, sir, I count my blessings."

In the afternoon, Dawson made his atonement pilgrimage to Dr. Botswe's house. Obi came to the gate but did not open it. He was cold, and his previous deference toward Dawson was gone.

"The doctor is not here," he said flatly. "You have to wait."

"When will he be back, please?" Dawson asked politely.

"About four o'clock."

"All right," Dawson said, glancing at his watch. Only about thirty minutes away. "I'll wait."

Since he was now persona non grata, he wasn't expecting to be invited in. He wasn't. Obi turned away and went back to his gardening or fixing things, or whatever it was he had been doing.

Dawson sat and waited while he thought dispiritedly about things. His concentration on people like Socrate, Austin, and Botswe seemed misplaced. *Maybe this murderer is just some lunatic roaming the streets of Accra. You might not just be looking at the wrong trees, you could be in the wrong forest completely.*

What should he do now? Should the surveillance continue, and for how long? As long as Lartey would tolerate it, Dawson thought, which would not be much longer. He was feeling deflated and listless. Maybe he was out of his depth. After all, he had never had a serial killer case, rare as they were in Ghana.

Botswe showed up about four-thirty in his lovely Infiniti. He glided into the garage. He had evidently spotted Dawson because Obi came out a few minutes later to tell him that the doctor would be able to see him now.

Botswe was at the window in the sitting room looking out onto the garden.

"Good afternoon, Doctor," Dawson said.

The professor turned slowly. "Inspector."

"How are you?"

"As well as could be expected, I suppose. Please, have a seat."

They both sat down.

"Dr. Botswe," Dawson began, "I owe you a big apology for my actions last night. I wanted to tell you how sorry I am. It was a complete blunder on my part."

"It was very upsetting, to say the least."

"Yes, I can see why. As I said, my humble apologies."

He nodded. "Apology accepted. On reflection, you were doing your job. Interestingly enough, you came to mind this morning."

"Why is that?"

"I was browsing through my book of Ghanaian proverbs and came across one that seemed apropos of your circumstances. It goes something like 'If you are on the road to nowhere, find another road.' Not to deliberately discourage you, but maybe we're not looking where we should for this killer."

Dawson noticed the word *we.* "You could be right in a way," he said, "but I think it's more that I haven't yet understood the message he's sending us in these murders. If only I could decode the message, I believe I'd be led to him."

"Yes. If it's all right with you, Inspector, let me ponder over it some more and call you in about a day with my ideas."

"That's fine, thank you. By the way, the book of proverbs you were looking at, is it *Three Thousand Six Hundred Ghanaian Proverbs*?"

"Yes. Are you familiar with it?"

"Yes. My brother Cairo sells it in his crafts shop in Osu."

"It's a terrific book to amble through, as well as a good resource."

Dawson stood up. "Thank you for seeing me with such courtesy, Dr. Botswe. It won't go unrecognized."

They shook hands. Botswe walked him to the door. Dawson had to give the man credit: he had scrupulous manners.

50

Daramani was home. He greeted Dawson like a long-lost brother.

"Oh, chaley, how I miss you," he said. "Why? Why so long you haven't come to see me?"

"Too busy. You know how it is."

"Sit down, sit down," Daramani said, moving some clutter. "Do you want something to drink? I can send someone to get you some Malta."

"No, thank you, Daramani."

"So how are you, my brother? You look tired."

"I am. I'm working a tough case."

"It's worrying your head, eh? You need to relax small-small. Because you don't smoke wee anymore, that's why you feel tense."

"Is that so?" Dawson grinned nonchalantly, but his heart-beat picked up with a tinge of excitement.

"Ah, but you yourself know that already," Daramani said.

"So can you help me?"

Daramani looked hurt. "But of course I can help you. Aren't you my brother, my friend? *Yes,* you are!"

He reached under his chair and brought out a small, covered box. He opened it up. There were the fat, neatly rolled joints.

"Here, I give you the biggest one," Daramani said happily. "Because I love you like my brother."

Dawson hesitated, wrestling. But it was too late. He was here. He took off his shirt and undershirt, hanging them outside the door so they wouldn't reek later. Bare-chested, he lit up with Daramani and sat back. He had forgotten how good it was. He had hoped it wouldn't be. He felt marvelous and loathed himself for it. *Why had he come?* He closed his eyes. A couple tears squeezed out for no reason he could fathom.

He was floating, very relaxed now. His mind began to free-associate.

If you are on the road to nowhere, find another road.

He laughed at that. It suddenly seemed funny. Daramani joined in his mirth for the hell of it.

But the Sankofa proverb was just as relevant to this mystery he was trying to solve. *It is not taboo to go back and fetch what you forgot.* Maybe he'd forgotten something in this case that he had to go back and fetch. That venerable bird with his head turned backward, like the one in Dr. Botswe's foyer. Dawson smiled. Generation after generation of schoolchildren learned about it.

His eyes popped open. *Head turned backward.*

He shot out of his chair.

"What wrong?" Daramani asked languidly.

"Ebenezer is the Sankofa bird."

"Oh, yeah," Daramani muttered.

Grabbing his phone, Dawson speed-dialed Cairo. "I need your help," he said.

"Sure, what's up?"

"Get out your proverb book. I'm looking for three different proverbs—one referring to the fingers, one to the knees,
and one to the tongue. While you're looking for those, I'll be
on the way down to the shop."

"Okay, I'll start right away and see you in a little while."

Dawson took one last puff of what was left of his joint and
then put it between Daramani's lips. "I've got to go."

"Why you leave me again?"

"No more wee for me," Dawson said, opening the door.
"Never again."

"Okay." Daramani laughed. "We'll see."

Dawson put his head back in. "Chaley, do you have any
chewing gum to freshen my breath?"

Daramani tossed him a packet of P.K. gum.

Cairo was poring over the book when Dawson arrived.

"Have you got anything so far?" Dawson asked.

"Man, there are a lot of proverbs," Cairo said as his brother
sat down beside him. He sniffed. "What's that smell? Have
you been in smoke or something?"

"Yes—tell you another time. Not important right now."

"Okay, here's the first one I've found. It goes, 'The knee
does not wear the hat when the head is available.' "

"What does that mean?"

"I'm not absolutely positive. I think it means, don't assume
a role that doesn't rightfully belong to you."

"That sounds about right. Give me another copy of the
book and I'll start from the back."

"Does this have to do with these serial murders you're investigating? You're all over the news today, I'm sure you know."

"Yes, only too aware," Dawson said sourly. "I don't want
to talk about it."

"Sorry. Carry on."

"So when this guy kills his victims, he stabs them in the back, mutilates them in some way, and then dumps them in or at some filthy location like the Korle Lagoon. I've been trying to figure out the meaning behind the mutilations. One of the victims, Ebenezer, had his head twisted around—"

"Twisted around?" Cairo said. "You mean twisted . . ."

"One hundred and eighty degrees, that's exactly what I mean."

"Broke his neck, in other words."

"Yes." Dawson paused. This was delicate territory. "Sorry, Cairo."

"Don't worry," he said, dismissing it. "I'm not sensitive about that anymore."

"So I thought, What is this murderer trying to tell us?" Dawson continued. "What's the message? He's not just killing people, he's *displaying* them in some way, so is there a lesson or moral he's trying to impress on us with that twisted head and neck? And then Sankofa hit me. That's an iconic Ghanaian symbol that represents possibly our most famous proverb. Dr. Botswe has a beautiful one in his house."

"Do you suspect him?"

"I did, but that's over. His alibis are established."

"I understand what you're saying about proverbs," Cairo said, "particularly Ghanaian proverbs that carry religious meaning. But *why* does this murderer have such a need to communicate that with us? What compulsion is driving him?"

"I don't know," Dawson said.

"Let's analyze this," Cairo said. "If I tell you a proverb, what am I trying to do? To pass on to you some kind of wisdom in a short, clever sentence, right?"

"Yes." Dawson sat up. "Wait a minute."

"What?"

"You said it just now, Cairo. When you state a proverb, you're trying to pass on to *me* some kind of wisdom, not someone else. All along I've been thinking the killer wants to tell *us* something, but it's not *us* he's trying to teach the lesson, it's his *victims.*"

"Oh," Cairo said, light dawning. "I see. Just a minute, though. What good is the lesson to his victims when they're dead?"

"That's easy. Whether traditional or Christian, so many people believe in the afterlife. The killer is sending them there branded with the proverbs, so to speak. Botswe called it right. It's messianic, apocalyptic."

They stared at each other for a moment.

"I hate to admit it," Cairo said, "but occasionally you're brilliant."

"It's you who's the brilliant one," Dawson said, laughing. "And while we're sitting around congratulating ourselves, we still have two more proverbs to dig up, so let's get to it."

They were quiet for the next fifteen minutes as they searched.

"Here's something," Cairo said. "Look at proverb number three-sixty."

Dawson turned to it. " '*Obi ntó ntasu ntó fam' mfa ne tɛkrɛma mfa,*' " he read. "Translation—no one spits on the ground and then licks up the spittle with his tongue. Lovely image, I must say."

"Meaning you don't defile yourself with what you've just defiled?"

"If that's what the killer chose, maybe he's saying the street children are sullied with the very filth they brought with them—immorality, disease, and so on?"

"Could be," Cairo said.

"All right, we'll take that one as a possibility. We have one more to go for the fingers."

"I think everybody knows that one," Cairo said. " 'No one points his left finger at his hometown.' In other words, be proud of your village, town, or country."

"The only problem with that," Dawson said, "is that it was the fingers of his *right* hand chopped off, not the left."

Cairo grunted. "Okay, never mind, then."

"What about this?" Dawson said. " '*Adeo kake loko adeo enyo.*' Meaning, we must count one before we can count two. It doesn't mention fingers itself, but he could be referring to counting on your fingers."

"Maybe," Cairo conceded. "A little subtler than the other two. So let's suppose we're right about this. How are you linking the street children to the Sankofa bird and the book of proverbs in Dr. Botswe's house?"

"I think I have the answer to that," Dawson said. "And that might mean I have the killer too."

51

Austin was thrilled that his long-hoped-for discussion with Dawson was finally taking place. They sat in the detectives' room. Austin seemed distracted by the noise.

"How do you work with all this going on around you?" he asked.

"We get used to it," Dawson said.

He and Chikata were seated at the table across from Austin.

"I won't take too much of your time," Austin said. "I just need a little information on the deaths of these youngsters. Let's see. The first one was Musa Zakari, then Ebenezer Sarpong, Comfort—I don't have her last name—and finally Antwi Boasiako. Correct?"

"Correct," Dawson said. He put the book of proverbs in front of Austin, watching for his reaction. "You know this book?"

Austin picked it up. "I'm not familiar with it. Should I be?"

"I believe so. You spent time reading it in Dr. Botswe's study when you babysat the house for him."

"I'm sorry, Inspector, but I'm confused. I've never seen this book before."

"Turn to the first bookmarked page and read proverb number three sixty," Dawson said.

"All right. It says, 'No one spits on the ground and then licks up the spittle with his tongue.'"

"Yes. Go to the next bookmark. What does the highlighted proverb read?"

"'We must count one before we can count two.'"

"What do these proverbs mean to you?"

"Em, well, nothing more than most proverbs mean to me."

"You took those proverbs and modeled your signature on them, didn't you? 'The knee does not wear the hat when the head is available.' That was for Comfort, so you gouged her knees out. Musa: 'Count one before we can count two,' so you chopped all his fingers off except the index."

"Wait a minute," Austin exclaimed in sudden realization. "Wait. Now I understand what you're saying. You think I killed all those people? On the basis of these *proverbs*? But Inspector Dawson, anyone could use any of these proverbs to fit with death. Watch, I'll turn to any random page and just read any proverb that pops out at me. Oh, look, here's one that goes, 'Everyone climbs the ladder of death.' Now just how fitting is that?"

Austin began to laugh, sounding like a hyena. Dawson stood up and grasped him by the collar, lifting him out of his chair and across the table until their faces almost touched. Abruptly, dead silence fell in the room as all the other detectives dropped what they were doing and turned to watch.

"Listen," Dawson said, his teeth clenched, "kids are being murdered, and I don't find it at all funny."

"Please, no, yes, I'm sorry, Inspector," Austin wheezed. "I didn't mean to laugh . . ." His scar had become moist and shiny.

Dawson let Austin go, shoving him back to his chair. As if a pause button had been released, the other detectives resumed work.

"I'm going to ask you some questions and you're going to tell me the truth," Dawson said.

"Yes, sir," Austin said, his voice trembling.

"Weekend of Friday, fourth June, where were you?"

"Fourth of June, fourth of June." Austin rubbed his head. "I can't remember that specific date, I'm very sorry, Inspector."

"Okay, try this one: night of Tuesday, twenty-second June."

"Oh, that's easy," Austin said, looking relieved. "I was at Dr. Botswe's dinner party."

There it was again: the dinner party.

"What time did you leave?"

"Actually, I stayed overnight."

"Why?"

"I was too drunk to drive. Both Dr. Botswe and I were drunk. I said I was going home, but he wouldn't let me. He made me sleep in his guest room."

"What time did you go to bed?"

"Gosh, Inspector, I really couldn't tell you. I have no recollection. I apologize."

"Can you prove that you didn't leave the premises sometime around two or three?"

"Inspector, I wouldn't have been able to even if I'd wanted to, because Dr. Botswe took my car keys away."

Dawson stood up abruptly. "Let's go. We're paying a visit."

Baidoo drove them to East Legon, Dawson on the passenger side and Austin in the rear with Chikata. They pulled into the driveway. Dawson hopped out.

"Wait here with him," he said to Chikata.

He rang the doorbell. Botswe opened the door, surprised to see him.

"Back so soon?"

"Yes, Dr. Botswe. Sorry to disturb again."

"No problem at all. Do come in."

Dawson stepped into the foyer.

"I won't take too much of your time, Dr. Botswe. It's about Austin. Did he come to your dinner party on twenty-second June?"

"Yes, absolutely. Why do you ask?"

"Do you remember what time he left?"

"The following morning. He was so inebriated that I wouldn't allow him to drive. I had him stay overnight in one of the guest rooms."

"Any chance he could have left the premises in the middle of the night and returned by morning?"

"How? I took his car keys away from him and kept them with me when I retired."

"Could he have sneaked into your room at some point to get them back?"

"With my door locked from the inside? Inspector, I don't want to infringe on your investigation, but if Austin is what you've come up with as a prime suspect, then you are really scraping bottom."

"Thank you for your time, Dr. Botswe," Dawson said tautly.

"You're very welcome, Inspector."

His hands jammed in his pockets, Dawson walked out

feeling ridiculous and deflated. Obi was in the driveway putting two yams, a bag of charcoal, and a small, brand-new charcoal stove into the back of his pickup.

"Good afternoon, Inspector."

"Afternoon, Obi."

"Please, is everything okay?" Obi said. "You look sad."

"Oh, not at all," Dawson said with forced brightness. "I'm doing fine, thank you. Going home?"

"Yes, please," Obi said, smiling. He gestured at the items in his pickup. "I will be cooking for my family this evening."

"So I see. Have a nice time, then."

"Thank you, sir. Good evening."

Chikata looked inquiringly at Dawson as he got back in the car.

"We're taking him back home," Dawson said quietly.

"So you confirmed my alibi, Inspector?" Austin said eagerly from the backseat.

"Yes, I confirmed it."

"Oh, that is really terrific. Thank you so much."

As Baidoo started the ignition, Austin said brightly, "On the way home, can I discuss the four murder cases with you for my paper?"

In unison, Dawson and Chikata replied, "*No!*"

52

Akosua had given in to necessity. Last night had been her first time as an ashawo at Nkrumah Circle. She had gone to the Beverly Hills Hotel with the client. It took him only about seven minutes to finish. For Akosua, it had been joyless and painful.

But here she was again tonight, soliciting at Nkrumah Circle. She had a kind of numbness of mind, hardly able to believe that this was what she was doing with her life now.

A pickup truck pulled up in front of her, and the driver called out, "Hello, beautiful one."

She leaned tentatively down to the passenger window.

"What is your name?" he asked her. He was good-looking.

"Jasmine." That was the name she'd decided on.

"Beautiful name for a beautiful girl."

"Thank you. What is your name too?"

"You can call me Chosen. Because I am."

"How can I make you happy, Chosen?"

"I want you to come to my house for the whole night."

"Why not let's go rather to a nice hotel instead?"

"I give you sixty cedis to come to my house, Jasmine."

Was he serious? That was an outstanding price.

"Look, if you don't believe me," Chosen said, "I give you twenty cedis right now if you get in the car, and the rest when we are finished."

Akosua got in.

Chosen smiled at her. "Thank you. Here." He gave her twenty cedis.

They drove off.

"I noticed you because you are so beautiful," he said.

She smiled shyly.

"Are you from Accra?" he asked.

"No, from Kumasi."

"You live on the street?"

"Yes. I was staying in my stepfather's house, but he told me not to come back there without money."

"Well, I think with the money you make tonight, you'll be able to go back, not so?"

"Yes, I think so," she said happily. She could hardly believe her luck.

He was driving on Ring Road West toward Obetsebi-Lamptey Circle.

"Where is your house, Chosen?"

"In Jamestown," he said.

Dawson was drowsily sprawled across the bed half undressed when Christine came out of the shower.

"Look at you," she said. "If I didn't know you, I'd say you were drunk."

Dawson grunted. "I'm defeated, not drunk."

"You'll be back in the saddle tomorrow. Go and have your shower."

Dawson rolled over onto his back. "You know those small charcoal stoves with the grate on top and the air inlet on the side?"

"Yes, what about them?"

"Did your mom ever use one of those in addition to her regular stove?"

"No, but my granny did. Why?"

"Today when we were leaving Dr. Botswe's house, his manservant Obi was loading up some stuff in his pickup and he had one of those stoves he said he was going to use to cook tonight. But later I remembered he had told me Dr. Botswe had bought him a gas stove years ago, so I was wondering why he'd need the charcoal."

"I have no idea," Christine said. "Why is it so important?"

"It's not really. My mind is just wandering."

"I remember Granny once burned herself with the grate of one of those charcoal stoves," Christine said. "Branded her skin with a pattern of lines that looked like jail bars."

Dawson sat up. "Jail bars," he repeated. *What was it about the bars of a jail?* He caught his breath. "Oh, no."

"What's wrong?"

"Oh, no." He leapt to his feet.

"What is it, Dark?"

Dawson pulled on his shoes but left his shirttails flying. "Have to go." He kissed her. "I love you more than you even know."

As Dawson moved off in Christine's car, he called Dr. Botswe with a question. Nobody picked up. Dawson's next call was to Chikata. No answer.

He was at Obetsebi-Lamptey Circle now. He took Ring Road West toward Jamestown.

Chikata called him back within five minutes.

"Is Baidoo close by with the jeep?" Dawson asked him.

"Yes, he lives in the same barracks as me, and the jeep is parked here."

"Meet me at Jamestown near the fire station—around where I took Tedamm down."

"What's going on?"

"Can't talk right now. Just come as quickly as possible."

Dawson slowed as he came to the edge of Jamestown east of the fire station. He pulled over to the side, mounting the curb, and got out his flashlight, although he didn't switch it on just yet. A nice sea breeze seemed to be directing the smell of the lagoon away from Dawson, which he appreciated. He ran to the second building along the border of the no-building zone. It was the shuttered Woodcrest Services gypsum and acoustic tiling factory. In a tight alley along its right side, Dawson saw a black pickup truck parked. He went to the front door of the factory, which faced the east bank of the lagoon. It was sealed with a strong padlock. No way he could get through that. *How do I get into this place?*

Dawson pressed his ear against the door but didn't hear anything. He trotted around to the left side of the building, praying, praying there was an opening somewhere.

He switched on his flashlight now. Thirty meters away, there was an overflow channel built off the lagoon to help reduce flooding in the rainy season. Agbogbloshie was on the other side of the channel.

Dawson turned his attention back to the building, walking along the wall with his flashlight on. *Not a single window.* But there was a door. It was wooden, shut solid with a dead bolt. He couldn't do anything with that either.

He jumped as he saw a massive rat appear from nowhere. God, how he hated rats. The creature scampered away. Dawson went a little farther along to see where it had come from. It was an opening in the wall near the ground, a spot where the brick had been damaged a long time ago and never repaired.

He knelt down and put his ear to the opening. He heard a slight whistle of wind, meaning there was cross ventilation. But thin as he was, the aperture was not large enough to get through.

He tugged at the edge of the hole, and some of the brick came away. Encouraged, he pulled and rocked the brick again, and came away with another piece. The hole was higher than wide. If he turned sideways . . . He got only as far as his hips.

He heard a woman moan. He strained his neck to look around and for the first time detected a faint light coming from a room beyond the one he was halfway into. He wriggled and rocked.

Shit.

He came back out a bit and removed his belt. Every little thing counted. He tried again, pushing with his feet and swiveling his hips . . . push, swivel; push, swivel.

He was through. The room was filled with the dark, rusty hulks of old machinery, and the floor was littered with metal and old raw material from the gypsum and tiling.

There was the woman's moan again. He moved as quickly as he could to the far wall without tripping on anything. He peeped round the corner to the adjoining room.

It was small and hot. Its floor was blotched with thick red paint. Dawson suddenly realized it was dried blood, like in an abattoir. A naked, gagged woman was tethered to the far wall, her back toward Dawson. Beside her on the floor was a butcher knife with a long, wide blade.

Obi was bending over the charcoal stove he had bought earlier, fanning the charcoal red hot. He picked up the grate with two pairs of tongs and turned toward her.

"Put that down," Dawson said.

Obi saw him, dropped everything, and bolted out of the room. Dawson followed, turning a sharp right. He knew where Obi was going. To the dead-bolted door.

By the time Dawson got there, it was wide-open and Obi was gone. Dawson came out, swinging his flashlight beam in an arc. *No one.* He ran around to the front of the building, but Obi wasn't there either. *Where did he go?*

Then he understood. The overflow channel. Dawson ran to the side of it and shone his flashlight. *Nothing.* And then he saw him. Obi was swimming across. His head bobbed up for a second and then ducked under for a long time. He was a strong swimmer, and he could hold his breath. Swimming after him was not the way Dawson was going to catch the man. He ran back to the car and jumped in. If he could drive around to the other bank, he would be there to welcome Obi as he got out.

He couldn't find the ignition key.

He leapt out again, alarms screaming in his head as he dug in his pockets.

What did you do with the key?

Shit. The hole in the wall. He sprinted back to the side of the factory. At the hole, he saw the key where it had fallen out of his pocket on the other side. He went partially through the hole and grabbed it.

But he had lost too much time. He shone his flashlight across the channel again and saw Obi getting out on the other side. He had slipped out of Dawson's grasp. Dawson let out a long shout of rage and frustration. And then, as Obi came up to the top of the bank, powerful headlight beams switched on and silhouetted him. Raising his arms, he slowly went to his knees in surrender.

"It's okay, Dawson," came Chikata's cheerful voice from across the channel. "We've got him."

53

"How are you, Obi?"

"Please, I'm fine," he said as Dawson and Chikata sat down opposite him. This time, he was in CID's only official interview room, for his capture had indeed achieved the status of "national importance."

Dawson studied Obi for a while. "What do you feel right now?"

He seemed puzzled. "I feel a little hungry."

Dawson grunted. "I see. You remember Akosua, the girl last night?"

"Akosua? She told me her name was Jasmine."

"Jasmine, then. What did you plan to do to her?"

"First to brand her with the hot iron grate of the stove. Then after that, I stick my knife in her back. One stab only, sir. Always just one stab."

"Why is that so important?"

"Everything has to be neat. Have you ever seen anything at

the doctor's house that looks *basabasa*? Never. Everything I do is neat and clean."

"But you never scrub the blood off the floor of your killing place."

Obi frowned. "Blood itself is purifying, Inspector Dawson. It is not untidy, it is a pure thing."

"When you kill, what do you feel?"

"Joy."

"Like the joy of the Lord?"

"Yes. He guides me in all things."

"He spoke to you and told you to kill Jasmine?"

"Yes."

"He also told you to kill Musa Zakari?"

"Yes, please."

"And Ebenezer Sarpong."

"Yes, please."

"Comfort Mahama."

"Yes, please. She too."

"Why do you believe God wants you to kill people?"

"Not people, Inspector. *Certain* people."

"Street children."

"*Certain* street children."

"Teenagers?"

"Teenage children of the street are a visitation of Satan and a pox on us."

"Why them in particular and not the young ones?"

"The small ones come with innocence. They have a chance to return to their villages, where they belong. Those that return will be blessed by God." Obi's face clouded over. "But those that stay have made a pact with the devil to do evil things. Fornication and prostitution, lying, cheating, and stealing. Worst of all, when they come of age, they begin to mate, producing offspring. Some of those offspring too will become fornicators, prostitutes, cheats, and thieves as they come of age. Look at the shame and filth they bring. Look at the venereal diseases. Have you not visited CMB and Agbogbloshie? They defecate like animals wherever they like, these people. They are dirty. No one wants to cleanse the city of them, so I have to. They are crowding our streets."

"But the doctor who you admire so much does not seem to agree with you about the street children," Dawson said. "He cares about them, does he not?"

"The doctor is a good man, but sometimes I feel sad about what he is doing. He is trying to cleanse the children by showing them a new way of living. But, you see, Inspector, it is too late. If you put a new cloth on a dirty bed, the bed is still dirty."

"Were you a child of the street?"

Obi stared at Dawson. "Please, the Lord blessed me when I was young and He took me out of the street. And He blessed me again and brought me to Dr. Botswe."

"Why can't you feel sympathy for street children when you were one yourself?"

There was a sudden flash of anger. Obi's voice rose and cracked. *"You don't call me that!"*

He stood up, and Chikata, at the ready, did the same.

"Sit down, Obi," Dawson said.

Obi did, hyperventilating. "Sorry, sir."

"It's okay. You say you sometimes feel sad about what Dr. Botswe is doing. You mean bringing the children to his home?"

Obi gripped the edge of the table so hard his nail beds turned bloodred. "Iniquity, sinfulness, and dirtiness defile such a home." His chin and bottom lip were quivering with emotion. "Have you seen the doctor's house? Have you seen how I clean it, how I make it more beautiful than even the best Lighthouse church? It is as a temple, Inspector.

"And then he brings this *filth,* this refuse from the streets to sleep in the spotless sheets I wash with my own hands. No. Those children do not belong here. They belong in the gutter or the latrine. That is all they are worth. Let them be there, let them roll in the Korle Lagoon and eat from it like the pigs."

Dawson shook his head slowly. "If there is a hell, that's where you are going. Dr. Botswe in heaven will never lay eyes on you there."

Obi inclined his head. "Dear Inspector, my heart is troubled for you. You know not of what you speak. Have you committed yourself to the Lord? Do you go to church?"

Dawson curled his lip. "You think any of this redemption nonsense is fooling me? You are a psychopathic killer pure and simple, Obi. All this religious speech you're making? False. Bogus. 'Commit yourself to the Lord.' You don't believe a word of it. You're a *liar,* just like any other psychopath. You dress up your murder in fancy language, but it's not even that complicated. You *enjoy* killing. Teenagers are the people you like to kill because they trigger the murder machinery in your soul."

They stared at each other across the table, neither of them blinking.

"They are so easy to get, these children," Obi said softly. "Just walk around the Novotel Lorry Park, or on Tudu Road, or around the old UTC building. You can find them there by the hundreds. Just pick one and go to him and ask, 'Do you want to make some money? Come and clean my house.' They are so poor, so desperate, and they will come with you. Even, you can just offer them a ride in a beautiful car."

"Don't you fear someone will see you take a child?"

"And so what?" Obi laughed hard. "Please, Inspector Dawson, let me tell you something you should know by now. Accra is a perfect place for murder. It is so dark and so quiet at night. Street people are sleeping everywhere. Who knows they are there, and who cares about them? Who will report anything? Everyone fears you, the police. They say if you go to report something to the police, you are the one who they will arrest. I could kill one of these rubbish children around the corner from where the other ones sleep and I could walk away without worrying. No one will care."

Dawson shook his head. He didn't want that to be true.

"When I throw such a person into the lagoon, or into the latrine or the rubbish pile or the gutter," Obi continued, "I can do it without any concern whatsoever. I go back to my bed and sleep without any problem. You think a policeman is going to come and get me? Ha."

Dawson leaned across the table and brought his face so close to Obi's that the man drew back.

"But Obi, my fool," he whispered, "that is exactly what I did. I came in and I fished you out."

Obi swallowed.

"It was you who was reading Dr. Botswe's book of proverbs and taking your cue from them," Dawson said. "Sankofa, the bird whose head is turned backward, so that's what you did to Ebenezer. 'The knee does not wear the hat when the head is available.' That was for Comfort, so you gouged her knees out. Musa: 'We must count one before we can count two,' so you chopped all his fingers off except the index. Right?"

Obi averted his gaze.

Dawson moved back again. "And last, 'No one spits on the ground and then licks up the spittle with his tongue.' You cut out Ofosu's tongue. A sweet boy who loved to talk and joke around. And you, cold-blooded, and vicious."

Obi was trembling. "But how . . . how did you understand what I was going to do with the charcoal stove?"

"Why do you need a charcoal stove? You told me yourself that Dr. Botswe bought you a gas one years ago. You needed the charcoal stove for the grate on the top. 'Everyone climbs the ladder of death,' the proverb goes. You were heating up the grate to brand the pattern of parallel lines into Akosua's skin. If you look at the pattern with the lines going horizontally, it looks like a ladder."

Obi nodded. "Yes."

"Why did you kill with proverbs?"

"Anyone can kill, sir, but few people can kill and leave a mark of wisdom on the body. Ghanaian proverbs are the wisest in the world."

"Leave a mark of wisdom on the body," Dawson echoed. "That's what you call all those mutilations?"

"Yes, sir," Obi answered. "Please, how did you find me?"

"I called Dr. Botswe to find out where you lived. He told me Madina—but then he said he thought you had told him that you had some kind of house in Jamestown. I knew it would have to be the most deserted section of Jamestown. The only area like that is near the lagoon, where putting up new buildings has been banned and old ones have been closed down. I have been passing that Woodcrest Services factory for years, and I never gave it a second's thought, but it is the only abandoned building that is completely closed, preventing people from seeing inside."

Obi's shoulders suddenly contracted and shrank, and he began to weep.

Dawson stood up. "Do you know why he's crying?" he said to Chikata. "Because he was caught. That's all he's sorry about. As for the people he has slaughtered, he feels *nothing* for them."

54

Dawson took Christine and Hosiah out for a celebratory dinner at Maquis Tante Marie. It was more than he could comfortably afford, but he didn't care. He wanted this to be special, and what was one more day of being broke? He surprised Chikata by inviting him to join them. Par for the course, one of the female waiters simply could not keep her eyes off Chikata, and par for the course, he got her phone number as they left the restaurant. Dawson and Christine exchanged glances and a sly grin.

Walking out to the car, Hosiah suddenly put his hand in Chikata's and said, "Uncle Philip, you can come to my house on Saturday and play with my cars if you like."

Chikata at first looked dumbfounded, and then a big grin burst out on his face and he laughed. "Well, I have to ask your daddy first, okay?"

"The answer is yes," Dawson said, smiling.

They said good night to Chikata, dropping him off at police barracks. Just after they passed the Ako Adjei Interchange,

Dawson spotted someone at the side of the street and pulled over.

"Why are we stopping?" Christine asked.

"It's Sly," Dawson said, his door already open.

He ran back to where the boy was standing.

For just a moment, Sly stared at him as he approached, unsure. Then his face lit up.

"Mr. Darko!" he screamed and began running.

Dawson knelt down, opening his arms wide. Sly joyfully threw himself into his embrace.

"I've been looking everywhere for you!" Dawson cried. "Where have you been?"

He held Sly at arm's length. The boy had lost weight, and his clothes were even more ragged than before, but that old spark in his eyes was still there.

"I don't live in Agbogbloshie anymore," Sly explained. "My uncle went to the north and left me and he never came back."

"So where do you live now?"

"Oh, well, just on the streets, you know. I walk around during the day and try to do some jobs, and then I find somewhere to sleep."

Dawson shook his head. *Sly is not going to be a street child.*

Christine and Hosiah had joined them.

"This is Sly," Dawson introduced.

"Oh, yes!" Christine exclaimed. "The boy we went to look for. How are you?"

"Please, I'm fine."

"Hosiah?" Dawson said, a touch apprehensively. He wasn't sure what the reception was going to be like. "Say hello to—"

"I already know about him, Daddy," Hosiah said in somewhat long-suffering tones. "I heard you and Mammy talking about him."

"Oh," Dawson said.

"Can you play soccer?" Hosiah asked Sly.

"Sure," he replied, grinning. "I can dribble paa, and I'm a good goalie too."

"I have a soccer ball at my house we can play with."

"They look sweet together, don't they?" Christine whispered to Dawson as the two boys talked. "He looks awfully hungry, though."

"His uncle left," Dawson said. "Deserted him without a word."

"Ewurade," Christine said, appalled. "So he's on the streets with no one at all to take care of him?"

"Yes."

They looked at each other.

"Well, we at least need to get him something to eat, poor kid," she said. "And then we can see what else we can do to help him."

"We may have to take a trip to the north to find his parents," Dawson said, "which might be easier said than done. Beyond that, unless we take him in, he'll become just like the other thousands of street children. And I don't think I'm going to like that."

"I know," she said, hooking her fingers around his. "I know you won't."

"Come along, you two," Dawson called out.

With the two boys in the backseat, Dawson was preparing to move the car into traffic when he realized he had a text message. It said:

Good news. Commitment from Dr. Gyan to make
your boy whole. Whatever you can afford.
     Call me. Dr. Biney

"Thank you, Jesus," Dawson said.

"What is it?" Christine asked.

He passed the phone to her. She read the message and let out a small shriek, throwing herself at Dawson and holding him tight. Choking with emotion, they said nothing as they stayed together in a long embrace.

Behind them, Sly shot Hosiah a puzzled look.

"They're like that sometimes," Hosiah explained. "You just have to be patient and wait for them to stop."

"Oh, okay," Sly said. It was fine with him.

Acknowledgments

First, I must express my deepest gratitude for the friendship and professional advice of Detective Lance Corporal Frank A. Boasiako of the Criminal Investigations Department (CID) in Accra. Meeting him was a result of a confluence of events that might even have been called providence. He is a treasure of information. Without him, many nuances and technicalities of the Ghana Police Service (GPS) could not have been detailed in this novel, not to mention the guidance and protection he provided as I explored the darkest recesses of nocturnal Accra. Any variations from reality should not be attributed to "incorrect information" from Frank but rather to the creative and editorial process in my writing of the story.

There are others at Ghana Police Service (GPS) headquarters I must also thank: my old friend Ken Yeboah, Director-General of GPS Legal Services, who helped me get in touch with the right people; Detective Deputy Superintendent of Police (DSP) Hanson Gove, who graciously allowed me to pick his brain while frequenting his office and the detectives' room.

Thanks also to DSP Solomon Ayawine, administrator of CID headquarters.

I'm very grateful to Joana Ofori of Street Academy in Accra for being so accommodating and helpful in setting up interviews and tours of some of the settings in this novel. Paul Avevor of Catholic Action for Street Children (CAS) in Accra coordinated my meeting with some of Accra's street children, and I thank him and director Jos Van Dinther for allowing me access to their organization and for giving me a tour of its premises. Thanks also to Theodora and Michael, the field-workers I went with to the gathering places of the street kids in town, many of which are represented in this novel. The children I met at both CAS and Street Academy were terrific, including Ernestina Marbell, whom I'm honored and delighted to be able to support through school.

My thanks to Colorado-Ghana Children's Fund's Edwin and Linda Vanotoo, whom I met in Sekondi-Takoradi and who helped me get in touch with the children they sponsor through their organization, and thanks to Mark, their fieldworker, who showed me around.

My friend and former classmate Professor Nii Otu Nartey, CEO of the Korle Bu Teaching Hospital, was instrumental in securing a tour of the Department of Child Health, where the nursing staff was extremely accommodating, in particular Juliana Adu Danso and Deputy Director Rebecca Armah.

Thanks also to Thomas Frimpong for welcoming me to the Police Hospital Mortuary and to the forensic pathologist and staff.

I'm grateful to Ethelbert Tetteh at Korle Lagoon Ecological Restoration Project (KLERP), who gave me a wonderful tour of the facilities and explained the technical intricacies of the pump station.

Seth Aheto took me through the bowels of Nima to places I would never have discovered without his assistance.

Samuel A. Mensah, general manager of Citi-FM, was kind enough to give me a tour of his radio station.

Thanks also to Bernard, my driver, who took me north, south, east, and west, to and through both the toughest and the loveliest parts of Accra as well as to the lush Western Region.

Of course, none of the foregoing would have been relevant if I did not have a book to write and get published. Which would not have been possible without the advocacy of and guidance from the best literary agent in the world, Marly Rusoff.

I count my blessings every time I reflect that a great publisher, Random House, and the Random House Publishing Group's wonderful trade paperback publisher, Jane von Mehren, have stuck with me in these challenging times when there is much upheaval in the publishing world and when nothing can be taken for granted.

An amazing amount of work goes into producing just one novel, and just like with a movie, the many talented people who bring it all together are often the unsung heroes. This time around, my editor was Jennifer Smith. An author in her own right, she is also a terrific editor with incisive perception, who, I might add, works with lightning speed—just the way I like it. Thank you, Jen, for seeing this through, and thanks also to my publicist Kristina Miller as well as the marketing team.

As with the first novel in the Darko Dawson series, *Wife of the Gods,* the production editor was Vincent La Scala. My gratitude to him, and a million thanks to skilled copy editor Susan M. S. Brown for her meticulous care with my manuscript. Thank goodness for copy editors!

Gloria Ampim, at the University of Ghana, was my cultural and ethnographic editor, and I'm grateful to have had the benefit of her guidance as she carefully reviewed the novel. Thank you, Laura McGough, Ph.D., at the School of Public Health, University of Ghana, for putting me in touch with her.

The proverbs quoted in this novel are taken from the book *Three Thousand Six Hundred Ghanaian Proverbs from the Asante and Fante Language*, compiled by J. G. Christaller, translated by Kofi Ron Lange.

Finally, I developed a deep respect for the industry and resilience of Accra's street children themselves, who withstand levels of hardship and poverty that would break most of us living in the Western world.

Glossary

(No emphasis is indicated for words whose syllables have little tonal difference.)

Agoo (ah-GO): requesting permission to enter, come through, or go past

Akpeteshie (ak-pet-eshee): homemade spirit, 40 to 50 percent alcohol by volume, produced by distilling palm wine or sugar cane juice

Ashawo (ah-sha-WO): sex worker, prostitute

Banku (bang-KOO): cooked fermented cornmeal and grated cassava

Basabasa (ba-sa-ba-sa): disorganized, chaotic

Bola (BOH-la): trash

Cedi (SEE-dee): the monetary unit of Ghana

Chaley (cha-LAY): familiar term for friend, similar to *buddy, bro, dude*

Chop bar: small eating establishment

CMB: Cocoa Marketing Board

Dabi (deh-BEE, dah-BEE): no (Twi, Ga)

Ɛte sɛn? (eh-tay-SEN): How are you? (Twi)

Ewurade (ay-wu-rah-DAY): God, as in the exclamation, "My God"

Ɛyɛ (eh-YEH): fine (Twi, in response to *ɛte sɛn?*)

Fufu (fu-FU): cassava, yam, or plantain pounded into a soft, glutinous mass and shaped into a smooth ball, usually an accompaniment to soup

Ga: language indigenous to the southeastern coastal region of Ghana in and around the capital, Accra; also, *Ga* people

Gari (ga-REE): Granular flour made from grated cassava

GPS: Ghana Police Service

Kayaye (KA-ya-yay): women from northern Ghana who make their living in Accra and other cities transporting goods on their heads when another means of transportation is unavailable. Also termed *head porter*. (Singular, *kayayo*)

Kenkey (KENG-kay): staple food made from fermented ground white corn and formed into a ball

Kwasea (kwa-say-AH): fool, idiot (directed insult)

Mepaakyɛw (may-pah-CHO): please (polite or deferential); Twi

Mmienu (MEE-yay-nu): two (Twi)

Nagode (na-go-DAY): thank you (Hausa)

Oware (oh-WAH-ray): count-and-capture game played with pebbles on a board with shallow wells

Paa (pah): very much, very well

Pesewa (PEH-say-wah): coin currency, 100p = 1 cedi

Sɛn? (sen): How much?

Shito (shee-TAW): hot pepper sauce

Tamale (TA-ma-lay): capital of the Northern Region of Ghana

Tatale (ta-ta-lay): pancakes made from a batter of ripe plantain

Tro-tro (traw-traw): minibus transporting several people

Twi (chwee): language spoken in Ghana by the Akan people, which comprise the Ashantis, Fantes, and others. The most widely spoken indigenous language in Ghana, with about 8.3 million speakers.

Wote Twi? (WO-tay chwee): Do you understand Twi?

KWEI QUARTEY was raised in Ghana by an African American mother and a Ghanaian father, both of whom were university lecturers. Dr. Quartey practices medicine in Southern California, rising early in the morning to write before going to work. His highly praised first novel, *Wife of the Gods,* was a *Los Angeles Times* bestseller.